9

Days 'Til Sunday

Lonnie Graves

EAKIN PRESS  Fort Worth, Texas
www.EakinPress.com

Contents

Preface v

Introduction vii

1. The Naughty Old Telephone Party Line. 1

2. The Real Reason We Moved to Town 23

3. The Stag Party Incident, A Night to Remember 30

4. Fate Interrupts the Plan 55

5. Two Fishes and Five Hush Puppies 73

6. The Surprise Shotgun Wedding 89

7. And Then, Momentarily, the Sun Came Out Again. . 102

8. Merry Christmas and an Unhappy New Year 125

9. Was it Suicide or Murder?. 135

10. Reconciliation 147

11. Eventide and One Last Call. 151

12. To Hell and Back 162

13. The Road to Recovery. 173

14. And Who Was Cousin Elberta?. 176

15. The Death and Eulogy of Pastor Ike 180

16. Nana Ella's Revelation 195

17. Jukebox Nick's Confession. 209

18. It's In the Bag 216

19. Nine Days 'Til Sunday 230

Preface

IT WOULD SEEM that Randall Carter, known to his family and friends as Randy, was a target of fate. It first pounced on him with fury when he was just finishing high school. That attack stirred a vicious rumor over the old party telephone line that Randy, a colored boy, was engaged in a secret affair with a neighborhood white girl. Such behavior was not only scandalous but also dangerous in Texas in the 1930s. The rumor, though an absolute lie, forced Randy and his family to move into town away from their comfortable country home.

A few days after the move, he was coaxed into going with some fellow graduating class members to a stag party. He had to be prodded because he was afraid these friends might try to tempt him away from his strong moral beliefs and position as a teetotaler. Unfortunately they convinced him to attend the party and tricked him into drinking something that tasted mild but was powerful.

Later that night, while intoxicated, he quarreled with his friends and left them to get home on his own. Fate took him instead into the home of a lady of questionable reputation. What happened that night was long kept a secret, and the lady disappeared from town forever with a black bag that contained incriminating evidence.

Randy decided to run from fate, to leave town and go to California. He told only one person, a close friend who was white. The friend begged him not to go, but he was determined. Nine days later fate slammed the door in his face and cancelled the California plans.

Randy confided the whole truth to his beloved Uncle Cephas who sympathized and took steps to rescue him. Fate, however, turned Randy's intentions to assist a friend in being neighborly into an adventure that threw him headlong into being the groom in a shotgun wedding. Rescue seemed a long way off.

His many problems with women made Randy decide to become celibate. Fate foiled his plans again with a beautiful girl who seemed his perfect soul mate and loved him in return. Then a tragedy occurred that affected him so much he renounced his religious convictions and fell into a deep depression.

Then Randy had an accident and almost died. When he finally recovered, he was a changed man. He became a preacher, telling people how he had been to Hell and back. Not only did he become a great preacher, but also an author, a successful business man, a director on the board of the largest bank in town, and educator and philanthropist. At this height of his achievement, suddenly the long forgotten black bag appeared. It held a document telling what had happened on that fateful Friday of his eighteenth year. Would the truth, when revealed, send him to his grave with shame and disgrace?

Introduction

DEAR READERS,

As most of it happened, I would never have imagined that my life story would be worth writing down. Some of it, for sure, seemed best kept to myself. As any preacher, of course, I have always used many examples from my experiences in my sermons. Only recently, however, have I realized the value of being wholly open.

It has taken a beloved young relative who looks at me with loving and admiring eyes and has sat with me through long winter evenings, patiently probing and gently pulling my story out of me to bring it before you. He is the one who has written it all down and seen to getting it into the form you are now looking upon.

From him I have learned that the truth, when seen in the light of love, not only can set us free, but can also bring us to a higher plane of knowing and experiencing the love of God and each other.

You will meet him later in this book as he becomes increasingly important to me and enters into conversation with me in the story. As the story reaches present time, he is as much a part of it as I, and he becomes the narrator. He is the reason the story must be told.

—REV. RANDALL CARTER

CHAPTER 1

The Naughty Old Telephone Party Line

WE WERE NEAR THE END of our school year and getting ready for our graduation exercises. I was a senior, and, along with my classmates, I was full of anticipation for that big event.

One morning in a classroom, a girl I had thought of for a long time as my girlfriend, surprised me with a note. She gave it to a girl cousin of mine in our first period class to give to me. Classrooms had a stricter setup back then. The boys and girls didn't sit together. The boys sat on one side and the girls on the other. There was definitely no note passing because the teacher would be watching and intercept. Anyway, at recess time, my cousin handed the note to me. She said to me, "You know who this is from."

I was anxious to know what the note was about. I went to a quiet place, and began to unfold it. She had a way of folding paper that made unfolding it like a puzzle. It was folded several times, adding to my suspense. I had to be careful not to tear it. Finally I was able to read it. I read it twice. It said "Hi, This is to inform you that I will not be going to the Junior-Senior Prom with you as we had planned. I've changed my mind. I have met another guy that I'm really intrigued with. As a matter of fact, I think I'm in love with him, so he is going to take me to the prom. I wanted you to know in plenty of time to get somebody else to take. I know it won't be a problem." She signed it YKW (You Know Who).

I was stunned, and didn't want to believe it. Nevertheless, I recognized her handwriting. It was definitely from my girlfriend, Maggie. We had been friends over the years, ever since we were, I guess, twelve years old. We were the same age. We

1

had always done things together, school functions, picture shows, the park, all the things kids like to do. We were a pair.

Incidently, my name is Randall Carter. They call me Randy. For the longest time, it has always been Randy and Maggie. We had always planned to go to the prom together. Because she had suggested it, I had asked my uncle if I could borrow his brand new Cadillac, and he had kindly consented. Now, just two weeks before the prom, she tells me that she is not going to go with me, that she is going with someone else. I was incredulous, my mind in a turmoil. I had no other plans.

Maggie was an outgoing person, quite popular. She could have gone to the prom with any boy at school if she had wanted to. She had it all, personality and good looks and she was always talking to boys. Yet she had passed them up and, all this time, it had been Maggie and Randy. I had so enjoyed our time together, took it for granted it would always be like that. Now to think she was going to the prom with this other fellow, saying she is in love with him! I hated to think about what my friends were going to think of me. I could hear them saying, "She's too fast for him!" I would be a laughing stock. I couldn't let it end with that letter. I had to talk with her.

When school was out that afternoon, I went to my locker. I had some personal things I wanted. I got out my dictionary, two blue ribbons, one of which I had won as her partner in a scholastic league spelling contest. We had won first place in the county. There were other things in my locker that were very special to me. I took them out of my locker. I walked with my things down the street to my friend's house and told him I was going to leave them there. I told him I had an errand to run, but I didn't tell him what it was about.

Maggie and I attended Booker T. Washington High School right here in Nelsonburg, Texas. This was in the early '30s. The white people had school buses to take them to their schools, but we had to walk to ours. Maggie's family lived in the country, two and a half miles from town in a community called Sugar Cane Point, which was generally a black community. There was an elementary school there but no high school. The high school children there had to go to school in Nelsonburg and so did I. I lived in the country on the south side of town about the same distance from school as she did.

2

Maggie had left school ahead of me, but I determinedly headed out, walking in her direction and caught up with her near the edge of town. I called to her and she said, "Hey, what are you doing heading this way?"

"I came to talk to you."

"Oh, I guess you want to talk about the note I wrote you."

"Yeah."

"What do you want to know about it?"

"I was surprised, for one thing, and I wondered if you were just trying to tease me or what. Do you really mean what you said on that note?

"Yeah, I mean it!"

"So you're not going to the prom with me?"

"No! That's what I told you on the note, isn't it?"

"Yeah. I guess I had trouble believing it."

"Why?"

"I don't know. I guess because we had all these plans that we'd made together. You'd seemed excited that I asked Uncle Cephus if I could drive his Cadillac and take you to the prom in style. I'll hate telling him I won't be using his car after all."

Uncle Cephus is the only uncle I have on my father's side, and he is so very good to me. When my daddy was dying, Uncle Cephus told him that he would see after me and my brother and sister. He seemed to take pleasure in being able to lend me his fine car.

"You can get somebody else, Randy!" Maggie countered, with a touch of exasperation in her voice. "There's plenty of girls who would love to ride in style to the prom with Randall Carter. I'm sorry, but this boy, this man that I've met has sort of swept me off my feet. He's twenty-three years old. He lives in Sugar Cane Point, and he is a nice guy. He's not bad look-ing, and his family has a new car, not a Cadillac, but it's a new car. I like the guy . . . I think I'm in love with him, and he re-turns my affection. You know, Randy, we're good friends and have been good friends forever, but this is serious. He and I, well, we're talking about getting married."

"Married! When?"

"Well, sometime in June. He asked me, and I said I want to be a June Bride. So, that's how it is."

"Well, I thought you were planning to go to college like I

am planning to go to college. That's the way we talked about it. Everybody assumed because we were the same age, in the same class, were going to graduate at the same time and had been together for so long, that we would get married and have a family. I guess I went along with the idea."

"Well, like I said, Randy, its nice to have a friend like you, but I've never had feelings like this before. I've got to go with someone I love. I don't think I'm going to go to college. I plan to just graduate and get married. I like the guy—I love the guy. I don't want to miss my chance. You can go to the prom with somebody else, but I don't want to risk losing the one I hope to spend my life with."

"OK, but this seems to be awfully sudden."

"Well, there are lots of cases of love at first sight. I don't want to be the reason for you staying home from the prom. You get somebody else to go with you. You can still drive your uncle's Cadillac. There are lots of pretty girls. I know Pastor Ike at our church thinks you are such a nice young man. There are many nice girls who go to his church. As well as he thinks of you, I know he would just love to pick out someone to go with you. You've got nothing to be ashamed of."

"You mean you think Pastor Ike has to pick out somebody for me?"

"Well, you know. You teach the little children and are secretary of your class. Randall Carter is the boy in the church and the community. I already hear that, when Pastor Ike goes to the convention in June, he's going to take you with him.

Like I said, he'll pick you out somebody."

"Why do you keep on about Pastor Ike? Why is he the one you think should choose someone for me?"

"Just because. He thinks you're going to be a preacher. I've heard him say it. 'One of these days, Randall Carter is going to be a preacher.' You study the Bible and are so involved in church business. Randall, I have no desire of ever being a preacher's wife. That's just not for me. I could not see myself sitting in church up on a front pew with a baby in my lap and one sitting on the side sucking on a bottle, sitting up there every Sunday in a long white dress down to my ankles, touching me nowhere except on my shoulders. That's not me. I want to have fun. So let Pastor Ike pick somebody else for you."

4

"Listen, Maggie! Your mother has told me more than once, 'Boy, you keep on coming to see my daughter because one of these days, I'm telling you now, I'm looking forward to you being my son-in-law.'"

"Look, Randy! My mama cannot pick for me, not even to go to the prom. I pick who I want."

"Why not? You are saying Pastor Ike can pick somebody for me."

"Well, that's different! Because, Randy, you see, you are still a teenager." You are still just eighteen years old."

"Well, so are you. You're eighteen; you're a teenager."

"That's different, too. An eighteen-year-old girl is grown, an eighteen-year-old boy is not."

"How do you figure that?"

"Girls mature faster than boys. It even say so in books. You've got a few more years of maturing before you're ready to get married. This other man is twenty-three years old. He knows how to be a man and treat a wife and all that kind of stuff. He is what I want. I'm going to let him take me to the prom. If mama doesn't like it, she's going have to live with it. If papa doesn't like it, I don't care. I am choosing what I want for my life. And, Randy, if you don't like it, that's just how it is. If you think you are going to change my mind by walking up here to talk to me, you are mistaken. You are wasting your time because my mind is made up. Now you're the first person I told. Nobody else knows yet. I told you so you'll have time to get somebody to go to the prom with you. You need to go ahead and accept what I've said and go on home now. I'll see you at school tomorrow."

"OK, I guess that's the way it is," I said, and I turned around and told her goodbye. Then I walked dejectedly all the way back to town

I stopped back at my friend's house where I had left my things. I left my school books there, but I took my dictionary, which was precious to me, tucked my other personal things inside it, and headed hurriedly for home. I still had chores to do.

When I was about three quarters of a mile from my house, I caught up with two girls who were walking home. I knew them and spoke to them, "Hi, Doris. Hi, Clara." They spoke to me too, and then I hurried on past them.

"Why are you running?" Doris called out from behind me.

"I'm in a hurry. I'm late, and I've got chores to do. I'm used to moving fast. I run track at school, you know."

"Aren't you tired?"

"No, I'm OK."

"Wait," Doris called out. "Won't you stay with us till we get to your house. Mr. Monroe's dogs always come out and scare us. We've been hoping someone would come along and give us a ride before we got there, but nobody has. We would really appreciate your company."

Incidently, Doris and Clara were white girls who were my neighbors. They went to a different school than I did. They were cousins and both lived within two city blocks from my house.

"That's not much farther. I guess I can."

"Thank you. We are really uneasy about going on past that house." It was Doris who was doing all the talking.

"OK," I agreed. I don't think those dogs will bother you, but I will walk with you. You all usually ride the bus, don't you?"

"Yes, but something went wrong with it when it was time to leave school. It's a nice day, and we thought we might get home sooner if we walked. What's that you've got in your hand?"

"Oh, It is some things I got out of my locker, things I don't like to leave at school over the weekend. It's my dictionary and some other things."

"What's that big piece of paper in your dictionary?"

"It's spelling words I studied. A friend and I participated together in the scholastic league spelling contest."

"How did you come out in the contest?"

"Oh, we won first place in the county. We lost by a few points in the district league."

"Can I see it?" Doris asked.

I gave her the paper and she scanned it. "Oh, yes," she remarked, "We had this same contest in our school. I didn't participate though. My, there are three pages of words here. I see you have some of them marked."

"Yes, those are the one that were difficult for me. I marked them to remind me to study those extra hard."

6

"Let's see if you can still spell them," Doris went on. "The first one here is *impeached*. Can you spell that?"

"I-m-p-e-a-c-h-e-d," I spit the letters back confidently.

"That's right!"

Then she looked at her cousin and said, "Clara, what does impeached mean?"

Clara hesitated and then said, "Well, I think it means when somebody has an office, a political office of some kind, and he does something against the rules he is supposed to follow in that office, then he might be impeached or put out of that office before his time was up."

"That sounds right," Doris declared. "Now, this next word is *extent*, e-x-t-e-n-t. Is that right, Randy?"

"That's right."

"What does that mean?" Doris went on.

Clara thought for a minute and then said, "Well, the next house we come to will be Randy's. When we get there, that will be the extent of his walk with us. Then, when we get to each of our houses, that will be the extent of the distance between his house and ours."

"OK!" Doris exclaimed. "You are good, Miss schoolmarm! Now the next word is *demeanor*. What does that mean?"

"I'm not sure. I've heard the word but never looked it up," Clara said thoughtfully. "I guess it means that, if somebody has a bad attitude, like they're mean and contrary and hard to get along with, and then somebody talks to them and convinces them to get a better attitude, that would be a change of demeanor."

"No," Doris countered. "I don't think that is a good enough answer. What do you say, Randy?"

"Well, I think that's close. I might not be able to do better than Clara, but, hey, I've got a dictionary. I'll just look it up."

"Well, how about you? That's just what we need," Doris said approvingly.

So I opened my dictionary and turned the pages till I found it. "Here it is," I announced.

"Let me see it."

So I held the book on one side, and she held it on the other, and we kept walking along while she read. "So Clara," she declared. "You were not wrong. It is about attitude and how you come across."

As we continued on, I noticed that we passed Mr. Monroe whose house was quite a ways farther up the hill just across from mine. His son, Jackie Ray, was my best friend. Any other day, Jackie Ray and I would have been walking home together. Mr. Monroe was out in his field plowing his corn field and had stopped to fix something on his plow. "Good afternoon, Mr. Monroe," I called and waved to him.

He spoke and waved back to me, and then Doris and Clara called to him too and said, "Good evening."

He called back to them, "Good evening Miss Doris. Good evening Miss Clara." Then we walked on. We had gone about sixty yards when Mr. Monroe called to me. "Can you come back here for a minute, Randy. I need some help with my tractor here. Will you help me?"

"Yes sir, I'll help you."

"I'll be much obliged to you."

I said, "Yes, sir." Of course I would help him. He was my neighbor and a dear friend of my family.

I looked at the girls and said, "I don't think I'll be long."

"We'll wait for you," they called out together.

"You all go ahead," Mr. Monroe called back to them. It's going to take a little while."

"We were afraid of your dogs," Doris said loudly. "We wanted Randy to stay with us till we passed your dogs."

"They won't bother you. My wife is right up there in the yard with them. She won't let them bother you. They don't do anything but bark anyway. You all go ahead. It's going to take a little while here."

"OK," Doris answered. "Randy, I will take your things home and give them to your mama."

"OK. I know you will take care of them," I said as I turned back to Mr. Monroe.

He had two wrenches, and he handed me one. "Hold onto this bolt and let me try to loosen this washer," he told me. The washer was tight, but, with me holding on, he was able to get it lose with one turn.

"Randy, he confessed, "I really could have done this myself. I had another reason for keeping you here. I wanted to talk to you without those girls here."

"Yes, sir?"

"Boy, don't you know you've got no business walking with those white girls in the broad daylight, walking like that, shoulder to shoulder? Some white man might come along and see you like that and jump all over you and choke you. No telling what they might do! You just don't do that kind of thing!"

"I didn't mean any harm. I was just on my way home, and they asked me to walk with them."

"Don't let me see you doing anything like that again. There's a whole lot of boys in the South, not only in Texas but other states too, that had to leave their homes, move away, because they were too friendly with white girls. Why, some of them are in their graves! You hear me! You don't do those kinds of things, not in east Texas!

"You must mind what I say because I don't want you to get in trouble. I promised your father when he was so sick, the night the doctor had told him he couldn't live, when he was so worried about how you and your sister and brother and your mama would manage without him, that I would help look after you and your family. He was just like a brother to me, your father. He was such a good man.

I made him a promise and I'm just trying to keep it now. That's all I'm trying to do. You're eighteen, aren't you?"

"Yes sir, I'm eighteen."

"And those girls are probably about seventeen. Son, I've been eighteen, and I understand that you might not think about these things. I'm not saying there is anything between you and those girls, but the Bible says that we should shun even the appearance of evil, and that's why I'm going to tell you this. You might not mean anything more than friendship with them, but it might appear to people that you do. Now tell me this. Why were they not riding the bus?"

"They said there was something wrong with the bus and they didn't want to wait for it to get fixed. It was a nice day, and they just decided to walk home."

"Why are you so late coming home? You should have gotten home when Jackie Ray did. He said you didn't show up when it was time to leave school."

"I had an errand to do while I was in town. That's why I'm late."

"I don't want you to think I'm nosy. I hope you understand what I'm trying to tell you. You need to do what you need to do because, you see, the school bus may be broke tomorrow evening. It could be late again. Do you understand what I'm saying?"

"Yes sir, I understand."

"All right, I'm just trying to help you. I just needed to tell you all these things. I'm trying to help your mama, too. I know those girls are your neighbors, and I know their parents, but you need to be more careful of appearances. Go on home now, and do your work. I don't want you to think Mr. Monroe is fussing at you. Like I said, I'm trying to help you because I care about you."

"I know, Mr. Monroe. Thank you. I really appreciate your interest in me."

"You're welcome. I think a lot of you, Randy."

"Yes, sir. I think a lot of you, too. I will head on home now. I have lots to do and not much time before dark."

I hurried on home and changed into my old clothes that I wore to do chores. It was spring and the days were getting longer. I had to get the cows in and milk them. Mama would get the milk and take care of it then, strain it and cool it. I had to chop fire wood. We didn't need the wood in the fireplace today, but I had to get some into the wood box out on the porch. We would probably have a cold spell again and the wood would be ready for another day.

When I got through with my chores, I went back in the house. My brother, Bobby, and my sister, Rose, had done their chores and were studying their lessons in the living room. I went on to my room without disturbing them, pulled my shoes off and lay down across my bed thinking about the day's events. I was still so disappointed and frustrated about Maggie breaking our date for the prom. I was already feeling embarrassed thinking how people would talk. Word would soon get out that somebody took away Randy's girl. She would show up at the prom with that other guy, and I would be known as a fool.

Then on top of that, it felt strange that Mr. Monroe jumped all over me about walking with Doris and Clara. I never thought about anyone thinking anything about me walking with my neighbors. My sister, Rose, and Doris and Clara were good friends, and Mama and their families were neighborly. Why should me being a boy make being friendly with them different. I felt rotten. It had been a bad day for me!

When Mama called me to supper, I said, "Mama, I don't feel like supper tonight."

"What's the matter? You must be sick; you always eat supper. Do you want some aspirin or something?"

"No, I'll be all right, Mama. You all just go ahead and eat. I guess I'm just tired or something. I had to walk a lot to talk to someone after school, and I just now got through with my chores. Just let me rest, and I'll eat something later on."

She went back to the kitchen, but after a while, I heard someone knock on the door. Someone opened it, and I heard Rose say, "Hello Doris. Mama, look who is here."

I heard Mama walk out there and speak to Doris. "What have you got there?" Mama asked her.

"My mama had a new recipe. I brought you some cake she made, a devil's food cake. She wanted you to try it. She said to tell you that it's not as good as your cake."

"Oh, now, Mrs. Smith makes fine cakes. I know it will be good."

"She sent four pieces, enough for all of you to have a piece."

"That is so thoughtful of her. I did not have time to fix anything sweet for supper. That will be our dessert. You tell her how much I appreciate it. I know it will be good. Tell her to save me that recipe, too."

"I'll do it. I have Randy's books, too. The school bus was being repaired this afternoon, so Clara and I walked home. He walked part way home with us because we were afraid of Mr. Monroe's dogs. Then Mr. Monroe kept him at his place to get him to help fix his tractor. Anyway, here are the books and things. We didn't see anybody to give the books to when we

11

came by, so I just kept them till when I knew you all would be home."

I heard my mama say, "OK, honey, I'll just put them right here on the sideboard."

"Where is Randy?"

"He's lying down. He said he didn't feel well."

"He seemed OK this afternoon. I hope he's not sick."

"He said he was just tired. I tried to get him to eat, but he said he would try to eat something later."

"I sure hope he hasn't got the flu. Some people in my school have been out with it."

Then Rose spoke up, a little quieter than the others were speaking, but I could still hear her. "I think I know what's wrong with him."

"You do?" Mama sounded real surprised.

"Now I don't want you to fuss at me, Mama. You always say it's not nice to listen in on our party line, but when I got home from school this afternoon, I picked up the phone to call my friend to ask something about our homework, and the first thing I heard was somebody saying Randy's name. Please understand that I just couldn't put the phone down then. Randy is my brother. Then I heard them say he had a fight today."

"A fight!" Mama and Doris exclaimed together.

"Well, they said he walked part of the way home with Maggie, and they were talking loud and not paying attention to anything going on around them. Somebody overheard Maggie tell him he would have to get somebody else to go to the prom with him because she was going with another guy and they had a big argument about it, and that Randy finally turned around and walked back toward town like he was mad."

"Oh, that's bound to have made him feel bad," Doris said, looking pained herself. "I don't know Maggie, but I don't think I would like her. The prom is such an important event in our lives, it seems unkind to break the date just two weeks away from it."

"Sure does," Mama agreed sounding sad.

"Most everybody will already have a date," Doris said. "But Randy has so much going for him. He is smart and nice looking and dresses so neatly. I'll bet any girl who doesn't have a date would love to go with him If I was a colored girl, I would like to go with him. He is such a gentleman and so considerate."

My brother, Bobby, got into the conversation at this point. "But you're not colored, and he's not white either!"

"Hush Bobby, "Mama admonished him.

"Well, it's the truth." Bobby tried to argue.

"Shut up," Mama raised her voice sternly. "She said if."

"I guess I'd better go on home for supper," Doris said. "You tell Randy I hope he gets to feeling better. I remember a song I've heard called 'More Pretty Girls than One.' Remind him of the truth in that."

"Thank you, Doris," Mama said appreciatively. "Tell your mama I thank her too and come back to see us soon."

"I will. I'll see you all soon."

I stayed in my room. The word was out. The old party line is working, and no telling who else knows.

Later Mama came to my door. "Randy, do you still feel bad?

"I'm all right, Mama."

"I still think you should try to eat something. Mrs. Smith sent us some really nice cake. Come on down and I'll warm you up some supper. It'll make you feel better."

So I went down and ate, but I didn't bring up anything about my situation, and she didn't ask. I just ate and went back to bed. Before I went to sleep I decided that I wouldn't try to go to the prom. I'd just tell Uncle that I didn't need the car. I didn't want to be embarrassed. I didn't want to see Maggie and that other guy. I'd just think about graduation. That is all that was really important.

The next morning I was up early as usual. Things were stirring in our house because Bobby and Rose and I all had to be ready to leave for school; after all, it was a two and a half mile walk to school.

I was out of the house ahead of Bobby and Rose, and across the street to Jackie Ray's house. Jackie Ray and I always walked to school together. He was a junior in high school, and was less than a year younger than me. We had been neighbors since we were babies. We were always together at school functions and when at home, when we weren't busy with our chores, we went off to hunt and fish together.

He was ready to go when I got there. "Let's go, man!" I urged as soon as he came to the door. "We'll get there a little early." So off we went.

Jackie Ray kept looking at me. "What you looking at me like that for?"

"Are you OK?" he asked me.

"Sure, I'm OK. Why did you ask?"

"You just look different for some reason."

"When I looked in the mirror a few minutes ago, I looked the same as usual to me."

"Well, I'll tell you the truth. My brother, it was Sam, my oldest brother, told me he was trying to use the phone yesterday, and, when he picked it up, somebody was on the line talking about you. Sam listened in and heard that you and Maggie had a fight and that she said she was going to the prom with some other guy. I didn't see you when it was time to go home from school yesterday. Somebody said you had taken off without talking to anybody and gone by your friend's house and then left there and walked in the opposite direction from home. That fit with what Sam said he heard on the party line because Maggie lives that way.

"Sam talked to me and said, as your friend, I should bring it up and see if I could help you feel better about it. He knew you would be upset."

"Man, I can't believe the word got all over town overnight! Well, it wasn't really a fight, and I'm not mad, but I'll admit I'm surprised and disappointed. I'm OK about it, but it has ruined how I looked forward to the prom, and I've decided I'm not going."

"Why?"

"I just don't feel like it, and I don't want to feel like everyone is looking at me and feeling sorry for me."

"I think you ought to ask somebody else and go on and hold your head up like nothing happened. There are lots of girls you could ask.

"For instance . . ."

"Actually, I've already been thinking about that. I know someone I would like to see you go with."

"Who?"

"You know my cousin, Minnie. She lives five or six miles away and goes to another school. She's visited us, been with my family around town. You've probably even seen her. She's pretty and smart and so nice. She is a high school junior, like me.

"I may remember seeing her with your family at church, but I don't think we were introduced."

"Last time she was here, she told me she had a boyfriend, but that he was joining the army and would be away. I think she said they might even get engaged, but I'll bet she would love to have a reason to dress up and go out somewhere different. Her parents never go anywhere except to church, and they pretty much expect her to do the same. I bet anything I could persuade her to go with you and her parents to let her.. I'm not just saying this because she is my cousin, but she is really good looking. She'll make an impression that will make you proud to have her for your date."

"I'm listening." It occurred to me for the first time that taking a good looking stranger who would really be noticed might make me feel less embarrassed about being dumped.

"If I suggest it, I think she might really go with you. Hey, we could double date and go together. You wouldn't have to worry about your uncle's car. We could all go in our car."

"I've never met her or spoken to her."

"You just leave it to me. I'm pretty sure I can make it happen."

"You let me think about it, and I'll let you know."

"How much time do you think it will take you?"

"Just give me until this afternoon. I'll tell you when we get out of school."

"That's a deal." he said smiling.

I really did think about it. The thing I thought most about was the tuxedo I already had. It was hanging in my closet, and it had been a gift. My aunt, my mother's sister, who taught in a black college in Austin, and her husband who worked for one of the college fraternities, had bought it for me as soon as they got my graduation invitation. They had often sent clothes to us, really nice clothes, that some of those rich fraternity boys had left behind when they left for the summer. I had gotten

15

most of them because they were usually my size. That was the main reason my friends thought I was so well dressed. The Austin aunt and uncle had no children of their own, and they had always doted on my brother and sister and me. They had always given us special gifts, things they knew would be important to us that my mother might not be able to afford. They had really outdone themselves with this tuxedo. It was no hand-me-down; it was brand new and had all the accessories, even a new pair of shiny black shoes.

My mother was so proud of that tuxedo, and I was, too. Mama was really looking forward to seeing me wear it. If it hung in my closet untouched, I would feel like I was letting everybody down.

I decided to make the effort to find a proper date, so on our way home from school I told Jackie Ray to see if his cousin would consider going with me.

"Do you want to just stop at my house and we'll call her today?" he asked me.

"No, that's long distance. You come on over to my house, and we'll call her from there."

So, later that evening, Jackie Ray walked over to my house and we placed the call. His cousin was the one who answered the call. "I've got someone who wants to talk to you." he announced. She questioned him about that, and he went on to tell her about me and that I was his good friend and neighbor. "His name is Randall Carter. We call him Randy, and he is graduating this year. I think you may have seen him sometime when you were visiting us. You know about the Carter family, our neighbors up the street. It's their son."

Jackie Ray took the phone from his ear and turned to me. "She'll talk to you. She remembers seeing you," he said as he handed me the phone.

I took a deep breath and took it from him. "How are you doing?" I asked, sounding as casual as I could.

"Just fine. How are you doing?"

"I don't want to impose on you, but I need to ask you something."

"What is it?"

"The senior prom is coming up right away, and you know I graduate this year. I really don't have anyone to escort to the

16

prom. I haven't asked anybody. Jackie Ray told me about you, and I remember seeing you. You're a very attractive girl. I just wondered if I could have the pleasure of having you as my guest at the prom. We could go with Jackie Ray and his friend."

"When is it?" she asked. I told her the time and date. "I thank you for asking me. I couldn't say yes right now. I will have to ask my parents. I don't know if Jackie Ray has told you, but there is someone I have a special relationship with, and I want to be loyal to him. He is away in basic training, and my life has been pretty dull lately. If you want me to go knowing those facts, I would like to go. It sounds especially fun that we would go with Jackie Ray and his friend. I think my parents will be more willing for me to go if they know that. I am really honored that you asked, but like I say, I will have to ask my parents."

"Would you please do that?"

"Oh yes, I certainly will."

"Can I call you back then."

"Sure, wait until about eight o'clock. I'll know something then."

"Thank you. I'll be calling you."

Well, that had been easier than I had expected. When I called her at the appointed time, I felt more comfortable about picking up the phone than I had taking it from Jackie Ray. Once again, I felt quite at ease talking with her. "My parents have given me permission to go with you and Jackie Ray and his friend," she announced. "They expect you to come inside to meet them and speak with them before we go though. They are pretty strict and old fashioned."

"Oh, I can appreciate that. I will be glad to speak with them."

So it was settled. I almost forgot the disgrace I had felt about Maggie's rejection.

I called Uncle Cephus, and he was very gracious and understanding that I was going with Jackie Ray in his car rather than in the Cadillac. The days flew by with much excitement about all the upcoming events.

On the day of the prom, Jackie Ray and I got haircuts. I also had a little mustache. My haircut and mustache trim was a graduation gift from my brother, Bobby. Mama and Rose got my clothes down and made sure there was not a wrinkle or piece of lint on them. Rose wanted me to have some cologne. She said that was going to be my present from her.

I was overwhelmed with all the attention. "Please," I protested weakly, "that's enough." I was really pleased though, and glad they seemed to be so excited.

About the time I got dressed the telephone rang. It was Jackie Ray. He said, "Hey, man, you ready?"

"Just about."

"I'll be there in ten minutes."

Mama made me look at myself in the mirror, and Rose put some of the cologne on me. Then we walked out on the porch to wait for Jackie Ray. Doris was waiting on the porch with a camera.

"Oh my, you're dressed up, Randy! You look so nice. I came to take your picture."

"I think they are going to have someone taking pictures at the prom."

"Well I want one for a souvenir, and I'll get one made for you, too. You need to have one made at your house. Stand down here in front of the house where there is light from the porch."

So I obliged her, and she backed away from me and aimed. "Now wait a minute, your tie is not quite straight. Let me fix that." She put the camera strap over her shoulder and walked toward me. She fiddled with my tie and backed away again. Now that's perfect. Say cheese," she ordered, and I did. The flash went off, and she motioned for me to stay still and took another one.

By that time, Jackie Ray had backed out of his drive and pulled into mine.

As I walked to the car, I noticed that Mr. Monroe and his wife were sitting on their front porch watching from across the street. Another man I knew was sitting on the porch talking to them. There was a horse tied to the fence post, and I gathered the man had come there on horseback. They had seen Doris over there taking my picture. I knew that man, and I sure was hoping he wasn't making something out of it. He was just like that, prone to drawing the wrong conclusions and telling them to everybody. He could be vicious.

I was concerned, but there wasn't anything I could do about it. I got in the car with Jackie Ray. We drove off and Doris and Mama and Rose all waved at us telling us to have a good time.

We picked up Jackie Ray's friend, and then went on to his cousin's house which was some distance away. We got out of the car and went to the door and knocked. Minnie came to the door and Jackie Ray introduced us. She was as pretty as he had said, and her dress was beautiful. She had on sparkling earrings and even a tiara. She brought her parents in and introduced them. Mr. Brady said he knew my father. "It's very nice of you to invite our daughter to your prom," he said kindly. "We are very careful about who she goes out with whether it is girls or boys. Knowing your family and that you are a friend of Jackie Ray makes us feel safe in letting her go with you. But understand that we expect you to respect her, and we always insist that she come home with the same ones she left with. We always want her to be home before midnight."

"Yes, sir. I will certainly respect her and will keep those conditions you have made. Jackie Ray will see that we do that too. I promise. You know, Jackie Ray suggested that I invite her. I thank you and Mrs. Brady for allowing her to go with me."

"You all go on, and have a good time, and be careful," he said with a smile that looked like he was satisfied with our conversation.

As we walked to the car, her mother called out to her, "Don't forget what I told you."

"I won't," she called back.

We went on to the reception. It was very nice, and I felt quite proud that Minnie looked so attractive. Friends came up and exclaimed over us. "Oh, Randy! How are you? Who is the lady?" I enjoyed introducing her. She was very poised, and her manners were perfect.

I did run into Maggie and her date, Charles Brown. I spoke to her and we briefly introduced our dates, but that was all. I never once asked her to dance.

19

The evening passed so fast. The whole event was beautiful. Minnie was a good dancer, and she seemed to really enjoy herself. The room was like a dream world with flickering lights and crepe paper streamers and balloons. The disc jockey played all our favorite music. There was punch and a long table spread with all kinds of finger food.

We watched the time and left a little before it was over. Jackie Ray had to get his date home, too. I walked Minnie to her door and told her, "You made my day. Thank you so much for being my guest. I really appreciate it and I had such a good time. I hope I can call you again sometime."

"That would be fine. I enjoyed myself very much. It was so nice of you to ask me, and it would be nice to talk to you again."

"It will be my pleasure. Good night."

Back home I had just carefully laid my new clothes on the bed to get them straight before I put them up, and the telephone rang. It was Doris. "Well, how was it?" she wanted to know."

"Oh, it was very nice."

"I'm so glad. You deserved it. I've been sitting here reading. You know, I'm always reading the *True Story* magazine before I go to sleep. I saw a light come on at your house and knew you must be home, and I just had to call and see how it went."

"We had a great time."

"Well, I'm glad. Goodness, you and Jackie Ray sure were dressed fit to kill with your formal jackets and black ties. I notice you folks sure do dress when you go out for a special occasion. You colored guys are sure more clothes conscious than the boys I go out with. You even dress better to go to school with your pants and shirts all starched and everything. It seems like our trend lately is to dress down and be more relaxed. I wonder why that is?"

"I don't know. I never thought much about it."

"Don't get me wrong. I admire you all for it. Now don't take offense at what I'm about to say. I think it might be because a lot of your people, after slavery, took service positions working for rich people. Then those people gave away their clothes all the time when they were still good, and you all got them and got in the habit of wearing fancy clothes like that. Now all of you take so much pride in looking good. I think that is great."

"I guess that could be the reason. I'll tell you right now, that prom really was a dressed up affair, and I'm not ashamed to say it. Oh, and how we danced!"

"Did you see your friend, Maggie?"

"Oh, yes, I saw her. She looked really nice, but I just spoke to her, and that's all."

"And the girl you were with?"

"Yes, she was lovely. I was really proud to have her for my date."

"That's great! You know, we may be different in some ways, and people want to put us on different sides of the fence, like white and colored are not supposed to socialize. But we're neighbors, and I think we ought to act like neighbors. I don't say things like that much. People don't understand me when I say things like that. They take it the wrong way."

"I'd better go," I said. "I think I hear somebody on the line!"

"OK, I'll talk to you later. Bye."

The next day was Saturday. I went out to get the cows in earlier than usual that afternoon since we would be busy getting ready for church in the evening. They were all as far down in the field as they could get at the edge of the fence. It was down about a city block from our house, I guess. Doris lived across the road near one of our gates. They had a big turkey pen under their house. They were raising turkeys to sell in the fall. Doris was out there feeding the turkeys. I spoke to her and walked on past to where the cows were looking over the fence.

They seemed to be watching two men over in the woods who had been hunting. The men were carrying guns, and one of them had a rabbit tied to his belt. I spoke to them, and after I counted the cows and saw they were all there and OK, I started moving them back toward the barn.

Doris called to me as I passed her house.

"Hey, don't you all have a phonograph and records that you play on it."

"Yeah, we do."

"Have you got the song, "Home on the Range"?

"I think so."

"Ours is missing for some reason. Do you think it would be all right if we exchanged some records for a while. I'd love to hear what you have that is different from ours. I'll bet you have some good blues."

"Yes, we do."

"Well, if you think it will be all right, tell Rose I will bring some of my records up there and exchange some with you all for a while. I've got some beautiful hymns that I'll bet your mama will like, and all of you will love "That Silver Haired Daddy of Mine.""

"OK, Rose and mama would probably like to listen to something different. I'll tell them. I've got to get on home now and get the milking done. See you later."

"Tell Rose I'll come right after supper."

"I will. She'll be glad to see you."

We did enjoy the records Doris brought. After supper that night we sat around in the living room and played them over and over and sang along. Mama said the hymns made her feel all prepared for church tomorrow. Some of the other records were some of the same ones we had danced to at the prom. I sat there feeling good, knowing I had done the right thing in going instead of staying home and feeling sorry for myself. I told my family about my night at the prom and how beautiful it had been.

CHAPTER 2

The Real Reason We Moved to Town

THE NEXT DAY we went to church. Mama didn't drive, and after Daddy died, we had sold our car. Bobby and I rode the horse, and Mama and Rose rode with some of the neighbors. Mama had gotten our dinner all ready on Saturday night. When we got home, she just got it out of the ice box and heated it up.

We were still eating dinner when someone knocked at the door. Bobby went to open it, and we heard him exclaiming, "Oh, Uncle Cephus! Come right on in."

"Cephus! You are just in time," Mama called to him jovially. "Let me fix you a plate."

"No thanks, Maybelle," Uncle Cephus told her. "I would love your dinner, but I already ate. Bessie and I just had dinner at a café in town. She didn't come, because she wanted to rest a while and do a few things. We have to go back to church at five-thirty, you know."

"Well, OK." Mama said easily. "Just have a glass of iced tea then."

"That I will do."

"Is anything wrong?" she asked.

"No, I just want to talk to you all."

"You want to talk now, or after we eat?"

"I'm in no hurry. There is plenty of time."

So we talked casually while we ate, but we were all curious about why Uncle Cephus had dropped in on us unexpectedly. After we ate, Mama got us all to go sit in the living room, telling Rose that the dishes could wait.

"I know I saw you at church," Uncle Cephus began. "But

23

I just barely had time to speak to you. I had to go on to a short finance meeting after church."

"I understand," Mama said expectantly. "Now, what's on your mind?"

"Well," he started hesitantly. "I came to talk to you about moving to town."

"I appreciate your interest, but what in the world has got you thinking about this now?"

"Well, as you know, before Joe died, I told him I would take care of you all, and I'm thinking that it is something you ought to do. I think it would be more convenient for you."

"It is kind of you to be concerned about us, Brother Joe." Mama sometimes called Uncle Cephus, Joe. His name was Josephus, and my daddy's name was Joe Nathan. She called both of them Joe. However, most people called my uncle Cephus. He was well known in town because he owned a funeral home.

"You know, Joe and I sacrificed a lot to have this house," Mama continued. "The old house was in bad condition, practically falling apart. We really worked to build this house, and it is quite comfortable. We are happy here."

"I understand that, Maybelle, I really do," Uncle Cephus went on. "Joe loved it here, and had a good life here. He suffered so much pain, and has gone on to where he is free of all that now. Your life goes on. Just think how much easier it would be for you and the children. You'd be closer to school and church and the grocery store. You wouldn't have to depend on your neighbors for anything."

"But think, Joe, I have my chickens and hogs; I have my garden, and there's the cows to think about. It would be so hard to give up all that."

"I know that, but listen to what I have in mind," Uncle Cephus went on soothingly.

"You know I have two rental houses. The people who lived in one of them moved out and went to Houston just recently. They had gotten behind about three payments on their rent. He had bought a car not long ago, because his wife was working in the next town. He offered to make a deal with me, to finish paying off the car and give it to me for his back rent. He and his wife didn't need the car in Houston because they both

24

got jobs near where they live. I accepted the deal because I wanted to help him.

"Now you know I don't need another car. Bessie and I both have cars, and a hearse with the business besides. I would give you and Randy the car, and you can live in the house rent free. I will even pay the utilities. I'll let Randy work for me at the funeral home evenings after school. When school is out for the summer it can be a steady job. He's smart; he can do some book work and wash the cars and things like that. He can take you back to the farm to see about your cows and chickens and all. You have a renter in that old house on your place. Let them move up to your house and take care of things for part of the rent. You really won't have to give up anything. You'll have everything you need in town, and you'll still own the farm. What do you think about this, Randy?"

"Right now, all I can think about is my daddy and how we were so close. We went hunting and fishing together all the time. He is so connected to this place for me."

"I know how you feel, but you've got to realize that he is gone now. You'll have the car. You can come back here whenever you want to and visit with your friends. You can leave your horse out here, and he'll be here for you to ride. I'd love to come out here and go hunting and fishing with you sometimes. Having you working for me will give me some extra time. Rose, what do you think?"

"I don't know. I'll do whatever Mama wants to do. I know the house. It is really nice, and I have a close friend who lives right next door there. We spend lots of time together at school. I could deal with moving just fine.

Uncle Cephus looked at Bobby. "And what do you think, young man?"

"I think it would be great. I'd like being near school. Do you think I could maybe make some money with a shoe shine stand when we get there?"

"I don't know why not." Uncle Cephus said smiling. "I'm giving Randy a job, but all of you can probably find things to do that will bring in some income."

Bobby frowned suddenly and looked up at Uncle Cephus. "Randy doesn't know how to drive, does he? How is he going to drive that car?"

"Yes I do," I chimed in. "I've been learning since I was fourteen. My friend Vernon Stewart has let me drive his car a lot of times. Nobody knew about it, not even his father, but he has picked me up and let me drive all over their farm. He has been a great friend to me, and I know how to drive pretty well."

"I'm sure glad to hear that." Uncle Cephus said approvingly. "Somehow I thought I might not have to teach you. I know several boys who have been driving their family cars for a while, and there is no place better than a farm to learn.

"See, Maybelle, everything is going to work out just that easy. Now I just hope you all will take me up on my offer. It is a great house, it has a carport, the streets are paved and there are sidewalks. It will be so much easier to get around to all the places you need to go. I think it will be especially good for the children to be closer to school."

"When are you thinking we would move?" Mama asked.

"How does Tuesday sound?"

"Tuesday! My land! I thought you were thinking about the end of the year."

"I just need somebody in the house. There are things there that need taking care of. There's a stove and refrigerator there. A house just needs somebody in it."

"I like my wood stove to cook on."

"There's a flue there and a fireplace. I've got somebody with a big truck that will come out here and move all your things. You can start packing your loose things, and I'll handle everything else. The house is clean and recently painted. The back yard is fenced. I just know you'll be happy there. Now, please, I just want to do right by my brother."

"Well," Mama said with a bit of a laugh. "I guess you've worn me down. It does sound like it might be the best thing."

"I'll tell you what, I have to go back to church tonight. Randy can go with me. The car is there at my place. I have the keys to it. He can drive it back here tonight, and tomorrow, when school is out, he can help you start bringing some things into town."

"Can I go, too?" Bobby asked.

"Yes, if it's OK with your uncle," Mama told him.

26

"OK, you boys come on. I need to get going," Uncle Cephus declared. "I'll see you tomorrow evening, Maybelle."

Bobby and I just couldn't believe it when we got to Uncle Cephus' house and he just took us inside and handed me the keys to the car. The ride home was a little wild, but there were hardly any cars on the road. That was before people had to have driver's licenses. Bobby sure didn't notice any driving mistakes I made. He was so thrilled with the car and our new prospects that he chattered all the way home.

The next two days passed like a whirlwind. Uncle Cephus was determined to get us moved, and by Tuesday night we were proud residents of Nelsonburg, Texas.

On Wednesday evening Uncle Cephus was showing me around his office and about some of the things he wanted me to do for him in my after-school hours. "I need to tell you something," he began on a serious note. "You're a good boy, you are respectful, and I am proud of you. You're about to graduate from school. You are smart and you don't mind working.

"I want you to know that I was aware of the rumor going around about you and that Smith girl, Doris, your neighbor. I didn't believe it because it just didn't sound like you. But I didn't ignore it either. It was hard to listen to people saying things about you that I knew weren't true, but they wanted to believe. Too many people try to make something out of a girl and boy just smiling and being friendly to one another. I had all the confidence in the world in you, but there are some people who had rather believe a lie than the truth. That is why lies spread so much faster than the truth, son.

"It was Mr. Cox who talked to me about it, and he wasn't gossiping and didn't believe it either. Just between him and me, he wanted me to be aware that there was a rumor going around that might be harmful to you. I was concerned and thought right then that the best thing I could do was get you out of that environment. I think you know that, too. That is why I was making such haste to get you moved to town. Those people out there can find something else to talk about.

"I felt uneasy about interrupting you and your family's living situation. If it had been up to your daddy, he would have gotten on his horse and gone around and told people to stop lying about his son. I just couldn't do that. I had to handle it my way. Do you understand?"

"I really do understand, Uncle Cephus, and I want you to know that there was nothing at all to that rumor. Doris has been Rose's friend for a long time, and Mama and Mrs. Smith are friends. Doris is just a kind, friendly girl who wants to be a good neighbor. She had no idea that being friendly with me looked any different to some people than being friendly with Rose."

"I know that. I'm not telling you not to be friendly with people. I want you to know something. Our family is respectable. We are responsible, and we own our property. That Smith family, they rent their property. Mr. Stewart owns it. There's nothing wrong with that; they're doing OK and they're good people. But there are some people, that no matter what your stand, what your aims are, how well you are doing, they are still going to label you that N word because that puts you below them. You hear me!"

"Yes, sir, I sure do."

"Don't ever let that keep you from going on with your life. I want you to aim high, and I am proud of you. I want you to always know that. I got you out of that situation to give you a better chance to do that."

"And I thank you, Uncle Cephus. I will not forget it. I hope I don't ever disappoint you since you have taken so much interest in me. I hope to measure up to your expectations."

"Good boy!"

"And I will finally say that all these rumors are just rumors. This is true. There was nothing to that thing with Doris and me but neighborly friendliness. But since people are saying these things, I will certainly be mindful and faithful to you for helping me take a step forward. We're going to settle in here and be happy and do well. I'm sure of it."

"Good boy! I believe it, and you're welcome. We'll talk again."

We really settled in and made the adjustment. Mama was, as usual, taking charge and making the best of things. She had her wood stove, and all the things that were dear to her. She was a wonderful seamstress and loved to sew. People in town discovered that and were always getting her to make this and that. Bobby invested in shoe polish and a shoe shine stand and was delighted with the business he got. Rose was happy having her friend, Peaches, next door. They were back and forth between both houses. We did go back to the farm often. Mama still planted a garden there and was always bringing greens and tomatoes and things back to people in town. The move was a good thing.

CHAPTER 3

The Stag Party Incident,
A Night to Remember

GRADUATION TIME WAS UPON US. As a matter of fact, it would be on Friday night and this happened on Thursday. The boys of our class had been saving some money so that, on this night before our graduation, we could have a stag party. There was this classmate we all called "Honey." His real name was Raphael. He was treasurer of our class, and he always had his own money, too. His mother worked for a very well-to-do white family in town, and his daddy worked on the railroad. He was their only child, and did he ever dress nice! And, yes, his pockets always jingled with money. He was nice looking, too, and he knew it.

I have to say this carefully. I don't want anyone to take it wrong. He had a little problem with me because of the clothes that I wore. Most of my classmates did not know that, as I have told you, my auntie and uncle at the college in Austin supplied most of my clothes. They sent most everything I could ever need, sport coats, trousers, shirts, shoes, even pajamas. Mama washed them or had them cleaned, and they were like new. I wore them proudly, appreciated them, but didn't talk about where they came from. That's why I was Honey's competition. People were always comparing us because we both dressed well.

Honey was the treasurer. He was going to buy all we needed for tonight's party. It was a responsibility he enjoyed very much.

I had some uneasy feelings about this party. You could say

I had cold feet. I had decided that I wasn't going. I said this to several of my friends. They worked on me though. Honey was one of the most vocal ones about it. "Come on," he urged. "This is the end! This is it! You can't miss one of the most important events of graduation. We're going to really have fun!"

My other friends echoed his words, refusing to let me act on my feelings. "Come on man. You are the star of our class. This is a once-in-a-lifetime event. You have got to come with us!"

I finally could not resist them. "Ok, I'll go."

Even Mama encouraged me to go, telling me that daddy would have wanted me to go and fussing about what I would wear.

"It's just a casual thing," I told her. "We're not even going to wear ties, just clothes like we would dress to go to school."

"OK, whatever you think. I just want you to have what you need."

"I do, Mama. It's all going to be fine."

So I picked out some clothes and prepared for the evening. It really was going to be sort of a big event. The president of our class, Ben Black, had a brother who lived in Houston, about thirty miles from Nelsonburg. I had not been to his home, but I had heard that it was quite a fine home. He had also graduated from our high school. He had moved to Houston, and between he and his wife, they had done very well. His wife was presently in California, and he was working a four to twelve shift in the evening. He said we could have the party at his house if we would respect the house and the neighborhood, and not cause any disturbance. It was a very quiet and distinguished neighborhood after all.

When I was about ready to leave, Mama came in my room. "I have something for you," she said smiling as she held out a box. "This is your graduation present. Open it."

I opened the box. Inside was a gold watch, a small gold pocket watch. "That's so beautiful, Mama."

"I've had it for some time. That was your father's. He bought it before he died. He wanted a good watch. When he was sick and we knew he wasn't going to live, he told me to save it and give it to you for your graduation. He wanted you to have something from him."

I took it out of the box and pressed the stem to open it. The face appeared. I snapped it back to close it. It had a beautiful design on the outside, and a gold chain. Almost at the end of the chain was something else in a smaller case, a compass. It was so unusual. Then there was a clasp to fasten to my belt loop.

I had a lump in my throat. "Mama!" I whispered. "This is so special. I am so proud."

"That's good. It would make your daddy so happy. I've saved it all this time, and now that your graduation is almost here, and you are going out for a festive evening, it seemed the perfect time to give it to you. You wind it and set it now. The hall clock has the time right."

I did what she said, tenderly, overcome with emotion. I felt as if my daddy was right there beside me.

"It's yours forever," she said. "To me, it is a precious family relic. Wear it with pride and dignity."

"I will, Mama, I promise I will always do that. I love you, and I love my father. I will treasure it as long as I am alive. Mama, thank you again. I will guard this watch with my life."

About that time we saw the headlights as the friends I was to ride to Houston with drove up. "Have a good time," Mama said to me as she gave me a hug.

"I will," I told her and I started out the door on my way to a big night in the city.

The sun was going down as we drove toward Houston. There were enough of us that we were going in two cars. My friends told me both cars were loaded with food and cold drinks, and that Honey had somehow managed to get us two pints of bootleg whisky. That news made me somewhat uneasy, but I kept quiet about it and decided I'd try to be a good sport. I could drink the cold drinks, or maybe even pretend to drink some whisky.

They kept on talking excitedly about what a singular occasion our graduation would be for us, and how we needed to celebrate as we never had before. They knew me pretty well, of course, and began trying to put me at ease about the liquor.

"We know you don't want to drink hard liquor," Honey began. "We're not going to get drunk. We're just going to have us some fun. We know you don't like beer either. We brought something special for you that you can drink. It'll be better than cold drinks."

"And what would that be?" I asked.

"It's called sloe gin. Have you ever heard of that?"

"No, I don't believe I have."

"It's a mild drink. I think you'll like it."

"Well, we'll see."

We were in Houston in no time and soon at the house where we were going to have this celebration. It really was a nice home in a first class neighborhood. It had a fenced back yard with a patio and bright outside lights. It felt homey and comfortable.

We carried in all our supplies, a big ice chest and food and drinks and all, and set them out on the patio. Honey was filling paper cups with ice and mixing drinks. He handed one to me. "Try this," he said smoothly. "See if you don't like it."

I did as he said. It wasn't bad. "That's OK. It tastes sweet."

"See, I told you you'd like it."

They had brought games. We played cards, dominos and checkers. Sometimes we were playing for money, and I even participated in that. Everyone was telling jokes. Some were rather ribald, I'll admit. I wouldn't have told them at Sunday School. I was feeling good though. I shook off all my tenseness, rattled the ice in my drink and joined in the merriment. I was having a good time.

A time or two I had some feelings that some of the boys were hitting the bottle a little hard, and that maybe we were getting too rowdy. I remarked that I was worried about the neighbors calling the cops, and things quieted down.

Soon after midnight, our president's brother came home. He sat down with us and drank a beer and asked lots of questions about some of his old friends who still lived in Nelsonburg.

We began to clean up after ourselves, making sure we were leaving the place as neat as we found it. Ben's brother seemed satisfied. We said our goodbyes to him.

I was feeling a little lightheaded. I had not known that the gin was going to affect me that way; it had not tasted strong at all. On my way to the car, I felt like I was walking on air. I did my best to act normal. I knew my friends would think it was funny if I was drunk. I was anxious to just get home and sleep it off. I relaxed when I got in the car. I felt I would be fine and soon home safe in bed until morning, when these strange feelings would be gone.

Our first stop was at Sugar Cane Point to let a couple of the boys out where they lived. Then we drove on toward town and were almost there. It must have been well after midnight when I heard someone say, "We've got a flat."

I felt dismayed. I was sitting in the back seat, and I knew I would have to get out because the tools to fix a flat were under the back seat. The other car that was following behind us pulled over. Someone from that car called out. "What's wrong."

"We've got a flat," I called back to them. I looked at my watch. It was almost one o'clock.

We began to pile out of the car. I was still feeling woozy, but I managed standing up OK. Three of us had been riding in the back seat. Honey was sitting in the middle, and he still sat there. He didn't want to get out.

Ben was the driver, and he called to Honey to get out. "All of my tools to fix this flat are under the seat," he told Honey. "You have to get out.

Honey's voice was slurred. "Aw, I'm tired," he growled. He didn't move.

"You've got to get out. My jack is under you. We have to get this car jacked up so we can get home," Ben told him.

"I'm not going to get out. Borrow somebody else's tools. I'm drunk. Just let me alone."

"Come on Honey," I coaxed. "I'll help you out." I reached into the car to get his arm.

"Take your damn hand off me!" He yelled.

"I'm not meaning to mess with you. I'm just trying to help you. I'm trying to help all of us. We need you to get out so we can fix this flat and get going or we are headed for trouble."

"I don't want your help. You ain't no help to nobody. You're just a looser. Your girlfriend, Maggie, I bet she is right now laying in someone else's arms like your old lady when she got you, you old mama's baby, papa's baby. How you like that? And everybody knows you're a damn Uncle Tom, white

34

on the inside. You like white folks better than us, and everybody knows it."

"Man, I don't appreciate what you are saying at all. Come out of that car!" I grabbed at both his hands and jerked him out of that car and knocked him away from me. He came right back at me.

"Cut that out!" Ben yelled at us. "Don't you know we can't disturb the peace around here. Look, you've got that boy's nose bleeding."

"I don't care if I do!" I yelled back. "I was just trying to be nice and help him out of the car, and he comes back with all that sass and talking about my mama. I don't appreciate it."

"Well hold on to your temper. He's not quite himself, you know, he's a little out of his head. You don't need to be hitting him." He grabbed me from behind and held my arms down so I couldn't go back after Honey, and somebody else got hold of Honey so he couldn't come after me.

"Let him go!" I demanded. "He needs his head knocked off."

"Take it easy; don't be such a hot head." Ben soothed. "Put Honey in the other car," he said to one of the other boys.

"Ok, I'll try to cool off, but this is one of those times I need to tell you what I think. You all took me out telling me what fun we were going to have. Well I don't appreciate this kind of fun. I think Honey tricked me into drinking more than I should have so he could make fun of me. I should never have come."

"I know, and I'm sorry for my part in it, and Honey will probably be sorry tomorrow, too. We'll keep him away from you for now. Just settle down a little and don't go crazy and do something you will be sorry for tomorrow."

"Well, you just think about this! Would you stand for someone to talk about your mama like that. And how does he know what Maggie is doing? That is none of his business. I don't care how drunk he is, he has no right to say such things."

"I know that, Randy. I'm just saying don't hit the boy. It's the drink talking. We need to just get this flat fixed and get everyone home."

"Well, as far as I'm concerned, you can fix it without me.

I'm out of here. I'll get myself home. I was trying to help and do the right thing, and everything turned ugly."

"Come on, Randy. You don't need to do this."

"Well, I am. You all can get the flat fixed without me. I just need to walk in this fresh air and get away from everybody."

So I took off, even though all but Honey were calling me to come back. The rage I felt just wouldn't leave me. I knew it was going to be a slow go because it was a dark night and I still felt a little woozy, but I figured the fresh air would help that.

I just kept putting one foot in front of the other, feeling myself up the road and on across the railroad tracks.

Instead of feeling better, I kept getting weaker in the knees, and boy, I really needed to lie down somewhere. But I managed to keep going. I was coming to some houses and was hearing dogs barking. I passed one house, and the next one didn't have a fence around it. There was a picnic table in the yard. Oh, man, if I could just get to that table and sit for a minute, I'd be ready to go on. I got there and laid down on top of that table. I could still hear the dogs barking.

Sadness came over me. I thought about Honey and my friends and thought, "Why did you do me like this? Oh, why did you do me like this?" I thought about Maggie too, and how badly she had treated me. I thought about paying them all back for all those wrongs they'd done me.

After I had been lying there like that a while, I felt my watch pressing against me, so I rolled on my side to get off it. I moaned a little because it was so hard to move. I heard a voice that sounded like it came out of a movie. "It's all right. It's all right."

Then I realized that someone was touching me. "Randy, is that you?" The voice said.

"Yeah, it's me. How did you find me?"

"What are you doing lying out here?"

"I don't know." I repeated over and over, still not knowing where or from whom the voice came from.

"Well, get up."

"I was trying and kept repeating, "How did you find me?" Somehow I thought this voice was trying to rescue me. It seemed like it was Maggie.

"Come on," the voice persisted. "I am going to take you into the house. Here, I'll help you."

She helped me up and steadied me with an arm around me. "I heard the dogs barking," she said. "I turned the lights on and looked out and saw you there. I didn't know what to think. I was afraid to look, but afraid not to. What in the world are you doing here?"

"I don't know. I just don't know," I said stupidly.

"Hey, you're squeezing me so tight," she said in an amused voice.

"Why can't I squeeze you tight?"

"Well, loosen up a little so I can get you in the door."

We got inside and she hooked the screen door back. "Now sit down here and relax," she told me.

"I don't need to relax," I declared. "I just need to have my way with you."

"Are you sure that's what you are in the mood for?"

"Yeah, I'm sure that's just what I'm in the mood for. You feel so good, and I want to just feel and forget everything else."

"But you are being so rough. Are you the Randy I know? You seem different."

"Yes, this is the Randy you know."

"Well, you said you wanted to have your way. I guess that is what we're doing."

"Oh, yes!" I sighed, and melted into her warmth.

Soon I lay on my back exhausted, and I guess I went to sleep. It was probably two or three hours later when I woke up. I realized I was not in my own bed. I was in a strange house. I felt around the edge of the bed until I touched a table and found a lamp to turn on. I felt confused. I saw my pants on a chair. I still had on my shirt and my socks.

I looked around some more. I saw another person in the bed. Shock ran through me. I realized I had been sleeping with an older woman who had a very shady reputation in our town, if you know what I mean. Her name was Lizzie Belle Bell, but I knew her as "Miss Tiny." This was not Maggie as I had thought last night.

"Miss Tiny" was a waitress I knew from a café called Dan and Dora's that I visited often with some of my school friends.

She was good to put up with us young folks, and had always been pleasant and accommodating to me. She teased me sometimes about being the quiet one in the bunch.

I was mortified when I recognized her. I thought I had to get out of there just as quick as could. I was putting on my shoes and she roused up. "Hi, lover," she said smiling up at me. "Are you feeling better?"

"Uh, yeah," I stuttered. "I've got to get going home."

"What's your hurry?"

"I just should have been home a long time ago," I said miserably. "Look, I am really sorry about this. I shouldn't have stayed here."

"You don't have to apologize to me," she declared. "You were a little rough, but you are an all right man. You were wonderful."

"I am sorry," I kept on. "I really apologize."

"No, don't apologize. That would spoil everything. Look, I took a little money out of your pocket, six dollars and some change. I was going to suggest that I take some and go get some eggs and things at the store so we could have breakfast together."

"No, no, no, I really have to get out of here."

"You don't want to stay and eat with me?"

"It's just that I should have been home long ago. People will worry about me. I really feel bad. I was confused when I came here, and I feel like I have mistreated you."

"You have done no such thing! I've seen you around town and thought you were a fine looking young fellow. I'd even thought about being with you like this. You don't owe me anything. Here, I don't even want to keep your money."

"Miss Tiny, you keep the money. Just please don't tell anybody about me being here. Please!"

She got out of bed on her side and walked over to me and put her arms around me. "You sure you don't want to stay with me?" she said, looking up at me with soulful eyes.

"No. I really can't," I told her quietly and firmly. "Please understand. My family might be missing me. I've just got to get out of here right now."

"I really would like to keep you here," she said smiling. "But if you can't stay, just hug me real tight like you did last

38

night, or this morning, that is, and kiss me. Then I'll let you go."

I just stood there.

"Is that too much to ask?"

"No," I said, finally doing as she asked. "Just please keep this to yourself, and I'll do the same. Goodnight."

"It's morning."

"I know, but it is still dark, and I need to get home before it is light."

I walked out the back door. A dog began barking just as it had done when I came here. I set out walking as fast as I could and finally got home. I walked around to where the car was parked. I kept a house key under the seat. I let myself in and went to the room Bobby and I shared. Thankfully, he was sound asleep. I didn't even turn on the light. I just undressed and crawled into bed.

Sleep did not come. I tossed and turned. It seemed forever until daybreak. I was thankful I didn't have to go to school. The seniors were out, but Rose and Bobby had to go.

Finally, I heard Mama down in the kitchen cooking breakfast, and soon she came up and called us to get up. I let Rose and Bobby go on down and took some time getting dressed and stayed quite a while in the bathroom trying to make myself appear normal. I splashed my face with cold water and used lots of mouthwash. I found a piece of chewing gum on the dresser and put that in my mouth. I didn't feel ready, but I went downstairs anyway.

"Well, good morning," Mama said cheerfully. "How are you?"

"I'm fine."

"How was the party?"

"Oh, it was nice."

"I woke up around one." You hadn't come in, and I was a little worried about you. I said, Lord take care of my child."

"Well, here I am. He took care of me."

"I sure am glad. Where's your watch?"

"Oh, I guess I left it in the pocket of my other pants," I kept my voice even, but inside I felt panic. I hadn't thought about my watch in a while. As soon as I could ease myself away and back upstairs I did. I looked in my other pocket, and sure enough, no watch. I tried to remember the last time I had seen it. It was when I was lying on that table in Lizzie Belle's yard. God in Heaven! Lizzie Belle had taken my money out of my pocket. She must have taken my watch. I felt sick at my stomach. Why would she do me like this?

My whole body felt tense. I must go see about my watch, but I sure didn't want anybody to see me going there in broad daylight. She was notorious. I had no idea whether she had a telephone. I doubted that she would. I moved quickly, calling to Mama that I needed get something in town, I was out the door before she could see me. "I'll be back soon," I called to her as I left.

I went to the drugstore and bought three newspapers. Then I drove out to where she lived. I got out of the car with my newspapers in my hand. My idea was, in case anyone came by, to pretend that I was going to sell her a newspaper. I knocked on the door. There was no response. I tried again. Finally I opened the screen and saw a padlock on the door.

I went around and looked in a window, then went to the back door. It was padlocked too. She must really be gone. I felt sick again. Where in the world could she be, and what was I going to do now. I must find that watch.

I went next door and knocked on the door. A man opened the door and looked at me. "Do you know where Miss Lizzie Belle has gone?" I asked him.

"She didn't say. She gave us the key and told us she was leaving town for a while. She is gone.

I went home and sat in the driveway and thought for a few minutes. I decided that I could drive to town and just see if I could see her anywhere. I went to the door and told Mama I was going to school to talk to one of my teachers.

I drove around for a while looking everywhere I could think of that she might have gone. I finally gave up and decided to go over to Uncle Cephus' place and wash his limousines.

I got to work and Uncle Cephus came out and greeted me, "Hi there, how are you?"

"Doing OK," I lied.

"How was your party last night?"

"It was just fine. I'm off school today, so I thought I'd come by and wash the cars."

"You didn't need to do that. It's your Graduation Day, and I know you must have been out late last night.

"Oh, I had to come into town anyway and check on something at school. I just had some time."

"OK. You know where the keys are, don't you?"

"Yes, sir."

"And you know where all the cleaning equipment is, I guess. You really don't have to do this today."

"I know."

"Well, I'll get on back in then. You go to it if that is what you want to do. Be my guest."

I got busy. I needed to work and get my mind off the watch until I could do something about it. I backed the limo and the cars out and got out the hose and all my cleaning equipment. It was about eleven o'clock, I guess. The sun was shining and things were really warming up. I began to feel hot and sweaty. My head began to hurt, and I felt funny in my stomach. I went in to get some cold water.

I got back outside, and began to feel even worse. I got in the limousine and just lay down on the seat. I had not been there long when Uncle Cephus came out and saw me like that. "What's wrong with you?" he asked, sounding alarmed.

"I just suddenly got a headache and feel bad in my stomach."

"Well, for goodness sake, get inside where it is cool and lie down on that cot in that back room."

I started to protest that I would be all right, but when I raised up, I had to hurry out of the car and throw up. When it was over, Uncle Cephus helped me inside and onto that cot. He ran to get me a cold wet cloth for my head. "What do you think is going on with you?" he asked.

"I guess I overdid it a little last night."

"I think you must have. What did you drink?"

"I didn't drink any whiskey."

"I hope not. Did you drink any beer?"

"No."

"Well, what did you drink?"

"I drank some peach brandy."

41

"Come on, you must have had something more than that."

"I did have something else. It wasn't hard liquor though, just something mild."

"What was it called?"

"Sloe Gin."

"Sloe Gin! How much did you drink?"

"Oh, I don't know. Just a few glasses. They had a half pint and mixed it with some fruit juice. I guess I drank most of the gin.

"Randy, sloe gin is a hard liquor, every bit as intoxicating as whiskey. That much would knock you for a loop. You must have been as drunk as a Bard Owl." Didn't you know you shouldn't drink it?"

"No, sir."

"Well, sounds like you have an awful lot to learn."

"I've sure learned one thing—not to drink any more of that stuff."

"We all have to live and learn. They say experience is the best teacher. Look, you just rest there until the sick feelings pass. A nap might take care of it. Tonight is a big night for you. You need to be in better shape in just a few hours. I'll take care of these cars. You relax a while."

"You are awfully kind to me, Uncle. I'll do my best to make it up to you.

I fell asleep quickly and woke up feeling much better. I stood up and smoothed my clothes. My head felt clear. Uncle Cephus must have heard me because he appeared at the door.

"How are you feeling?" he asked.

"So much better," I assured him.

"In that case you'd better get going. I'm sure you have lots to do before the big event."

"Yes, you're right about that."

"Before you go, I have something for you—a graduation gift. I'm very proud of you for reaching this milestone in your life. I know you have worked hard and been a good student." He reached into his inner coat pocket and handed me an envelope. It was a window envelope, and I could see it held a greenback.

I opened the envelope and there was a stiff, new fifty dollar bill. I was overwhelmed. In all my life I had never held a fifty dollar bill. "Oh, Uncle," I exclaimed. "You didn't have to do this!"

"I wanted to. Brother Ike is taking you to California. I know he is taking care of the trip, but I want you to have spending money. He shouldn't have to pay for your food, and I want you to be able to buy some things that will help you remember this special time of your life."

"I thank you so much. You have given me and my family so much already. I hope I can pay you back some day."

"Well, you don't have to pay this back. It is a gift from my heart. You are like a son to me.

"Thank you, Uncle.

"You can pay me back just by being a good boy and growing up to be a man with pride and ambition. Finish your education, and I will be so proud of you and more than paid in full for anything I've done for you.

"You go on home now and get all fixed up for tonight. I want to see you looking good when you walk across that stage tonight. I want to see you toss that tassel and look at your diploma."

"I'll do that, Uncle, and I thank you again. I'll see you tonight."

"I'll be there."

I headed home feeling on top of the world. As I pulled into the carport, I heard a horn honk. I looked back and saw it was my good friend, Vernon Stewart. I hurried toward him. "Get out and come on in, man," I said warmly. "It is so good to see you."

"I don't have time to stay but a minute," he said decidedly. "You come sit in the car with me. I have something for you."

I went around the car and got in beside him on the passenger side. "What are you talking about?" I asked him.

"It's a graduation present from Cindy and me. Reach over into the back seat and get it. I didn't wrap it."

I looked back there and saw a brand new two suiter. "Oh man!" I exclaimed. "That is something I really need. How did you know?"

"Everybody needs luggage. You are going to be a traveling man, going away to school and all. Look, it has a key so you can keep it locked. Congratulations on your graduation. You are going to graduate tonight, aren't you?"

"I'd be surprised if I didn't."

"I'm not sure if I'll get there, but I wanted you to know that Cindy and I are so proud of you. She would be here right now, you know, but it is nearly time for our baby to be born. She needed a little rest before we come to your graduation."

"Thank you. I love this luggage. You have been such a good friend to me. I so appreciate all you have done for me.

"You don't need to thank me. I'm the one who should be thanking you."

"I don't know what for."

"Well, I know, by the way, did I hear you are going to California after graduation?"

"Yes, my pastor is going on a mission out there, and he wants to take me with him. He thinks that I have the potential to be a preacher. He plans on working on that with me. I don't really know about that, but I do plan to go with him."

"When are you going?"

"A week from Sunday. We'll leave right after the morning service."

"That sounds great. California is a beautiful place. There's lots to see out there."

"I'll bet."

"What are your plans when you come back?"

Well, I plan on working for my uncle this summer and then going to school in the fall, but I'm really torn. Can I trust you with something?"

"Sure. Why not."

"I'm thinking seriously about not coming back from California."

"Where did that idea come from?"

"Vernon, you have been such a good friend. I know I can trust you with this. Understand I haven't talked to anyone else about this. It is something that has just occurred to me. I want to do better for myself. I don't want to depend on my Uncle. I did get a scholarship to a school, but it is not going to take care of all of my needs. I have some friends and some kinfolk out there. I think I just want to stay out there and go to work. I know if I work hard, I'll make some money."

"I thought you really wanted to go to college."

"I'm thinking that will come later. You know my mama is getting older. I need to help her and my younger brother and sister. I feel like I can stay out there a little while and send for them to come live with me. Mama's always done so much work in the garden, in the fields, cooking, cleaning and staying up and sewing all night. I know she's doing well enough here, but I feel like I have this duty to my family. I think my daddy would want me to take care of them. My brother and sister are still in school. They need to be in a place where they will get more advantages."

"What do you mean? We have good schools here."

"Look, I know I can say this to you. Please think about what I'm saying and try to understand. You may not even have realized how many differences there are between our schools and the schools for the white children here in this town. We get their old discarded books. There is hardly a clean place in them to write our names. The state supplies new books for them. That just doesn't seem fair, and surely you have noticed that the colored children walk to school no matter how far from it they live or what the weather is like, while the whites ride."

"But you are finishing. You won't be there any more."

"I know that, but my brother and sister are still there."

"But you live in town now and have a car."

"Yes, that's true. I don't want to sound bitter and complaining, but I want to be in a place where my children and their children will have things better. You know something, I had never been inside of a school bus until about two winters ago. It was a terribly cold day. Mama was going to keep us all at home, but my friend, Jackie Ray and I loved to go to school and would always brave the weather. I dressed warmly and went to his house like I always did, and he was ready, too. We probably made the walk to school in record time. About lunch time it started snowing. It just kept coming down. It was a real snow storm.

"People who could came and picked up their children. They went ahead and let us out early and Jackie Ray and I started home. Man, it was blowing cold, and the snow was getting deep enough that it was hard to walk. We had made it

45

about a mile. We were walking by Mr. Wilson's house, and he spotted us. He came out on his porch and called us. "Boys, you come in here and get out of that weather! It is too bad for you to be walking home. If nobody comes for you, you can spend the night. We'll make room for you. You don't need to be out in this."

I was thinking that Mama would be worried about us. I hesitated. "Well . . ."

"Well nothing. Just get on in here! It's dangerous to be out in that."

We obeyed and started toward his house, but, just then, a school bus approached. Mr. Wilson saw it coming and went out and waved it down.. The driver opened the door, and we could see there were only two boys on it.

Mr Wilson recognized the driver. "Mr. Watts," he said. "These boys here were walking home, and I don't like them being out in this terrible weather. I was going to keep them here, but their families will be worried about them, Your bus is almost empty and you are going by their homes. Will you please let them ride?"

"Uncle Wilson, I have no problem with it, but I have to do what they tell me to do, you know."

"I understand, but this is an unusual situation. Let them ride."

"All right, I will let them ride, Uncle. Just don't say anything about it."

"So we got on that bus. Like I say, that was the first and last time I was ever on a school bus. He took us home and let us out. "Don't say anything about this, boys," Mr. Watts said. "I don't want to get fired from my job. Somebody might object to me taking you on the bus. Jackie Ray and I both said we would keep it quiet and we thanked him.

"The next year our school rented a Greyhound Bus to take us to the state fair in Dallas. We were going to the fair on the day they, at that time, called Negro Day. I really couldn't understand why they ran the fair for three weeks, and there was only one day, that Monday, set aside just for Negroes to attend the fair. I wondered why we couldn't go on any day. The school took us on the Greyhound, though, and I really enjoyed it. There was a high school football game played early that day

46

and later a college game. We stayed all day, and I enjoyed it all. But the fact that it was Negro Day and that was the only day any of us could have gone to the state fair still bothered me."

"It doesn't seem right to me either, Randy," Vernon declared. "I guess it is something we have just inherited. It happened before we were born."

"But does it have to stay like that? You know, my grandfather bought three hundred acres of land. I don't know how he managed to do it. He and my grandma must have worked awfully hard to do that and then grubbed stumps and did everything themselves to make the land ready to farm. My daddy and my two uncles and my Aunt Ella in Baltimore inherited that land. My daddy and his younger brother have died. My uncle Cephus has done really well. He has added fifty acres to that land for more pasture. He's had that land divided up. He owns two rent houses in town and a mortuary. He pays his taxes every year. Mama pays her taxes every year, yet none of us can vote. The Smiths and the Whites, your sharecroppers, our white neighbors who live in houses you own, pay no taxes and get to vote. We have no say even about the local sheriff and judges and so on. It just isn't fair! Now please understand me when I say I want for myself and my family the same privileges that other people have."

"You have a point, Randy, and I have to say that I agree with you, but you need to know that there are so many people in California, both black and white, who are in worse shape than people right here in Texas. You think about all you have here in Texas. You have property, your house and farm. Don't think that California is the pot of gold at the end of the rainbow. You know there is no such thing as that."

"Yeah, I do know that."

"Sometimes you have to invest where you are, fella. Look at the people around you. Lots of your friends are going to school and becoming teachers."

"I know that, Vernon, but other than that and farming or maybe selling insurance, what else can colored people do here besides sweeping floors and washing windows and working on the railroad track and such as that."

47

"Think about that speech. I know you remember it, that one by Booker T. Washington."

"I sure do remember it, 'Cast Down Your Buckets Where You Are.' When I won the Scholastic League speech contest here and went down to Fairview to the finals, a girl from La Grange won using that speech. I couldn't forget that."

"That was a great speech. He encouraged people to stay where they are and work hard to make the changes they believe in."

"It sounds good, but I know people who think white people paid him to write that speech because they were losing all their farm workers to industry in the north. People just want to go where they can do better. Now, I don't know if Washington was paid to write that speech, but I'm just saying, there is another side to that argument."

"Well, it may be for somewhat selfish reasons, but I want you to stay right here in Texas. I think you can be a part of making this a better place. I believe in you. You've got a good head on your shoulders. You want to make something of yourself. I want to see it happen."

"Vernon, your friendship has meant so much to me. In my heart I want to do whatever you want me to do, but surely you understand what I'm trying to tell you. Do you remember that the first time I ever went to a movie, you were the one who took me? You bought my ticket and everything. Our tickets cost the same, but I had to go around and enter by the door in the alley and go upstairs where there were no cushions in the seats. You would have taken me to eat with you in a restaurant after the movie, but I couldn't go sit in a restaurant. You got us take outs, and we ate in the car.

"You know, there is a story about two black boys who were watching a train go by. One of them said, 'I wish I would be a white man when I grow up so I could drive a train like that.' The other one said 'I don't. I want to stay black and be able to drive it.' That is all we want, not to be just like you, but to have the same privilege."

"Randy, I believe change is going to come. Look how your grandfather and your uncle Cephus worked hard and changed things to make it better for your family. You and I and others who want change will have to work for it. It will happen."

"Yes, but when? What if I don't live to see it?"

"I believe you will. These things take time. Be a little patient. Because of your grandfather's work and your parents, you have graduated from high school. They didn't get to do that. You might be letting them down if you move away."

"It is hard to be patient. You have to admit that a dollar bill in my hand and one in your hand have different values. You can do more with yours than I can with mine."

"I can't deny that. You do have a point, but let me ask you something. Have you got another reason you want to leave Texas?"

"I'm telling you lots of good reasons."

"Yes, but I have a feeling there is something else. You are going to have opportunities either here or in California. Have you even thought about how your mother is going to feel about your plan. Do you think she is really going to like the idea of moving away to California. Your folks have a lot of land here. Think of those colored people up in Limestone County. They recently discovered oil on their land, and they are all rich now. They've put money into their schools and county projects. The whole county is thriving. Land is always valuable, and sometimes more than we know."

"First of all, I think I can convince Mama that it will be for the best, and as for that Limestone County deal, we certainly can't expect to get lucky like that. Truthfully, I guess there is something else that has influenced my decision, but it's a little hard to talk about. Please, this has to be in confidence."

"You know you can trust me."

"Do you know why Uncle Cephus moved us to town?"

"Well, I guessed it was so you could have better opportunities, and he has got you working for him."

"That is only part of it. There is another reason."

"What is it."

"This is hard to say, but there was a rumor going around on the party line that I was interested in Doris Smith. People made it sound like we were having an affair, but it was definitely not true. Uncle Cephus wanted to get me away from that situation. He moved us to town in a big hurry. We'd been neighbors with the Smiths for years, and my sister and Doris were always good friends. Our families were in and out of each others' houses, borrowing things and just being neighborly. People just had to make something out of that. I know you know how that is because you told me about Doris liking you. I had known she had a crush on you. I used to see her walking down to your house before you got married. Remember telling me that your father didn't like her coming around.

"Yes, I certainly remember that. I thought of her as just a kid. I didn't have a problem making myself scarce when she came around."

"Well, I never even thought she was chasing me. She was just eager to treat our family as equals. You know how she is, sort of intense about everything."

"That describes her well. I heard that rumor about you and Doris, but I never believed it. You have a girlfriend, don't you?"

"Well, I did. You probably remember meeting her a few years back before you were married. You were out with a date and came by the park where we were having a nineteenth of June freedom celebration. You saw me walking hand and hand with Maggie, and you stopped to shake my hand. I introduced you to her by her given name, Maggie."

"Yes, I remember. What about Maggie? Are you still going with her?"

"No, it didn't work out. She broke up with me just recently."

"The same thing happened to me with the girl I was with that night. Those high school romances don't usually work out. You'll find someone else like I did. I am very happily married to Cindy.

"But Randy, back to the thing about you and Doris. Like I said, I had heard that rumor. I didn't believe it about either you or Doris. I didn't think badly of her, even when she had that crush on me. That was just a childish thing. She and her family are good people and good neighbors. Our whole community is like that. We stick together and help each other.

"You may not have heard this story, but one day I was at the store. There were three young men I had never seen before outside playing dominos. They were looking down past our fence and I overheard them talking about how they'd like to go fishing in the river down there.

"I spoke to them and told them that we let people fish down there and that the gate was not locked. I cautioned them to be careful of the cows and not disturb them and to keep the gate shut. They thanked me and I went on.

"But later, Mr. Smith, Doris' father, came and told my father he had heard that those boys had been drinking and talked loud about how they were going to fish all night in our river and that they were going to find a black boy to take with them and were going to hold him captive and abuse him some way.

"As soon as Mr. Smith heard that, he came straight to my daddy. I was there and told daddy that I had spoken to them and told them that they could go through the gate to fish, but they hadn't said anything about a black boy to me.

"Daddy immediately got me to drive the car and had Mr. Smith come with us. We went straight back to that store, and the boys were still there playing dominos. My father and Mr. Smith walked right up there where they were and spoke to them. 'You see that young man sitting over there in that car?' my father asked them. He tells me he told you it would be all right for you to fish in the river inside our fence.'

"'Yes,' one of them agreed. 'He did tell us that.'

"'And so you may. I let people fish on my property as long as they respect it and don't trash it or bother my cows. I heard a rumor, however, that you talked about taking a black boy down there and doing something bad to him. I'm telling you anything like that better not happen. You'd better hear me, or you will be in big trouble. We will be watching you. You are welcome to go fishing, but you are not going to do any harm to anyone who lives in our part of Texas. We have never in my lifetime had any such lawlessness in this county. We are peaceable people. I don't think I have to worry about it, but if I have anything to do with it, we never will. My river is a place for my cattle to drink, not a place for crimes.' With that, he and Mr. Smith turned around and walked back to the car, and the fishing party was cancelled.

"You see what I am trying to tell you, Randy. There are good people here, both black and white. I think that story is a good example of how people around here think and how we care about each other. But I have to go now. I plan to see you tonight unless the baby decides to be born. Enjoy it. And by the way, if you get out to California and find out you don't like it there. Call me. I'll see you get back here. Daddy would hire you to work for him anytime."

"Thank you, Vernon, for the gift and for being my friend. Tell Cindy I love the suitcase."

"I will. She is your friend, too. Bye now."

I waved to him and went on into the house. Mama was there and saw me bringing in the luggage. "Oh my!" she exclaimed. Is that from Vernon?"

"Yes, we've been talking out in the driveway for a while."

"I saw you all out there. Vernon is such a wonderful young man. I am so proud you have such a special relationship with him."

"I am too, Mama. He is the best. I'd better get back here and get ready for tonight. It will be time to go before we know it."

"Don't forget your watch," Mama reminded me.

I'd been expecting her to ask about the watch, but my heart almost stopped when she did. I had been thinking about what I would say, and I knew I couldn't lie to her. "Mama, I hate to tell you this, but the night of the stag party, I drank some stuff I didn't know was so strong. I got sick and had to lie down. The watch was uncomfortable against me the way I was lying. I took it out of my pocket and laid it on the table there. I wasn't thinking and left it there. I know where it is, and I know I can get it back, but not before graduation. I am so sorry. It was important to both of us that I should have it today, but there is no way I can. I hope you can forgive me. I have let us both down."

"I do forgive you, but I am really disappointed. I'm thankful you know where it is. There is nothing we can do at this late time. There will be other important times you will be able to wear it. I'm counting on that. You need to hurry and get ready now."

Graduation was held in our church. It was the biggest black church in town, and it was packed with people. Mama and Rose and Bobby were there in their finest Sunday attire. Uncle Cephus and Aunt Bessie were sitting with them. One of their daughters had come all the way from Florida to be at my graduation. My Uncle and Auntie came from Austin. Mr. Smith was there with his family, and Vernon and Cindy had made it too. I was really proud to see them all out there just for me.

I scanned the audience looking for Lizzie Belle. I had thought she might come, but she wasn't anywhere in sight. I really wondered where she and my watch might be.

My music teacher had given me a solo to sing. She was a great teacher, so positive.

She had a way of getting the very best out of me. The words of the song really spoke to me as I started to sing them. I was feeling them in my heart. The song began like this: "I've done my work; I've sung my song; I've done some good: I've done some wrong. Still I shall go the way of the Lord." It made me think about my recent mistakes and how much I wanted to make up for them. I put my heart and soul into singing that song. When I finished the audience gave me a standing ovation. That made me feel so good.

It also made me wish my father could have been there. He had wanted so for me to have that watch to wear tonight, to have a part of him in my pocket as I walked across that stage and turned my tassel. That wasn't to be, and I felt so sorry about that.

There was a party for the seniors after graduation. I went for a little while, but my heart wasn't in it. I left and went home quite early to be with my family. I was full of memories and thoughts of living up to all that my family and friends expected of me. I felt strong determination to right all my recent mistakes.

The next day the first thing I did was go to a gift shop to buy a wedding present for Maggie and her fiancé. I planned to have Mama take it to them when she went to their wedding. I was planning to be away in California. I believed this would show Maggie my good will and a better attitude than I had when I last saw her.

Who should I run into while I was shopping? There was Honey, and I felt glad to see him. "Hey man," I greeted him jovially. "I didn't get to talk to you at graduation because we were sitting so far apart, and I left early from the party. I wanted to apologize to you for my behavior after the stag party. It was wrong of me to hit you. The sloe gin got to me, and I lost my head."

"You had a right to get angry," he said sheepishly. "I was trying to needle you."

"Well, you did a good job of that. It was talking about my mama that got me. You know you wouldn't have liked it if I had said something like that to you."

"You're right. I was acting like a fool, and I am really sorry. It is me who owes you the apology."

"Well, I'm sorry I lost my temper. Can we just shake it off and be friends again?"

"Sure. I was hoping you would think that way."

So we shook hands and all was well again between us, and I felt good about that. I felt this was progress in turning over a new leaf in my life.

The next thing I did was go to my job at the mortuary. I worked hard straightening things up in the office, getting familiar with the files, and making sure everything was in order. I wanted Uncle Cephus to see that I could do a good job for him and be very responsible.

My trip was a week away, but when I went home, I couldn't resist starting to pack some things in my new suitcase. Rose came into my room and observed what I was doing for a few minutes. "My land!" she exclaimed. "What in the world are you doing packing all that stuff. You are not going to be gone that long, and besides, you'll need some of that stuff before you go."

"Now you just leave him alone," Mama admonished her.

"But he is packing enough for two, and he'll have to take it all out before he goes."

"Let him enjoy himself. He is so looking forward to this trip. You just quit fussing about nothing. He is going to be all right. That boy is going to be just fine.

CHAPTER 4

Fate Interrupts the Plan

THE WEEK PASSED BY QUICKLY. I had stayed true to my plan of showing Uncle Cephus what a good worker I could be. Everything had gone well, and I was so looking forward to my trip. When Saturday came, I had everything in order to leave the next day.

Before bedtime, I noticed my head was hurting and I wasn't feeling well. I chalked it up to the excitement about tomorrow and the extra energy I had been putting into getting ready. I went on to bed early thinking that would take care of anything I might be coming down with.

I woke up about four the next morning feeling worse. I got up and went to the bathroom. It was painful to urinate.

I got back in bed, but slept fitfully. I awoke at dawn and had to urinate again. It was painful as before and the urine looked cloudy. I felt feverish.

This was not something I wanted to talk to Mama about. I needed to talk to a man. Uncle Cephus would surely know what to do about this. I put on my clothes and drove over to Uncle Cephus' house. I rang the door bell twice even though I hated to wake him and Aunt Bessie.

It was Uncle Cephus who came to the door. He had his bathrobe and house shoes on. "Randy!" he exclaimed. "What are you doing up and out so early?"

"I felt badly about coming so early, but I have a problem I need some help with."

"Let's go in my office. We can talk there." Uncle seemed to understand that this was no small problem. "What is it?" he asked as we were sitting down. "Do you need some more money? It's OK if you do. Like I told you, I don't want you depending on the pastor for anything."

"No, that's not the problem. I'm not feeling well."

"Is that so? Now that I think about it, you don't look too well. What seems to be going on with you?"

"Well, I have been weak and feeling feverish since last night, and I have been urinating more than usual and it is painful. It looks cloudy, like there are some particles or something in it. I'm supposed to leave here in a few hours. I was hoping you could tell me something to take to make me feel more able to go."

"Son, you have an infection. At your age, when you have been healthy all along, I tend to suspect you could have something like gonorrhea. Have you had sexual relations with anyone lately?"

"Well, yes."

"I'm afraid that is your problem. We'll have to do something about that. Aspirin will take your fever down and make you feel a little better, but you have to see a doctor."

"What doctor can I see?"

"You can't get in to a doctor today. It's Sunday. You'll have to go tomorrow."

"But what about my trip to California."

"I'm afraid you'll have to forget that. If you go to California, you are just going to feel worse. This has to be seen about. I'll take you tomorrow to a doctor friend of mine whose practice is in Houston."

"I was going to help Pastor Foster drive."

"I have to put my foot down. You just can't go. The doctor might even want to put you in isolation with what you have got. You could be contagious. Reverend Foster can get along all right without you. I know it is a disappointment, but you just can't go. Now I have to ask you, have you had sexual contact with more than one girl?"

"No, sir."

"We will have to get in touch with her. She may not have the disease, but she could be a carrier. She has to know that, and she might have to be isolated too. The health department is strict about these things. This disease can be dangerous if left untreated, and it can't be allowed to spread. We'll just have to call Pastor Foster and tell him you can't go."

"I sure hate that, but I guess you are right."

"Have you told anybody else about your symptoms."

"No."

" Do you want to call Pastor Ike, or shall I?"

"I'd rather you did it," I said firmly and gave him the number to call. I really didn't want to have to tell Pastor Ike.

I was glad I had let Uncle do the calling. He was very diplomatic and let the pastor know that I was just sick enough not to be able to go but not seriously ill. He just told him we didn't know yet what was wrong, but that I had a fever and needed to see a doctor tomorrow. From the conversation it sounded like Pastor Ike was taking it well, but then he wanted to talk to me.

I told him pretty much what Uncle had, but I also told him how much I regretted not being able to make the trip. "I trust Uncle Cephus' judgment though and have to do what he thinks is best. You and he are the main men in my life since my father died," I told him affectionately.

"Yes, you need to do what your uncle suggests," he said. "There will be other church conventions. Next year it will be somewhere other than California, but wherever it is, you can be sure I will take you if you can go."

"Thank you Reverend. I probably won't see you in church. I guess I shouldn't come with a fever, but I surely wish you a good and safe trip."

"Thank you. You say a prayer for me, and I will say one for you, and I will see you when I get back."

When I hung up the phone, I turned to Uncle Cephus. "I'd better get on home. Mama will be getting up and be looking for me."

"Well, stay just a little longer. I still need to talk to you. Bessie would fix us breakfast."

"No, I'd better get on as soon as I can. Mama won't know what has happened to me."

"Well, look me straight in the eye and tell me one thing."

"Yes, sir."

"Now look me straight in the eye and tell me the truth."

"Yes, sir."

57

"Is this girl you had relations with someone I know?"

"Yes, you know her."

"Do you know where she is?"

"No, I don't. I've been trying to find her."

"When did you last see her?"

"It's been a week."

"Do you know where she lives?"

"Yes, sir, but she is not home. I've been checking."

"Well, it is important that we find her. What is her name? Was it Maggie?"

No, Maggie broke up with me, and we never had relations. It wasn't a girl."

"What do you mean? You haven't been messing with boys, have you."

"Oh, no. I mean it was a woman."

"A woman! You say I know her?"

"Yes, sir. You know her."

"Well, tell me her name."

I hesitated. I just couldn't get the name out. Uncle didn't let up. "Come on," he urged. "If I'm going to find her, I have to know her name. You said I know her."

"Her name is Lizzie Belle. You know, the one we call "Miss Tiny."

"Lizzie Belle Bell?! Don't tell me you've been bedding her. You know what people say about her. She's a prostitute for sure, and the rumor is that she has crossed the color line. What in the world were you thinking about? Where did this happen?"

"At her house."

"At her house? You went to her house? Boy, you are sure surprising me this morning. I never would have thought you would do anything like this. Why she is old enough to be your mama. I could understand it happening with Maggie or some young girl, but I always believed your standards were too high to do anything like going to bed with a prostitute. How much did it cost you? I know that is what she is about. She is about money."

"Six dollars."

"Well, six dollars sounds like a bargain these days. I don't know; I don't know! You are full of surprises today!"

"Uncle, I don't know what to say, but I have to try to explain. It wasn't like you think."

"Well how was it then?"

"To begin with, it was the night we had the stag party. I was high on that sloe gin. We had to get out and change a flat when we were almost home. My friends were about in the same shape as me, and I got in a fight with one of them. It was Honey. He was needling me about Maggie breaking up with me, and talking nasty about what she might be doing with someone else. The hurt Maggie caused me was strong on my mind. I was thinking about her, and I decided to leave them all and walk on home.

"I set out walking even though I was weak in the knees. I came to this yard that had a table near the front, and I just had to lie down. I probably went to sleep, and then all of a sudden, someone was out there with me waking me up and pulling me toward the house. In my stupor, I honestly thought it was Maggie. I remember telling her that I wanted to hurt her like she hurt me, and she told me to go ahead if that is what I wanted to do.

"I don't know how many hours it was before I woke up and realized I wasn't at home. I found my pants on a chair and my shoes by the bed. That's when I saw 'Miss Tiny' lying there in the bed. That was the first time I realized that I had slept with her.

"I knew I had to get out of there. I started dressing, and she woke up. She was all smiling and friendly. I started apologizing and telling her I didn't know what I was doing. She cut me off and told me I didn't have to apologize, that she'd always thought I was something special because I was always nice and polite to her. She even wanted me to have breakfast with her.

"She knew I just had six dollars. She had been through my pockets. She was going to take that just to buy food to make us breakfast. I told her I had to go home, but I insisted that she keep the money. I still felt like I had taken advantage of her in that I thought she was someone else, and I begged her not to tell anyone I had been there.

"And you know, Uncle, she insisted I give her a hug and a kiss before I left. She clung to me. She was trying to make me stay, and I got aroused again, but I was back to my senses. I knew I had to get out of there, and that is the truth."

"Well, that is quite a story," Uncle declared. "I have to believe it is true, and I do understand. I know you need to get on home so your mama won't be worried about where you went. Go on, and tomorrow I will take you to the doctor. Your mama will probably want to go, but I'll have some reason to keep her home. You go on, and I'll see you tomorrow about nine o'clock. Meanwhile I will look for Lizzie Belle."

"Another thing, Uncle Cephus, I think 'Miss Tiny' has Daddy's watch that Mama gave me for graduation. I wasn't used to wearing it, and I must have taken it off there. I treasured that watch. I've told Mama I know where it is and will get it back. I am so worried that I might not."

"All we can do is try. I know lots of people, and I will ask around. You go on home, and try not to worry so much."

Sure enough, Mama had been looking for me and was a little put out that I had gone off without telling her. I explained that I had to go talk to Uncle Cephus and didn't want to wake her. I told her I hadn't been feeling well and that Uncle had talked me out of going to California. She was surprised and got a worried look on her face. "What's wrong?" she asked.

"I've just got some fever and have been feeling weak. It is some kind of infection. We already called Pastor Ike and told him I won't be going with him. He is OK with that. Uncle is going to pick me up and take me to a doctor he knows in the city."

"I'll go with you," she said firmly.

"Uncle says he will talk to you about that. I don't feel so bad that I can't take you to church. Pastor Ike told me to stay home because I could have something contagious. I really don't feel like sitting in church anyway. You go on and get ready. I won't have any problem taking you."

I got her to church and came home, but I was restless and couldn't lie down. I had heard about an herb doctor in the Sugar Cane area. I thought he might be able to give me something that would make me feel better until I got to the medical doctor. Back then we called an herbalist a "two-headed doctor."

I wanted to look respectable and mature because I was going to have to ask directions of someone. I didn't know exactly where to find this doctor, and I didn't really remember what name I had heard him called. I thought I remembered that "Pepper" was part of his name.

Anyway, I dressed up in a new graduation shirt and a nice hat that we called a jitter-bug hat at that time. I put on sun glasses, and thought I looked presentable.

I drove to Sugar Cane Point and saw three men talking outside a café there. That seemed a likely place to ask directions. I stopped and got out of the car. I walked up to the men and politely asked if they knew of an herbalist in this area named Dr. Pepper-something.

"Oh, you are talking about Dr. Peppard," one man spoke up. "He lives near here, actually over in Post Oak."

"Can you direct me to find him?" I asked.

The man who had spoken up gave me detailed directions. Since I was a little familiar with the territory, I understood just where to go. I handed the man a dollar bill and he thanked me. That was a courtesy that was expected in that day and time.

On my way there I passed the Live Oak Chapel. There were cars there and horses and wagons. The morning services had begun. I felt drawn to go in. Maybe it would be easier to pray there where people would not be so familiar. Maybe in that situation, I could think less about my guilt and remember the Lord's promise of forgiveness. On the other hand, I did not want attract notice to myself by walking in late. Besides, I was on another mission.

Dr. Peppard's office was in back of a building that housed a tavern called The Oak Hideout. When I arrived there was only one car there, and Dr. Peppard's office was locked. I went back around to the front and found the proprietor of the tavern who was cleaning up from the night before. He told me that Dr. Peppard was out of town for the weekend and would not be in before Monday.

I was disappointed. There was nothing to do but get back in the car and go home. Passing the church again I once more felt the pull to go in, but I knew I was not appropriately dressed, and Mama would be looking for me to pick her up shortly. On the way back to Nelsonburg, I thought a lot about what my friends were going to think when they heard I hadn't gone to California after all.

The next day, Uncle Cephus arrived right on time. Mama was geared up to go with us, but Uncle Cephus handled her smoothly. He told her Aunt Bessie needed her to come help her choose some paint and material to redecorate the dining room. He promised her that he would take good care of me and ask the doctor all the right questions.

The receptionist recognized Uncle Cephus and called him by name. He introduced me to her and told her that I was the patient. She kept us with her to fill out a questionnaire about my medical history and had us sit to wait our turn. It was not long before she called us into the hall to a room where we waited for Dr. Johnson.

Dr. Johnson came in and went straight to my Uncle and shook his hand warmly. "It is so good to see you," he exclaimed. "And this is your nephew, Randall?"

"Yes, my brother's oldest son. My brother died a few years back, and Randall has become like my own son."

The doctor gave me a cup for a urine sample and then had me get undressed. He examined me carefully and thoughtfully. "Been sowing some wild oats, have you?" he asked in a way that was more kind than sarcastic. I nodded, hanging my head in embarrassment.

"Now, don't feel badly. You are certainly not alone in this situation, and you did exactly the right thing by telling your uncle and not letting this thing go. I think we can take care of this quickly with a shot and some pills. I can let you avoid isolation. I know your uncle, and I know he will hold you to following my directions. You must take all the pills according to directions, come back to see me in a week, and, until you do that and I pronounce you cured, avoid any kind of sexual contact. Can you do that? My reputation as a doctor could be ruined if you don't do exactly as I say."

"I most certainly can," I said emphatically.

"The other thing is that we must get in touch with anyone you have recently had sexual contact with. We can't allow this thing to get passed on to anyone else. Can you put me in touch with any or all of those contacts."

Uncle Cephus spoke up. "We have already tried to reach her. She seems to be out of town. All I can do is keep trying until I find her. I'll make it my responsibility to do so."

"I'll trust you to do that. It is possible that she does not have the disease but is a carrier. It is very important that we get in touch with her."

Dr. Johnson gave me the shot and prescription. He cautioned me to rest and avoid any strenuous activity. He said my symptoms should improve within a few days, and if they did not, I should come back at once. He stressed again the importance of avoiding sexual contact, and I told him that in no uncertain terms I would do as he said.

"I would really like to talk with your uncle for a few minutes. We haven't seen each other in a while. Would you wait in the outer office while we do that."

I did as he asked, relieved to be by myself to be quiet and think. I did wonder what they might be saying about me though.

We stopped at the drug store and, though I objected that I had money, Uncle Cephus insisted on paying for my medicine.

"You keep your money," he said. "You'll need it. You are going to have to stay away from work this week. I'm keeping you on the payroll, but you stay home and do what the doctor told you. I feel responsible for you. You have to realize the seriousness of this situation."

"I promise you, Uncle. I will be ever mindful of my responsibility in this thing. I won't let you down. I feel so thankful to you for your help and guidance. You don't have to worry for a minute that I would do anything foolish. Please, just trust me in this."

My symptoms improved quickly, and in a few days I felt like going into the office and doing some desk work. I even signed up for a business course Uncle Cephus wanted me to take in Houston that I would have to drive to on week nights. I felt like myself again.

Saturday afternoon came, and Uncle had a funeral in one of the nearby towns. I stayed a little later than usual in the afternoon to put the office in order and lock up for him.

I was anxious to get home because I knew there was a ball game going on up the street from our house. I was a member of the Nelsonburg team. I had joined it after we moved to town, and I usually played in all the games. We were playing

Sugar Cane Point, and they had a really good team. In general they were bigger than our boys.

Our team was the Nelsonburg Bumblebees, and their team was the Sugar Cane Cougars. We were very competitive, and this was a grudge match for us. As I walked home I saw there were lots of cars at the field. Both teams had plenty of supportive fans. I took the car home and walked to the field because it was close by, and I didn't want to have to look for a parking space.

We had a good playing field. A big league team had used it earlier to practice in the winter months, but they had a new place in another town and had left the field to us. There had been talk about putting a school building on it, but that had not yet materialized. For the time being, it was our ball field.

So I walked down our street until it dead-ended into another one. I walked on across that street onto some property that belonged to an elderly lady I had always called Aunt Molly. She was sitting out on her porch watching the ball game. I called out to her. "Hi there, Aunt Molly."

"Well, hello there, Randy. I'm sitting here watching this good game. I thought you would be playing."

"Well, I've been a little sick and haven't been given the go ahead to play again yet. I'm going to watch it though."

"Take care, and have a good day," she called back.

I walked on up her side of the street, and I noticed a car coming toward me. It was weaving and making a funny noise. I ignored it because one of my friends was close by in left field. I called to him and asked the score.

"They're one ahead of us," he said.

"Then some of the other boys noticed and began to call to me. "We need you, Randy. Hurry up."

I had no intention of playing any ball. I had my instructions from the doctor, and I had promised to do what he said. I was getting along great. My symptoms had almost disappeared.

Suddenly I noticed the car again. It was coming closer, then it swerved and was coming straight at me. I moved over into the ditch, but the car seemed determined to hit me. The more I moved away from the road, the more directly it came at me. There was a picket fence right there by the ditch that surrounded Aunt Molly's rose garden. It was not too high, so I leaped over it. Something on my clothes caught on a fence post as I was going over. There was a rip, and I fell forward on my face into a rose bush. The car jumped the ditch and crashed into the fence and came to a stop near me.

People came running from the game thinking the car had hit me. Someone was shouting, "Call an ambulance!"

I felt stunned. I could feel a cut or deep scratch on my leg where my pants were torn from getting caught on the post. People were gathering around me. I could hear some of my ball team friends asking for people to move aside so they could get to me. Someone was wanting to pick me up, and then someone else said not to move me because I might have a broken bone. I soon realized I wasn't hurt much and rolled over and reached for a hand to help pull me away from that rose bush.

I was scratched and bleeding, but it was mostly from the rose thorns. Someone asked if I was OK, and I said I was. I noticed the errant car was sitting still. It had stopped just after it broke the post I had caught my pants on.

Rose and her friend, Peaches, came running up and both were crying. Bobby was with them calling anxiously, "Brother, brother, are you all right? Shall I go get Mama?"

"I think I am fine," I assured him "Just stay here for now."

Someone was helping the driver out of her car. It was a tall, brown-skinned girl I had never seen before. Someone got out on the passenger side, and I realized it was my friend, Buster.

The girl came over to me. "Are you all right?" she asked in a frightened voice. "I am so very sorry."

"I think I'm all right." I could tell she had not intended to run me down. Buster came up then and looked me over with concern. "I'm so sorry, Randy. I'll be glad to take you to the doctor."

"I don't think that is necessary. I'm just scratched up."

"I know the car didn't hit you, but you fell pretty hard. Are you sure you're OK?"

"The rose bush broke my fall," I said, managing a laugh.

The girl continued to apologize. Buster said, "She was trying to watch the game and drive at the same time. I think she hit the accelerator when she meant to hit the brake. "Are you sure you don't want me to take you to the doctor."

"I'm sure. Like I said, it is just scratches and bruises, and I was scared out of my wits."

"I am so thankful," the girl said. "It was my fault. I was distracted and not paying attention."

Another lady walked up just then. "You'd better be glad he is not hurt," she said angrily. "If he were, you would sure be in trouble. Were you trying to run over him?"

"Oh, no, ma'am. I had no reason to do that. It was an accident. I've never seen this man in my life."

"Well, it sure looks strange to me. It looked like you were meaning to hit him."

"Honestly, I don't know him. I meant to put my foot on the brake and somehow missed it."

"Well, you'd better be telling the truth because this is my man."

"Believe me, I had no reason to do him harm."

I looked at this woman who had just claimed me. I was astonished. It was Lizzie Belle Bell. I had never heard her talk in this belligerent manner before. She didn't sound like herself.

Another woman who was standing beside her said, "Don't pay any attention to her. When she is drunk, she lays claim to every man around. That boy is not her man. Lizzie Belle, you'd better hush and go home."

"I can stay here and say what I want. This is a free world. Yes! I like that man, and I don't have to go home."

"Well, you are making a fool of yourself. That boy doesn't care anything about you!"

Someone said, "Take her out of here. She is crazy!" Then someone else did grab her hand and start pulling her away.

"Take your hands off me," she yelled, and jerked her hand away. "I said what I mean, and I'm not taking it back."

The first lady who had chided her turned to me and apologized. "I'm sorry, sir. She is not herself today."

"It's OK," I said. It didn't seem like a good time to ask Lizzie Belle about my watch. About that time Aunt Molly walked up. "Is he all right?" she asked nobody in particular.

I answered her myself. "I'm fine, Aunt Molly." By that

time, I was really sounding like I knew what I was talking about.

"He's one of my boys," Aunt Molly told the crowd around. He has helped me with my yard and gotten groceries for me. I have to watch after him."

About that time Mama came running up. She looked frightened. I ran over to her to assure her I was indeed alive and well. She needed more convincing. She wanted to find someone we knew who had a car here to drive me home.

Somebody said, "Mrs. Carter, it could have been a lot worse. He is lucky to be alive!"

"I know that and I'm thankful," she replied.

Buster was still standing there. "This car has some dents in it, but it will drive out of here fine. We'll take you all home in just a minute."

"I can walk," I insisted. "I'm just scratched up. I'm fine."

"Well, if you want to walk, I'll walk with you," Buster insisted.

"Maybelle," Aunt Molly, who used to be a nurse before she retired, spoke up. "I've got antiseptic and bandages right up here in my house. Bring him up here and get him cleaned up and treated before you go home."

"Aunt Molly, I'll get this fence fixed back as good as new for you," Buster said. "I'll come tomorrow and bring paint and everything to get it done right. I'm really sorry about all this."

"I'm sorry, too, but I'd rather this fence had gotten hurt than the boy. Nothing is harmed that can't be fixed."

Mama thanked Aunt Molly for the offer, but said it was only a short walk home, and we had all the supplies we needed there. Then Buster, Mama, Rose, Peaches, and Bobby all walked home with me.

"I'll check up on you tomorrow," Buster told me. "I'd still be glad to take you to the doctor and pay for it. It was my fault. I was helping her to drive, and I should have taken over when we got near that ball game and all those people."

"I'm fine, man. Thanks for being so concerned. I think a little soap and water and iodine will take care of me. I'll see you later."

I heard Rose out in the hall on the phone. She had called Pastor Ike, who was just back from California, to tell him about the accident before he heard it from someone else. She went into detail telling him about how frightening it was, but assured him I was OK and that he didn't need to come over.

After she hung up, the phone rang again. It was Uncle Cephus. He apparently had already heard the news. She let him talk to Mama. She told the story again, and added that she didn't know the girl who was driving the car, but that she was with Buster. Uncle Cephus knew Buster.

Soon after Mama hung up the phone, it rang again. I heard Rose answer. "Brother, it's for you," she called to me.

"Who is it?"

"Margaret, Maggie."

"Just a minute. Let me get my robe on."

I put on my robe, went into the hall, and took the phone from Rose and answered it.

"Are you OK, Randy?"

"Goodness, word travels fast. Yes, I didn't get hurt much. I'm OK."

"Are you sure?"

"Yes, I'm sure. I walked home from it."

"I heard you got your leg broke."

"No. The car came close to me. It didn't even hit me. I wouldn't be walking if my leg were broken."

"Well, did you leg get hurt?"

"Yes, just some scratches from Aunt Molly's rose bush."

"Well, who was the girl? I heard she ran you down."

"I'd never seen her in my life."

"Well, it sounds strange to me."

"I don't even know her name. She was with Buster."

"Didn't she and Lizzie Belle Bell have some words about you."

"Sort of."

"What do you mean 'sort of'? I heard that Lizzie Belle said you were her man and was bawling that girl out."

"Where did you hear all that mess?"

"I don't think it's mess. Didn't she say that?"

"Well, yes, but they said she was drunk, and that she always talks like that when she's drunk. I don't know why I need to be here having this conversation with you. Like I said, the girl driving the car was a stranger to me."

68

"You seemed so upset and carried on so when I broke up with you. I felt bad and embarrassed because of what our friends were thinking of me. Now it sounds to me like you've been messing around with a teenage girl and Miss Lizzie Belle Bell. I heard she is a prostitute, the most notorious woman in town. Everybody says so, and that she is as old as your Mama. All this time I've been putting myself down because I broke up with that 'nice' Randy Carter who cared so about me, and now I hear this. I am really surprised! I just can't believe I had all this confidence in you, and you have made me feel like such a fool."

"Look, Maggie, I'm sorry you are feeling like this, but you are going on gossip and you don't know the whole truth. I'm in the middle of cleaning up from this accident, and it is not a good time for me to talk to you."

"Well, I thought you might appreciate me having enough sympathy to check on you and ask if I can do anything to help you."

I do thank you, but I am getting all the help I need here at home. My injuries are small compared to what they might have been. I'm really OK."

"You're sure?"

"Yes, I'm sure, and I do appreciate you calling.

"I don't think you do!"

"Well, I do, and all I can say is I'll come out smelling like roses, and my feet will be in forget-me-nots. Goodbye." With that I hung up the phone.

I shook my head in disbelief as I went back to my room. I couldn't believe all the gossip and confusion over this incident.

In a few minutes the phone rang again. I heard Rose answer and exclaim, "Nanna Ella! Oh my goodness."

That was our aunt in Baltimore, my father's and Uncle Cephus' sister. I couldn't imagine that she would have already heard the news there. But sure enough she had, and soon Mama was talking to her telling her the real story.

I heard Mama gasp, "You heard he got killed! You know I would have called you before now if he had. No, Heavens no, you don't need to come down here! It was at a ball game, and the car came close enough that, from a distance, it looked like it hit him, but it didn't. He is just scratched up from falling on a rose bush. He is fine.

I'll let you talk to him."

"Here I go again," I thought as Rose called me to the phone.

"Honey, I thought you'd been killed," Aunt Ella declared.

I assured her I was OK and told her to say hello to Uncle Tony for me. I thanked her and told her I loved her. I was getting accustomed to the anxious calls. I wondered who would be next.

It was Vernon Stewart, as always my friend and mentor. He was so relieved when I told him I was not badly hurt. He expressed regret that I had missed my trip to California and hoped his wish that I stay in Nelsonburg hadn't caused me bad luck. I assured him that such a friend as he could never cause me trouble.

After talking with Vernon, I went back to my room and my thoughts turned to Lizzie Belle. I sure did need to talk to her. I had never seen her in the kind of condition she was in tonight. I had never heard her curse or be loud and aggressive like that. If I could just see her I would apologize again to her and ask her about my watch. Surely she had it or knew something about it.

I was thinking that I would get up early in the morning, before anyone was up, and go to her house and see her. On this night things were too up in the air. Nobody was going to let me out of their sight. I couldn't believe how the news had traveled even in our little town and how things had gotten twisted out of reason. There was nothing I could do about it tonight. Mama fixed me a late supper, and I went on to bed.

I didn't sleep well, and easily got up at dawn. I dressed and left the house, walking down all the alleys that led me to Lizzie Belle's house. I knocked at the back door, but no one came. When I went to the front door, I found the screen unhooked, but the padlock was still there. She must not be home. I went back to the house, and no one knew that I had been gone.

A few days later, Buster and another man came to fix Aunt Molly's fence. The man was Mr. Levy, Buster's employer. Buster's family lived and worked on Mr. Levy's farm as sharecroppers. They had brought all the supplies they needed to do the repairs.

Before they got started, Buster came to see me. He brought me some barbequed ribs. He told me the girl who had been driving his car that night was named Sylvia. Her mother had fixed the ribs for me. She just wanted to do something nice for me because of the accident. I offered to help him fix the fence, but he said he had plenty of help.

He explained to me that Sylvia and her mother, Mrs. Malvo, had recently come to live on the same farm where he lived, and they too worked for Mr. Levy. They had come from Louisiana, and were just looking for a new life. They had stopped in town to eat and just happened to hear that Mr. Levy had recently lost his cook and housekeeper. One of the sharecroppers had died, and his wife, who had been Mr. Levy's helper in his house, moved away to be nearer her children. Mrs. Malvo had applied for the job, and Mr. Levy was happy to give her employment.

Sylvia and her mother were now Buster's neighbors, and, since Sylvia had just turned sixteen, Mrs. Malvo had asked Buster to teach her to drive.

"I should never have let her drive there while the ball game was going on," Buster said sheepishly. "I just wasn't thinking. She wasn't expecting the crowd either, and it got her distracted. Again, I'm so very sorry."

"I didn't come out so badly," I assured him. "I am practically healed. I have to tell you though, that accident brought me all kinds of trouble that had nothing to do with my injuries. Gossip had me dead from being run over, and then someone said I had a broken leg. Another person said I was driving and wrecked with another car. Those stories flew all over town, and my auntie in Boston even heard it before we could call her and tell her I wasn't hurt bad. Say, do you know Lizzie Belle?"

"Yes, I know her. She sure seemed to be showing out that night."

"Well, some people said she was drunk, but I had not known of her drinking or acting that way before."

"Well, no. I used to see her down at the Ninth St. Café sometimes. People who knew her down there called her 'Miss

Tiny.' I haven't seen her for a long time, but I never saw her act anything like that."

"You haven't seen her since then have you?"

"No, I haven't."

"I hope she didn't upset Sylvia."

"I don't think so. Sylvia hasn't said anything about it other than that she thought that lady must have been crazy. I've still been working at teaching her to drive, but I've been keeping her on the farm.

CHAPTER 5

Two Fishes and Five Hush Puppies

A WEEK OR SO LATER, Buster came to see me again one morning before I went to work.

"You're really looking good," Buster said. "Your scars are all cleared up."

"Oh, they were just scratches, superficial things. I'm fine, and you and Mr. Levy sure did a good job fixing Aunt Molly's fence. I know she is pleased."

"I'm glad of that. I've been meaning to come back to see you," Buster continued. "My wife and I planned to go to a movie and take Sylvia with us. We were going to ask you to go along, but we didn't get to go that night because of a rain storm. I came today though, because I wanted to ask you a favor."

"What is it? You know, if it's something I can do, I will."

"Well, you know, Sylvia's mother, Mrs. Malvo, has been so very nice to me. She is always fixing us stew and barbeque and all kinds of good food. She loves to cook, and she is a wonderful cook and a great person. She wants to go fishing. She is off on Saturdays, and she wants to go fishing in the river. Mr. Levy has a pond on the place, but she likes to fish in the river. I thought about some land your uncle, Mr. Carter, owns, and I wondered if he would mind if we went fishing there. Would you tell him about the situation and ask him if he would mind?"

"I don't think he would mind at all. He lets people go down there. He does keep the gate locked, and he wants that tended to and the place left just as it was. I'll be glad to ask him."

"If it is OK with him, will you go with us?"

"I will certainly ask him. Tomorrow is Saturday, and we don't have a lot to do on Saturday"

"I sure will appreciate it."

"When do you want to go?"

"We could probably go tomorrow, if you can get it worked out."

"I'll sure talk to him. Give me your phone number. I'll give you a call tonight and let you know what he says."

"That sounds great."

So that evening, before I left work I told Uncle Cephus about the lady and Buster wanting to go fishing on his place.

"Sure they can," he said. "When do they want to go?"

"How about tomorrow?"

"Are you going to go with them?"

"Well, he asked me to, but I wasn't sure whether you might have something you wanted me to do tomorrow."

"Oh, nothing at all. Are you feeling up to going fishing?"

"I think so."

"You know you have to cross the creek to get to the river. I have built a bridge over that creek, but the last hard rain washed out the tracks where you go down to the bridge. You won't be able to drive across it till I get it fixed. I'm planning to do it right away but not by tomorrow. You can park near it and walk across. When you get to the other side, it is only about a quarter of a mile to the river."

"That's great. I've walked lots farther than that to go fishing."

"You go then. That will be a good break for you. You have been working hard, and getting over an illness and an injury at that. Are you sure you are up to it?"

"Yes, I feel pretty good."

"You are due to go back to the doctor Monday, you know."

"Yes, I know. I've been doing what he told me and keeping all my promises to you. I feel sure I will get a good report."

"I'm glad to hear you say that. Fishing will probably be good for you. Look, I've got the keys to the gate right here. I'll give them to you right now. There are three keys on it. You know the one to the gate, and this one here is to my boat that is chained to a tree down there. This other key is to my little hide-away cabin down there."

"We won't be needing those. We're just going to fish on the bank for two or three hours."

"Well, they are all on the same ring. Just take all of them. I hope you all enjoy yourselves and catch some nice fish."

"I appreciate that.

I called Buster that night as I had promised. "I got the OK from my Uncle," I told him. I guess you all have some lines and poles to bring. Uncle gave me the day off, so I can go with you."

"That is so great! I can't thank you enough for arranging it."

"What time do you want to go?"

"Pretty early if it works for you. I'd like to be there by at least nine o'clock.

"That is good for me, too. I'll meet you at your place and we'll go from there. Tell me how to get there. I know about where it is, but I don't know your house."

Just come into the gate and through the cattle guard. It will be open. You know where the big house is, don't you."

"Yes, I know that house."

"You just come on past it and keep going straight. Our's will be the next house; it is white. You can't miss it."

So the next morning, I got Mama's fishing poles and a can full of earthworms. I even caught a few grasshoppers and put them in a jar. I found Buster's house easily. He and his wife Gertrude were ready to go when I got there. He had me to follow him to where the Malvos lived in a nice, well kept, small house. His wife went in. I stayed in the car and Buster got out and came to talk to me.

Sylvia came out on the porch and waved. "We're about ready," she called to us. "Mama will be out in just a minute."

We waved back and assured her we were not in a hurry. Buster kept thanking me for making the arrangements for the outing, and I kept telling him I was so glad he had suggested it and invited me along. There was not much I liked better than going fishing with friends.

Sylvia and Gertrude came out of the house. Sylvia was carrying a big basket. "Sylvia, why don't you ride with Randy," Buster suggested. "All these poles and things take up lots of room in the car."

Sylvia got in the car with me. "I'm sorry Mama is so slow," she apologized. "She has fixed so much for us to eat, and she keeps doing something more. We haven't got anything to drink though."

"We'll stop in town and get something," Buster volunteered. "You all have brought all this food. I'll pay for the drinks."

"You all were so kind to invite me to go along," I spoke up. "I should pay for the drinks."

"You don't have to do that," Buster hedged.

"I'm going to eat a lot of this food you all have brought. It is the least I can do."

"Well, if you insist."

"I do insist," I said firmly.

"Well, why don't you and Sylvia go on ahead and get the drinks. Gertrude and I will wait for Mrs. Malvo, and we will meet you at the gate to your Uncle's farm. That will save us some time."

I was agreeable to that, so I drove off with Sylvia and we stopped at the store. I got plenty of soda, and she suggested we get some cookies as she wasn't sure her mother had made any. We loaded the provisions in the car and drove on to Uncle Cephus' farm. I unlocked the gate and drove inside, and there we waited, and waited.

"What do you suppose is taking them so long?" I asked Sylvia. I was beginning to feel uncomfortable with the situation of sitting there with this girl I hardly knew.

"I told you she wasn't ready, and she is a slowpoke, like I said."

"Maybe I'd better turn around and check on them. Buster may have had car trouble."

"No way. He's got a good car. They'll be here in a few minutes. You have to understand my mother. You will learn about her. Everything has to be just so with her. Why don't we just walk on down to the river? Buster knows how to find this place. He'll see the truck here and come on down."

"I think we should wait. It is a walk to the river. We have to cross a bridge over a creek, and it is a ways from there. They might not find us."

"I just can't wait to get down there and go fishing. It is hot here in the car. I think we should just go on. They'll find us."

"It's a half mile past the bridge. I just don't feel good about leaving them to find us."

"Look, I know my mother. She is itching to go fishing. She will be here and they will find us. I have never been fishing in my life, not even in a pond. Let's get out of this hot car anyway, and let me walk around and explore."

I could agree to that. We crossed the bridge and explored around both sides of it. She asked me the names of trees and plants. Still there was no sign of Buster. Sylvia got bored quickly. She wanted to head on down the path. "Look," she said. "There's a nice sandy path going on down there. Let's go on. I'll carry the poles and on bag of drinks. You can carry the basket and the other bag."

I was uneasy, and she knew it, but she kept on after me until I gave in. "Let me walk down first and take part of the supplies. Doing it all at once is too much for the two of us. You wait here, and I'll come right back, and we'll take the rest of the stuff down together." I hoped by the time I got back, Buster and his crew would have arrived.

Sylvia was still alone when I got back, so there was nothing to do but walk down to the river, and that is what we did. Uncle Cephus had made the place like a park. There was a nice bench to set our things on down there.

I walked with Sylvia down to the water, carrying the poles and my bait jar. She grabbed a pole and threw the line right in. "Wait, you have got to have some bait," I told her. "A line with just a hook won't catch anything but an old shoe or a root or something."

She pulled the line back up and let me bait it. Actually there were two hooks, and I baited both of them. I showed her about the cork, and told her if it began to bob and if she felt tension on the line, there would likely be a fish on it."

She threw her line out in the water, but it didn't go out far enough from shore. I had her to try again. Her next try satisfied me, and I showed her that she could stick her pole in the bank and just watch it. If the cork bobbed, then she could grab it and pull the line in. Fishing was too new to her for her to do it the easy way. She wanted to hold the pole. So I told her she was all set, and went to bait my hooks.

When my line was ready, I told her I would go far enough down stream that our lines would not get tangled, but that I would be close enough to hear her if she had any trouble. "Before I go downstream, I think I'll walk up the hill and see if I see any signs of the others," I told her.

I walked up and looked and listened. There was no sign of anyone. I had a bad feeling. I just felt like I shouldn't be alone with this girl. I was about to go down to tell her we had to go back and check on them. Just at that moment, I heard her calling, "Help! Oh, help!"

"I started running back. "What is it?" I called to her.

"I've got something on the line!" she shouted excitedly. "I can't seem to get it out."

I hurried down the hill and helped her pull out a large catfish. "You really got lucky!" I told her.

She was jumping for joy. "What are we going to do with him?" she asked.

"We're going to take him off the line."

"Will it hurt him?"

"Hurt him? Not that I can tell. You have to take the hook out of them." I got the fish loose and put it in Uncle Cephus' fish box that he kept out there and set it down into the river. It would let water in to keep the fish fresh and alive for now. There was a chain on it to pull it back up.

Sylvia was so excited, and ready to try again. I baited her hook and took off up the hill again to look for Buster. Still he wasn't there. Sylvia was yelling again that she had something on her line. Sure enough she did, a three or four pounder. "You must be having beginner's luck," I told her.

"I can hardly wait to show Mama and Buster and Gertrude."

I hadn't noticed until now that clouds had been gathering. The wind hadn't been blowing, in fact, it was very still and humid. As I was getting this fish off the hook and putting it in the box, I felt a few drops of rain.

"Look, Sylvia. We'd better go to the car. You may not know about the weather in Texas, but I do. Storms come up really fast here. It could set in and rain hard just any time now and make the river rise. Buster will know not to even come across the creek and down here now. We need to get out of here."

"Can't I catch just one more. The river can't come up that fast. It is only sprinkling."

"I don't think so. You have two already. Sometimes people fish all day and don't catch any. There'll be other times. My uncle doesn't mind us coming down here. We need to go."

"What about my fish."

"I'll get them. We won't leave the fish."

"Pretty please, can I try just one more time?'

"No!"

"You're mean!"

"I am not mean. I'm doing what is best for us both. The clouds are getting darker and darker. We are going up that hill and across the creek to the car."

"Are you fussing at me."

"No, I'm not fussing at you. If it doesn't rain, we will come back later. For now, though, pull that line out of the water."

"You are being so contrary."

"You are the one who is contrary. Now get that line out, and let's get moving. I mean it. We'll leave the poles down here, and I will take the basket. I'll let you get the soda water."

"What about my fish."

"I'm going to get the fish."

I found a forked stick, and lifted the fish out of the box with it. It took a few minutes to hook them together and tie some line to the hook so I could carry them. I had them in one hand and the basket in the other. By then it had started to rain, and there was a big thunder clap. "Grab that soda and come on," I yelled at her.

We started up the hill. Lightning flashed and the thunder boomed louder. The wind started to blow, and rain was falling faster.

"I left my hat down there!" she cried out, and started to turn back.

"It is too late to go back," I told her. "Here take my hat. It will help you see."

The rain got heavier. It seemed impossible to go on. Uncle Cephus' cabin was just ahead. We headed for it and got up on the porch where the rain couldn't hit us. I found the key and opened it up. "Get on in here, Sylvia."

I was so thankful Uncle Cephus had given me all the keys. I don't know what we would have done if we couldn't have gotten out of that storm. It was pitch dark inside, however. We couldn't see a thing. I knew where to find the fireplace and that there were first aid supplies and matches on the mantle. I felt my way to the fireplace and found the matches. I lit one and then another until I found the lantern. I got it lit. It made a decent light for us. I found a straight chair and told Sylvia to sit down.

"Whose house is this?" she wanted to know.

"It belongs to my Uncle Cephus. He calls it his hideaway. He comes down here when he wants to get away from the business and the phone and all. He comes down here to fish on holidays and sometimes brings his friends along. He has a barbeque pit out there. They bring food and lawn chairs and have picnics. Sometimes he and his wife come down and just spend the night. They have it well furnished. It is their home away from home.

"The reason it is so dark in here is because there are shutters that hook from the inside to keep out thieves, and there are screens under those to keep out insects. The shutters can be opened and the windows to let in light and air. He has spent quite a bit of money on it. It is an old house, built maybe as early as 1900. He bought it and fixed it up."

"It is nice, as well as I can see in this dark."

"The kitchen is great. You won't believe how well it is stocked. Anything you could want to cook with is right there. There are utensils, pots and pans, all kinds of canned goods, anything you can think of that you might need."

"That's really something."

"I think so, too. We're really quite safe here but as soon as the rain stops, we'll have to get out of here. It won't be fit for us to go back to the river today. I sure wish we knew what happened to Buster and his wife and your mama. That is a mystery I wish was solved. It looks like they would have let us know something after all this time. It's past dinner time, and we've heard nothing. Buster is a pretty dependable person.

I'm sure we will hear something soon. I still wish we had turned around and gone back."

"Well, I don't. I am so glad I caught those fish."

"I'm glad you did, too."

I opened the door back up to see what was going on outside. The wind had changed, but the rain was still coming down.

"I'm not going out in that," Sylvia said emphatically.

"I know. We'll stay here until it is not falling so hard."

"Are you cold?" I asked her."

"No, I'm OK."

I'm going to look in the closet and see what Uncle Cephus has got that we might need. I found another hat and a raincoat. "Look here!" I exclaimed. "Put this on and we'll make a run for it."

"I want my fish!"

"OK, I'll go find them." The fish were outside where I dropped them. I picked them up and went back to where she was waiting on the porch. I motioned for her to come on, and we headed up the hill toward the car. We had a big surprise when we got to the creek. It had risen until the bridge was covered with water. We couldn't even see where the bridge had been.

"Can you swim?" I asked Sylvia."

"Oh goodness no!" she replied.

"We really need to get across. I can swim really well. Maybe we can walk upstream and fine a narrower place to cross, and I can help you."

"No! No! I will not get in that water!"

I felt urgently that we must get to higher ground. Hoping someone would be nearby, I began to call for help. When no answer came, I called louder, but to no avail.

"Surely someone will come and look for us," I told her. "I could swim across, but I can't leave you here. Let's go back to the house and wait for a while. There is no point in staying out in this rain."

We walked back to the house, and again I unlocked it and lit the lamp. I tried making conversation to pass the time, but it was awkward. Sylvia and I hardly knew each other. The wind was now coming from the north, and the rain was still falling pretty heavily.

After some time had passed, perhaps as much as an hour and a half, I felt we needed to go back up to the creek and make some kind of effort to get out. Again, I put out the lamp, locked things up and urged Sylvia into the raincoat and up the hill. Again I called for help over and over again. When I was almost exhausted and about to give up we heard a voice. "I'm coming. I'm coming."

"Thank God!" I cried. "Here we are!"

"I'm coming," we heard again. Shortly someone appeared on the other side of the creek. It was Buster.

"Where have you been? We've been waiting for you for hours." I called to him with all my exasperation in my voice.

"We had some trouble," Buster called back."

"What kind of trouble?"

"Mrs. Malvo got real sick."

"Is she all right?"

"Well, it seemed like she was having a heart attack or something. We started to the city to take her to the hospital, but she took some kind of pill and got better and wouldn't let us take her on to the hospital. Coming back, all this big rain storm came up, and we had to stop several times because it rained so hard. I took her on home, but I was afraid to leave her right away. The storm knocked down trees and knocked out all the power. Then Gertrude was worn out with all of it, and I had to take her home. I got here as soon as I could."

"You've got to get us out of here."

"I don't know how. It is going to be dark before long. There is no way I can get a boat down here tonight.

"I need to be with my mama," Sylvia spoke up. "Are you sure she is all right?"

"She seems fine. She sure did scare us though. I'll check in on her before I go back home."

"We can't stay here. You have to get us out," I demanded. I couldn't believe he was just going to leave us.

"I just don't know what I can do right now. The house is down there. You can just spend the night there. I will get somebody to help me get you out first thing in the morning."

"It is just not right for Sylvia to have to stay all night with me in this situation. We hardly know each other."

"Randy, this situation can't be helped. I know you, and I know that Sylvia is safe with you. Sylvia, Randy is a good Christian man. I know he will take good care of you and not take advantage of you in any way. You could not be in better care than with him. You can take my word for it."

"I don't like this," Sylvia protested. "I really want to get home and take care of mama."

"I just don't see any other way," Buster said helplessly. We won't have to tell anyone you all stayed down here. I'll get you out as soon as I can, but I have to leave now."

"Buster, you can swim. Why don't you swim over here and stay with us. It would look better if there were three of us."

"I can't do that. I need to see about Mrs. Malvo, and get back to Gertrude. You all will be all right. Now do what I tell you, and I will be back soon."

Then he was gone. I was speechless and felt betrayed, but what could I do? Sylvia and I were quiet as we walked back to the house. Once more I unlocked the door and lit the lamp.

"It's cold," Sylvia grumbled.

"I'll make a fire. You keep that coat on until I get it going."

Uncle Cephus kept plenty of wood and kindling. There was kerosine to get it going quickly, and I did just that. I found two more lamps to light. Then I looked in the closet and found Aunt Fannie's bathrobe. "Here Sylvia," I said, handing it to her. I'm going in the kitchen to start cleaning the fish. You get your wet clothes off and put this on. We'll put some chairs in front of the fireplace and get them all dried out for you. You call me when you are ready, and I'll help you get them hung out."

"All right," she agreed.

I took a lamp and went into the kitchen and began to work on the fish. It was not long before she called me, and we found three chairs to hang the clothes on. After that I lit the wood stove and put out a pan to catch some rain water. I cut the fish into pieces to fry. I found the frying pan and a half gallon of cooking oil. I found meal and salt and pepper to get the fish ready, and then got the oil hot and put the fish pieces in to fry.

I had watched mama make cornbread and hush puppies all

my life, so I thought I could make us some hush puppies to go with our fish. I mixed up the rest of the meal and other ingredients I remembered mama using. I had to find another pan to fry those in. I remembered the little boy in the Bible story of the loaves and fishes. There was not a lot of meal, but I figured I could get at least five hush puppies out of it. I would give her three and I would take two. My appetite was not great. I was still angry and disgusted that Buster had left me in this situation.

I found some packages of Kool-Aid and made one of them up with some of the rain water I had caught. I found a can of pork and beans. I found silverware and plates to set up the kitchen table for our meal. I felt pretty good about this meal I had prepared. "Come on in here, Sylvia," I called. "I've fixed us dinner. I have cooked your fish."

"I'm coming," she called back. "Can I wash my hands?"

"There is a pail of water out on a shelf on the porch. Here is a wash basin. You can pour some of it in and some soap. I will get you a towel." I found a towel and handed it out to her.

"I'm ready," she said shortly.

"I asked her to have a seat at the table and laid the food out on it. "Let's say the blessing, and then we'll eat," I said to her. I bowed my head and thanked God that we had this safe place to keep us warm and out of the rain and that we had food to eat.

"Do you really believe in God?" she asked me.

"Why, yes. Don't you?"

"I don't know. I have never been one to go to church. I guess I have only been to church a few times in my life. I guess I believe in a power in nature, but as for the God they talk about in church, I have some questions about that."

"What kind of questions?"

"Some things in the Bible just don't make sense."

"Like what, for instance?"

"Well, just like that place where it says God fed all those people with just two fish. You know what I'm talking about, don't you?"

"Yes, but that was Jesus, God's son who came to earth as a human being."

"Do you believe he fed a thousand people with those two loaves and two fishes?"

"The Bible says it was five thousand."

"Oh, Randy, please! I just can't buy that. It doesn't sound reasonable. You really believe that?"

"Yes I do."

"And all the leftovers they picked up?"

"Yeah, the Bible says twelve baskets full."

"I just can't believe that."

"I think there are a whole lot of things we have to believe on faith. There is a whole lot we don't understand. We can't understand why the hail and the rain came down out of the same cloud today."

"Nature did that."

"Well, God controls nature."

"OK, have your way. Let's eat."

"OK. I still say it was God."

We ate, and afterwards she thanked me. "You cooked nice. I enjoyed that dinner," she told me.

"I'm glad you liked it. You go on back by the fire. There are some magazines in there you can look at. I'm going to clean up in here. I want to leave the kitchen as clean as I found it."

"I'll help you."

"No, you just go see about your clothes. I'll get this done in a hurry."

I knew what to do. I got everything cleaned up and put away. I locked the back door and carried the lantern back into the room where the fire was burning brightly.

"It's hot in here now." she said.

"Yes it is, and the screen door is even open. But now that it is dark, we'll have to close the door. Some wild thing might try to come in." I closed the door and locked it. I walked over then to examine her clothes to see how dry they had gotten and went to the fireplace to spread out the coals so the fire would go down since it was so hot. She was lying on a bed, but she got up and came over where I was standing.

"Randy, I want to thank you for being so nice to me."

"You are welcome. It was nothing. I'm sorry we got ourselves in this situation, but we have to do the best we can with it."

"I do feel like I owe you some gratitude."

"I accept your thanks. I'm glad to be able to do things that will make this less unpleasant."

"I really want to do something in return for your kindness."

"Oh my goodness, Sylvia. You don't have to do anything. I'm just glad we have a place to stay and be safe, and whatever I can do to make it less of an ordeal, I want to do. Your thanks is certainly enough."

At that moment, to my astonishment, she untied the robe and it just fell off her.

I caught my breath, and my next reaction was to avert my eyes.

"What's wrong?" she asked.

"I just don't think this should be happening. Buster told you I would take care of you and respect you. It is what is expected of me."

"You have been so nice to me. The least I can do is share my body with you."

"It would haunt me all my life that you could think you had to pay me this way just for being nice to you."

"It's not about paying you. It's this situation, us being here together. I'm not a virgin, and I am older than you think. I am eighteen, and I know about these things."

"I don't feel right about this. I'm afraid we will be sorry."

"Why? I want to. I have really come to like you in these last few hours. Nobody will know. I'm not going to tell anyone."

"There are other reasons. I just can't do it."

She moved toward me. I had on a pair of Uncle Cephus' overalls that I had put on while my clothes were drying. They were too big for me. Sylvia put her hands inside them and held me against her and pressed her body close to mine. "Your lips are saying no, but your body says yes," she murmured.

"I can't, Sylvia. It has nothing to do with your age or experience or that anyone might find out. I just can't."

"Are you saying I don't appeal to you? Your body is saying that I do."

"It's not that. Please believe me. I have to say no. It is not that you are not attractive. You are, but I have to say no."

"Well, you are the stupidest man I ever knew about." She whirled around and marched back to the bed and got in it. She turned her face into the pillow."

I didn't know what to say, so I just didn't say anything. I lay down on the couch, but I hardly slept at all. I think it was the worst night I ever spent in my life. I thought about all the bad things that had happened recently and how I just couldn't seem to live up to my ideals or be the person my family needed me to be. I worried about daddy's watch some more. At least Mama had stopped asking me about it, but I imagined she was thinking about it and seeing me with disappointed eyes. When dawn came I was up, went to the kitchen and put on my clothes that were still damp. I wanted to be out of there.

I called Sylvia and told her I would be in the kitchen while she put on her clothes. As soon as she was ready, I said, "Let's go."

We were out the door and I locked it behind us. She followed me up the hill without saying a word. The creek water had gone down some. We could see the bridge. "We've got to go across that bridge," I told her. "Come on, I will hold on to you so you won't fall."

We got across. The car was still where I had parked it. I opened the door for her to get in, then got in on the other side. I worried that the car might not start easily after all that rain, but it did. I breathed out thanks to the Lord for that. I took it slow up the winding road, all the way to the gate.

I parked outside the gate, and walked back to lock it up. About that time, Buster drove up. "I'm glad to see you," I told him.

"I promise I did all I could," he told me. The town is still torn up from that storm. Did you all make it all right?"

"Yes, we did all right."

Buster spoke to Sylvia then. "How did you make it?"

"Not too well," she answered listlessly.

"Are you sick?"

"No, it was just a bad night."

"What's wrong?"

"Do you really want to know?"

"Of course I do."

"Well, this man raped me last night."

"That can't be. You mean he forced himself on you?"

"Yes, two times he did."

"Girl, what are you saying?" I exclaimed.

"I'm saying what you did to me last night. You know you did it!"

"Why are you telling this man a lie like that? I never bothered you."

Sylvia turned to Buster. "Get me out of here," she demanded. "I don't ever want to see this man again."

"Buster, I never did such a thing."

"Well, the girl ought to know what she is talking about."

"No. There was no sex at all last night."

"You didn't coax her into it."

"No. Nothing happened at all."

Sylvia started crying. Then she got out of the car and started vomiting. "It must have been those fish he cooked," she sputtered. "Get me out of here. I need to go home."

Buster got her into his car. He looked at me and spoke angrily. "Randy, you sure have surprised me. I never would have expected such from you. He got into his car and drove off.

I was thinking as I walked away from the gate to my car about all the things that had been happening to me. I had done what I thought was right, what I had to do to keep my promise to the doctor and Uncle Cephus. I wanted to have a clear conscience when I would go to the doctor on Monday. Now, what in the world was I going to say. Would anyone believe me?

CHAPTER 6

The Surprise Shotgun Wedding

I COULDN'T BEGIN TO THINK about how this drama would unfold. Sylvia had told this tale to Buster, and now she would tell her mama. There were going to be repercussions. I wasn't sure what the possibilities were. Could I be arrested for something I didn't do? I was frightened.

I drove home slowly, not really wanting to get there, wishing time would stand still.

But time moved on, and I arrived at my house. I told Mama about the creek rising so I couldn't get home and having to stay at Uncle Cephus' cabin, but I didn't tell her everything.

She was relieved to see me. "You sure had me worried, but I knew you couldn't get home in that storm. I just hoped you had found shelter."

Nothing had happened when Uncle Cephus came to take me to the doctor on Monday. He asked me about the fishing trip, and I told him about Sylvia catching two fish and us getting caught in the storm, but I didn't let on about all that had happened. If he had heard anything, he sure didn't let on. He didn't ask any more questions.

The doctor's examination was routine, and he said everything looked fine. "You kept your promise, didn't you?" He said, and it didn't even sound like a question.

"Yes, I did," I answered promptly.

"You are doing well, but you're not a hundred percent cured. Continue to be careful, and I will see you in about a month."

"Yes, sir."

After that time passed. I heard nothing more about the incident. I thought maybe Sylvia had decided not to make an issue of her story. One day, about a month later, Mama wasn't feeling well. I had decided to stay home from business school because Rose and Bobby had gone to Vacation Bible School. Mama had something of a heart condition, and I felt I should not leave her alone. Uncle Cephus was out of town, and she couldn't have called him if she got to feeling worse.

By that time I had made some friends at the school and was sharing rides with two brothers named John and James Mason. They lived in a community north of Nelsonburg. On alternate weeks they would pick me up and drive to class each class night, then the next week they would stop, leave their car at my house and I would drive. I called John that night, since he was the one driving, to tell him I wouldn't be going, but promised him I would be able to drive the following week.

Mama was lying down, and I was reading in the front room. I heard a car come into the drive. I got up and went to the door and looked out. It was a car from the Sheriff's Office. Two men got out and started up to the door. Then another big car pulled in. Buster was driving it and it looked like there were other people in the car, but I couldn't see them. They just sat there.

I spoke to the men as they came on up to the door. "Good evening," one of them said. "I am Sheriff Neal. We are looking for Mr. Randall Carter.

"I'm Randall Carter, " I told them.

"We need to speak to you," said the Sheriff.

I knew all I had been worrying about was about to take place. Why had Sylvia waited so long to make trouble for me, and what was it going to be.

"It's like this," the Sherif began. The white man out in the car is Mr. Levy. I take it you know him."

"Yes, sir, I do."

And you know Buster, who is driving his car."

"Yes, I have known him for a long time."

"You know the girl, Sylvia, who lives on Mr. Levy's farm."

"Yes, I have known her for a short time."

"Well, Mr. Levy has just taken Sylvia and her mother for Sylvia to see the doctor. The doctor says she is pregnant. She says you recently forced yourself upon her, and the baby is yours. They believe that it is your duty to marry the girl so she can keep her self-respect and the baby will have a legal father."

"You must have the wrong person!" I told them. I have not had that kind of relationship with Sylvia."

"Didn't you spend the night with her down on the river in your uncle's cabin about a month ago on the night of the big storm?"

"Well, yes I did, but nothing like that happened."

"You took her down on that river when you knew a storm was coming up, didn't you? And you deliberately kept her down there while the rain made the creek rise. Just the two of you stayed all night down there, right?"

"Well, it wasn't exactly like that."

"I know you want to deny it, but Mr. Levy will tell you what the doctor said. You'll have to make up your mind what you want to do about it."

"I've already made up my mind. I am not marrying that girl. I can't be that baby's father, and that is the truth!"

One of the officers went toward the car and motioned for Buster to come join us."

Buster came up looking very uncomfortable. We looked at each other and spoke. "Now Buster," the Sheriff addressed him. "Tell us again what the girl told you when you went to Mr. Carter's fence the morning after the storm."

"Well, she told me she wasn't feeling well, and then she told me Randy had raped her.

"Did she say how many times?" the officer asked him.

"Yes, she said twice."

"And what did you say?"

"I just told him I was disappointed in him. I had promised her the night before that Randy was a nice Christian young man who would treat her with respect. I had to leave them down there together because there was no way to get them back across the creek just then. The water had covered the bridge over so we couldn't even see it, and Sylvia couldn't swim. Randy begged me to get them out, but it was getting dark, and I had to get back to check on Sylvia's sick mother and tend to my family. I couldn't get back till the next morning. I couldn't get into it any more with Randy because Sylvia got sick and started crying and vomiting. I just put her in the car and took her home."

By that time Mr. Levy had gotten out of the car and walked up to where the officers were talking with us. He had been listening to what was said. He spoke up after Buster finished talking. "Sylvia and Mrs. Malvo have lived on my place for a while now. The house they live in is very close to mine. I would notice if they had visitors. I have never seen any boys coming around there. Buster's family and Mr. Draper, an elderly man, are my other helpers. Sylvia stays at home and helps her mother. I just don't think she's been seeing any other boy. She doesn't drive, and when she goes away from the farm, it is always with her mother or Buster and his wife. I have always heard that Randy is a good boy, but it is my place to protect Sylvia and her baby. I want him make this right for them. I insist on it! It isn't right for him to father a child and leave her to raise it alone." I would say the same if he were a white boy. I am backing Sylvia and her mother."

"Well, Randy," the sheriff said quietly. "Are you ready to come with us and marry this girl?"

"No sir. I am not guilty."

By this time Mama had come to the door. "Randy! Who are all these people? Are they trying to arrest you?"

"Is he your son, ma'am?" the sheriff asked gently.

"Yes, he is."

Mama listened as the officers tried to explain what was going on. Then she went out to the car and spoke with Mrs. Malvo and listened to her. When she came back to the porch where I was still standing with the officers, she looked directly into my eyes and spoke calmly. "Son, tell me the truth. Could you have fathered a child with this girl?"

"No, Mama. We did have to spend the night together at Uncle Cephus' cabin the night of the big storm. I told you about how the creek rose, and we couldn't even see the bridge to get across. But I never even touched her in the way they are talking about. She slept in the bed, and I slept on the couch."

She looked then at the officers. "I know my child," she told them. "He says he is not responsible for this girl's child. I have never known him to lie to me. I believe him."

92

"It's natural that you would, Ma'am," the Sheriff spoke up. "You are his mama, but all these other people who know about the night they spent together believe the girl. Mr. Levy and her mama say she hasn't had any boyfriends around, and the doctor says she is pregnant. The girl says your son raped her twice. If he doesn't marry her, we will have to take him in. He will face rape charges and possibly have to go to the penitentiary."

"Look," Mama said to the Sheriff. "Give us a little time here. I need to talk to my pastor, Reverend Ike Foster. If I call him, he will be here in five minutes. He is a good friend of our family, and I really need to talk to him."

"We can't wait long ma'am, but see if you can get him here right away."

Mama went in to make the call. I just stood there and stared toward the car where I could now see Sylvia sitting. She was looking back at me, but I couldn't read her look at all. The car must have been getting hot, and they probably wanted to hear what was going on. Mrs. Malvo and Sylvia got out of the car and walked toward the porch. I stared at Sylvia as they came toward us, but she did not look up.

Mama came out and said Pastor Ike would be right over. She had let him know it was an emergency. The five or six minutes it took him to arrive seemed like a lifetime to me, but then he was coming up the walk and his wife, Ella Mae, was with him. He looked around at the officers and all the people who were gathered around. "What's wrong?" he asked anxiously. Mama and the officers filled him in. I stood by quietly with tragedy written all over me. While they were talking, he kept looking at me with concern.

"Randy, would you tell me your side of the story?" he asked me gently.

So I took a deep breath and told him all about the day that Sylvia and I were going fishing with a group of people and why we wound up alone and had to spend the night at Uncle Cephus' cabin. I was careful to tell him that Sylvia and I barely knew each other when we started out, and that I certainly had not been sexually intimate with her, much less raped her.

He held my eyes with his and asked me if I was telling him the truth.

I looked back at him steadily. "I promise you I am telling the truth," I said firmly. "They are accusing me, but I am not guilty."

Pastor Ike turned to the Sheriff. "I know this boy well. I've known him for a long time. He comes to my church and he has always been an upright Christian young man. He is a respectful and moral person. If he says he didn't do it, I have a hard time believing otherwise."

"Thank you, Reverend. I understand what you are saying. Nevertheless he is young. You've been a boy yourself, and you know the power of a boy's desire for a young woman. You have experienced it yourself. It's why we got married. Think about it, this nice looking girl, and them stuck all night in a cabin. You have to understand the temptation. She said he attacked her. He raped her. I have to handcuff him and take him in if he says he won't marry her."

"Please don't take my son!" Mama moaned.

Sister Ella Mae came to Mama and put her arms around her. "Sister Maybelle," she spoke soothingly to Mama. "Come on in and lie down. Ike will take care of this. He won't let them take Randy." She turned to the Sheriff and frowned at him as she whispered, "This lady has a heart condition. You don't want to upset her."

"Yes, Mama," I said, looking thankfully at Sister Ella Mae. "You go on with her. I'll be OK."

"Yes, Sister Maybelle," Brother Ike agreed. "We'll get this worked out somehow. I promise you that. You go in and rest."

As soon as the women had gotten inside, Brother Ike turned to me. "Randy, you have a problem. It is her word against yours, and these people are believing her. You shouldn't risk going to prison. Your mama needs you. She is not well. I'm not judging you. I'm just saying you need to weigh the consequences of what you do here. You've got a situation where your back is against the wall. The evidence is circumstantial, and you can't prove your innocence. I'm not suggesting that you have to stay with her forever, but taking all things into consideration, it might be best if you just go ahead and marry the girl. I'm your pastor. I'll be with you all the way. It won't mean you have to live with her. You can decide about that afterward. But I think you do need to go ahead and marry her. Can you do that?"

I was taken aback. At first I couldn't say a word, then I finally spoke, "But Pastor Ike, it is not my child."

"I believe you, and it is your decision to make. You are, however, in a situation where the right choice may be unfair to you, but considering all things, I have to strongly suggest that you go ahead and agree to this marriage. We will have to wait till tomorrow. You have to get a license and all. I will help you through it. I will take you to town to the court house, and I will do the ceremony."

"I guess you are right," I agreed. "I'll do what you suggest."

Pastor Ike then turned to the Sheriff. "I'll take responsibility for the boy. Just please let him stay here tonight with his mama. He would have been in Houston at Business School tonight if she hadn't been feeling poorly. I will have him at the courthouse at nine o'clock in the morning to get the license. Then if he wants me to, I'll do the ceremony."

"I trust you, Reverend. I know you to be a man of your word. Will that be acceptable to you?" he said, turning to the others who were waiting there. Sylvia, Mrs. Malvo, and Mr. Levy all seemed relieved and nodded.

"I'll come to the wedding and be a witness," Mr. Levy said. "And Reverend, I am a church-going, Bible-reading man. I hope you understand that I just want to see justice done."

"I understand your point of view," Pastor Ike answered. "But you must understand too, that I know this boy, and the evidence we have here is her word against his. We are going to see this marriage through because the law is telling us we must. I feel there is some question as to whether he is guilty. As his pastor, however, I have advised him to comply with what the law is expecting of him. We will see you tomorrow."

"Be sure that we do," the Sheriff said pointedly. "If you are not there it will be my job to find him and pick him up. We will see you tomorrow at the Courthouse."

I moved nearer to Sylvia and whispered angrily, "You should be ashamed of yourself!"

Pastor Ike pulled me away from her. "Let it alone," he said and pulled me toward the house. "We need to get in here and see to your Mama. If something happened to her because of this, you wouldn't be able to live with yourself. Your family needs you to be with them. That is the important thing here. An unfair marriage is better than jail."

Mama was lying quietly on the couch. "I saw she took her pill and got a cool cloth for her head," Sister Ella Mae told us. "She seems to be all right now."

"I'm awake," Mama said, opening her eyes and moving to sit up.

"You just lie there, Sister Maybelle," Pastor Ike told her. I want you to trust me and let me take care of this problem. I have advised Randy to marry this girl rather than risk jail and a trial. I believe what he tells me, but this will assure that he will be at home with you. You leave it to me, and I will see that he will be with you, and life will go on as normal. I have to go back to church right now, because Bible School is about over."

"I do trust you, Pastor. It was so good of you to come so quickly and try to get things straightened out. I just couldn't handle it. It was such an unexpected shock. You have helped us so much, and I thank you from the bottom of my heart."

"Sister Maybelle, I'm just happy I could help. Randy is a good boy, and you need him. I'll get all that business taken care of tomorrow. You don't worry. I'll have Randy back here by afternoon."

Sister Ella Mae spoke up then to her husband, "You go on, dear, and I will stay here a while. You can come back and get me after you are done at church. I could even spend the night here if I am needed. We'll decide about that when you get back. You can bring Rose and Bobby back when you come to get me."

"I was going to get them," I said.

"Well, you won't need to. I'll bring them," Pastor Ike said decidedly. "It will be best if you stay right here until we go to town in the morning."

I did some thinking while he was gone, and when he came back, I asked if I could get the marriage licence using my middle name, which was Iglehart. It was the last name of the midwife who had delivered me. I knew of no other Carter who had that name. I had never used the name because I didn't like the sound of it. No one who read the wedding license notices in the newspaper would know who that was, and they wouldn't know Sylvia's name either, because she was new to the community. Everyone agreed that it sounded like a good plan.

When Rose and Bobby had come home, they had stayed in the living room. I asked Mama and Pastor Ike if we should tell them what was going on. Both Mama and the Fosters thought we should tell them. We called them to Mama's room. Rose looked worriedly at Mama and asked if she was all right. Mama had her to come sit by her on the bed and told us all that she was feeling better. We pulled up a chair for Bobby. Pastor Ike did the talking. He started out just telling them I was going to get married the next day.

"Married!" Bobby exclaimed. "To who?"

"Bobby," Rose said sharply. "You should have said 'to whom.'"

"OK, Miss English Teacher, I'll say 'to whom.' I hope it is not Maggie."

"No, it is not Maggie," Pastor Ike said. "You tell them, Randy."

"It is Sylvia," I said. "She is the girl who almost ran over me at the ball game."

"What!" Rose squawked. "What is this about? You haven't been courting her!"

"I'll try to explain," Pastor Ike began. As smoothly as he could, he told them the truth. He told them how we had to spend the night at the river during the storm and that now Sylvia was expecting a baby and saying I was the father, that it was her word against mine, and that I would go to trial and might have to serve time if I didn't marry her. "He is getting married tomorrow so he can come home to be with you," Pastor Ike told them. "If anyone ever asks you about it, you don't know anything. You are not going to be there. Do you understand?"

"I guess so," Robert answered looking grim. Rose just nodded and looked troubled.

"I promise you I will have him back home tomorrow afternoon, and he will be with you as always. It will be OK. Don't look so worried."

"Uncle Cephus is out of town, or I would want to go tell

him about this right now," I said. "He will not be back until tomorrow. I will just have to tell him after it is over and done with. I'm sure he would agree that we have no other choice. I wish he were here, but he is not."

We decided that Sister Ella Mae would come back tomorrow and stay with Mama until we got home. Mama seemed pretty much herself by now. She was concerned but not as agitated as she was earlier. Pastor Ike and Sister Ella Mae went home then because everyone was weary. After being sure Mama was settled in for the night, we all went to bed. I slept fitfully.

The next morning Pastor Ike and Sister Ella Mae arrived punctually. I had already been up, ready and pacing the floor. I wanted it over with. Pastor Ike and I did not talk much as he drove me to the courthouse. Mr. Levy, Buster, Mrs. Malvo, Sylvia, and the Sheriff met us there. We got the license. We agreed to have the ceremony down in the city park. It seemed less public than at the courthouse. When Pastor Ike came to the part where he asked if I would take this woman to be my wife, I hesitated. "The answer is 'I do or I will,'" he said to me.

"I will marry her," I finally said. I hardly remember the rest of the ceremony. At the end, he said, "Salute the Bride." and I just walked away. I went up to Mrs. Malvo and looked directly at her. "Ma'am," I said to her, "I have no wish to cause you trouble or pain. If I have, I ask your forgiveness. I want to give you my respect. I want you to know, however, that I am not guilty of what I'm accused of, and to that I swear. I don't have anything else to say."

"Thank you for that," she said in return.

That was it. It was over. I got in Pastor Ike's car. "I don't know how to thank you. I'm sorry you had to go through all that, but I am so grateful to you for helping me and standing by me."

"I'm your pastor, son, and your brother in Christ. You owe me nothing, not even thanks. I am privileged to serve my members, and you are a special friend. Just keep your head up and be the man I know you to be. You know, Satan is always at work. You've just gotta keep overcoming."

"I guess I'd better go talk to Uncle Cephus. I dread having

to tell him, but I noticed when we passed his house that he is at home."

"I'll go with you."

Uncle Cephus couldn't have been more understanding. He listened and never once did he question my honesty in the matter. He just shook his head in sympathy.

"So much for my luck with women," I told him finally. "As for Sylvia, I hope I never see her again. Maggie was a big disappointment, and now this. I feel like I never want to get involved with anyone again."

"You can get a divorce from Sylvia, and put all this behind you," Uncle Cephus suggested.

"I don't want to make it easy for her. I have no intentions of getting involved with anyone else anyway. Let it be her problem. All I want to do is get my education and do what I can to learn about your business and help you. If she meets someone and wants to get married, she can get the divorce. Then I'll probably give her a hard time about letting her have it. Why should she find happiness after the way she treated me?"

Uncle Cephus and Pastor Ike both smiled at that. "You're young," Uncle Cephus began. "Most young people have disappointments and bad experiences that turn them bitter toward life and love for a while. Someday you will meet someone who will make you believe in both again. It happened to us, didn't it, Pastor?"

"Indeed it did," the pastor said. "Randy, think of your mama and my dear wife who is there with her. There are many good women in this world who bring up good daughters. There is one somewhere who will bring you lots of happiness. It will happen."

"I'll try to believe you, but right now I don't even want to think about another girl. I just want to get my education and help my family."

I threw myself into my studies and worked hard at excelling in school. I still worried about people finding out about my unfortunate marriage. What would Maggie or Honey think? Would they want to think the worst of me and believe the lies that Sylvia had told about me? Then I would tell myself that it didn't really matter what they thought. I was married. That gave me an excuse to avoid the courting game. Life was going to be strictly business.

Going to school with John and James every week had become routine. They were really nice guys. John was the older one who always drove their car. He was a jovial fellow who liked to joke around and tease. James was just a little more than a year younger than John. He laughed at his brother a lot, but he was quieter, more inside himself. I liked both of them. We usually ate dinner together. We took food with us or occasionally stopped at a café before we went to class. We spent enough time talking together that we were getting to know one another pretty well.

One evening we were headed for school and John was driving. I was in the back seat. "Hey, Randy," John spoke up. "I'm curious about something. I don't want to be nosy, but James and I have both told you about our girlfriends, and you have never mentioned one. I hope I'm not offending you by asking, but you are a good looking guy and an outstanding student. Surely there is someone special in your life."

"Actually, not at this time. You might say I've been burned."

John didn't react to my last comment. He turned to his brother and said, "You know, I would like Randy to meet our cousin, Margaret. They would have some things in common. I'll bet they would like each other."

"John, I've thought the very same thing myself. One makes me think of the other. They are both reserved and serious about their future. They should really meet sometime. Randy, would you like to meet her? You two could be made for each other. "

"I'd be glad to meet anyone in your family, but you've got to know that I'm just not looking to go courting now while I'm in school. I'm just trying to prepare myself to help my uncle in his business and do all I can to help my mother and brother and sister. My dad died young, and I'm sort of the head of my family now."

"Well, I just want you to meet her," John asserted. "She is really nice looking, and she has a head on her shoulders. She is in college, and I think she is going places. I think you would find her inspiring."

"I'll be glad to meet her, but don't expect any fireworks.

Don't build me up to her. It might make her mad at you. She will not think I'm as great as you do, and if she did, she might be wasting her time."

"She is going to Prairie View College right now and won't be home for a while," said James. "But, one of these days, I hope you get to meet her."

"Oh," I guess I sounded relieved. "Someday I probably will."

In a few weeks though, Margaret's name came up again. "You'll get to meet her now," John said eagerly. "You still want to, don't you?"

"Well, sure. You all have been great friends. I'm honored to meet any of your family."

"One day soon we will work something out," he promised.

About a week later we heard that a strong hurricane was moving into the Gulf of Mexico and was approaching the Texas coast. We were pretty far inland, but we would feel the effects of such a storm after a while, maybe tonight. Mama sent me to the store to get candles because we could expect the electricity to go out.

As I walked out of the house the clouds were beginning to gather and there was a nice breeze. It felt good, for recent days had been too hot.

CHAPTER 7

And Then, Momentarily, the Sun Came Out Again

I DECIDED TO WALK to the convenience store that was not far from the house. Mr. Marshall was the proprietor there, and made a fuss over seeing me. "Look who's here!" he exclaimed. "Why, Randy Carter, I haven't seen you here all summer, not even to buy gas."

"I've been going to school, and that has been keeping me pretty busy."

"Yes, I'd heard that, and I was glad to hear it. Sit down here and talk to me a minute. I want to catch up with you."

So I chatted with him for a while, telling him about school. Then I remembered what I came for and asked about the candles.

"Sure, I've got candles," Mr. Martin said. "How many do you want."

"Oh, a half dozen or so, I guess."

He showed me where the candles were, and I picked up some and was paying him for them. "Who do you think will win the World Series?" he asked.

"I'm not sure at all. You're an American League fan, aren't you?"

"I am that, how about you?"

"I don't know what I am. I love to watch the games. I like to see a good team win, and sometimes I am for the underdog."

Someone came in just then and announced that it had started raining.

102

"I'd better put a move on and get home," I spoke up. "I wasn't very smart to walk up here."

"I'll take you home in a few minutes," Mr. Marshall offered.

"Oh, no. It isn't raining that hard. I don't mind getting a little wet."

"Sure you don't," he agreed. "You are young and fit. Grab yourself one of those caps over there."

"That's a good idea," I said gratefully. "I'll pay you for it."

"You just count that an early Christmas present," he told me.

"Why, it is just July!"

"That's quite all right. I just want to give it to you. Go on and take it. Now, you don't wait so long to come back and talk to me. I like to see you."

I assured him that I would be back soon. I walked out under the canopy where the gas pumps were and looked out from under it at the sky. The rain was not heavy yet, but the clouds were moving in more. The wind was stronger than when I came in. I paused there, looking up at the sky. I had a fascination with clouds. I noted that a car drove by, but kept my eyes on the sky instead of looking to see who it was.

"Randy Carter," a voice rang out. "You're going to drown like a chicken! A chicken will look up at the sky and let rain run down its nose until it drowns."

I looked where the voice came from. It was John Mason. The car he was driving was different from the one I was used to. It was new.

"That is a beautiful car," I told him. "When did you get that?"

"Actually just today," he replied. "I was coming to your house to show it to you and chat with you a while."

"I came to the store to buy candles in case the electricity goes out."

"Well, it's raining. Why don't you go with us to run a couple of errands, and I will take you home. We are really not going to be gone long."

"I have to say it would be a privilege to ride in this brand new car."

"Well, then, get right in," he said invitingly and got out

and opened the back door for me. I did as he said, and at the same time James, his brother, got out of the other side and got in the back with me. I hadn't seen the girl who had been sitting between them. She moved over to the passenger side of the front seat.

I looked the interior of the car over. "This is some car!" I exclaimed.

"Will you quit talking about the car?" John said in a pseudo-cross voice. "There is something more important here than this car. I want you to meet my cousin here. Miss Margaret Mason, meet Mr. Randall Carter."

Margaret turned around and smiled at me. "I am pleased to meet you, Randall. These cousins have been talking a lot about you lately."

"I am very glad to meet you too, Margaret, and I hope you don't mind my saying so, but you are even more beautiful than they led me to believe. John and James, my friends, I thank you for giving me the privilege of meeting your cousin."

The brothers both seemed pleased with themselves. "We just felt we had a calling to get you two together," John said with a big grin.

I was very interested in talking to Margaret, but I guess I felt shy about that and started a conversation with James about sports. That was what we talked about most of the time on our way to our classes.

John had other ideas. He was clever at helping me past my shyness. "Hey, there are four people in this car," John scolded. "You two are hogging the conversation."

"We're willing to be inclusive," I retorted. "You pick the topic."

He got Margaret to tell us about her plans and the things she was studying in school. We got to the place where they had bought the car. They got out to complete some papers they were supposed to fill out. I stayed in the car with Margaret and told her about my studies and my job with Uncle Cephus, and we talked a little about our families.

John and James soon finished their business and got back in the car. "We have one more place to go," John announced. He drove on to a nice part of town and turned into the driveway of a nice looking large, white building. A young lady in a white uniform walked out and met us. I got the impression this was some kind of nursing home.

She spoke to John in a very familiar way, and he said "Hi, Honey."

"When did you get this beautiful car?" She asked.

"Just yesterday," he answered.

"I hope to get to ride in it soon."

"You bet you will." John assured her.

She suddenly noticed the rest of us in the car. "Oh, Margaret, how very nice to see you. Aren't you looking great!"

"Well you are one to talk about somebody else looking great, Becky. Nobody beats you!"

John's face was beaming as he introduced Becky to me.

"It is a pleasure to meet you," I told her. She was certainly a most beautiful young woman.

"I hope to be Mrs. John Mason one day," she told me proudly.

"Then you are both lucky," I told her. "John will surely be a good husband. He is a great friend to me."

"Yes, and you keep thinking that way and don't get any ideas about her yourself," John said teasingly. "She is going to be my girl forever!"

"Congratulations to you both," I said warmly.

"We'd better be on our way. We all need to get home before this storm comes in," John told Becky. She kissed him and we all exchanged pleasantries and hoped to see each other again soon.

We started back to my house. My attention again turned to Margaret. Her looks and intelligence impressed me so much. She seemed almost too perfect. I wondered what I was going to discover wrong with her. I asked myself if I would see a club foot when she got out of the car.

James spotted a drugstore with a soda fountain on our way and wanted to stop. We all went in for a soda, and I insisted on paying for them all. It made me feel important to show them I had a job and could treat them. Even though I still wanted to think that there was something wrong with every girl I might meet, there was part of me that wanted to show off to Margaret.

And as for Margaret, any notions I had about her having

any physical defects vanished. She was a dream walking. She was tall and slender and carried herself beautifully.

Conversation flowed easily as we sat there sipping our sodas. Then John and James said they wanted to look at the magazines and left Margaret and me to ourselves for a spell. She put me at ease, seemingly interested in any subject I led us into.

It was raining again when we got in the car to head back to my house. Margaret and I just sort of naturally got into the back seat together this time. John had to drive slowly because of the rain. Margaret and I talked and talked, but the ride was entirely too short for me. I wanted to talk to her forever.

"We're here," James told me because I seemed oblivious of that fact. "Your mama will be expecting you to get on in out of the rain, and we'd better get on home."

"I've really enjoyed getting to know you a little, " I told Margaret. "May I ask you for your phone number?"

She had something to write on, and we exchanged numbers. I told her again how much I enjoyed meeting her and that I would call her. I told John and James how much I thanked them for the nice afternoon. As much as they had made an effort to get me to meet Margaret, now they were making teasing remarks about my obvious reluctance to get out of the car. "Better get in, your mama will think you've drowned," said John.

"I see some girls in the window," James told me. "They are wondering why you have been out here so long."

Finally I did get out of the car, but my eyes were still glued to Margaret's. "You are about to forget something," she said. She handed me the package of candles I had completely forgotten.

"Thank you." I told her. "I'll be talking to you soon." I was oblivious of the rain as I walked slowly to the door, turning often to watch the car disappear.

James was right. Rose and Peaches had been looking out the window. They wanted to know all about who I had been with. They had seen that there was a girl in the car and that I had been sitting in the back seat with her. I told them as little as I could get by with.

I went to my room so they wouldn't notice how keyed up

I was. I felt all this energy, but all I wanted to do was call Margaret. She wasn't even home yet. I didn't think it would be appropriate for me to call her the same day she gave me the number. I would have to wait at least a day or two. It would be a long distance call at that, but I didn't care.

The next night, when John and James picked me up for school, I thanked them again for letting me meet Margaret. They assured me that she was just as happy to meet me and that they were pleased with themselves for getting us together. I was so encouraged that I called her the very next day.

It seemed almost like she had been waiting for my call. It was so easy to talk to her. John and James had told me that she lived with her grandparents on their farm. I asked if I could come to see her sometime and meet them. She encouraged me to do just that and told me how dear they were to her and that I couldn't help but like them. I learned that her mother and John and James' father were brother and sister.

"I would like to come and see you and meet your grandparents," I told her. "When would be a good time for me to come."

"Come sometime this weekend. I think we have some plans on Saturday, but Sunday would be a good time. Could you come Sunday afternoon around three o'clock?"

"Yes, that sounds fine. I will look forward to it."

I was really excited about seeing her again. I floated through the week. On Saturday I called her again just to make sure it was still convenient for me to come. She told me to come on, that they were expecting me. I could hardly wait for the next day to come.

I was very careful in dressing for my visit. I wanted to look my very best. I had gotten a haircut and moustache trim the day before, and I had washed and shined up the car. I was out to make an impression on her grandparents.

I found her house easily enough from the directions she had given me. I parked in front and went up and knocked on the door. I was expecting that she or one of her grandparents would answer my knock, but it was a young man instead. "Hi, I'm Randy Carter," I introduced myself. "I was invited here by Margaret Mason. Is she here?"

"Yes, she's here, come in," he told me and then called

Margaret to tell her I had arrived. "I am Randall Mason," he spoke to me again. "I am also called Randy by my friends and family. Isn't that a coincidence?"

"Yes it surely is," I said, shaking his hand just as Margaret appeared.

"This is my brother, " she said. "I guess we'll have to use your last names to keep you straight. Do come on in and make yourself at home, Randy Carter. I am so glad to see you."

"I'm glad to meet you, Randy Carter," Randy Mason said to me, and he conveniently disappeared to some other part of the house.

"Let's go sit on the porch," Margaret suggested. "My grandparents are out there."

Mr. and Mrs. Raphael Mason put me at ease at once. They laughed about my name being the same as their grandson's. They talked like they were expecting to have me around some more because they, too, discussed how they would address the other Randy and me to distinguish one of us from the other. They recognized the Carter name, of course, because they knew Uncle Cephus. Everyone anywhere near Nelsonburg knew about Uncle Cephus. I told them that my father had died, and that Uncle Cephus treated me like his son, and I was working for him. That seemed to make a good impression on them.

"You have made a nice friend," Mr. Mason told Margaret, and then they discreetly withdrew to give Margaret and me some time alone.

How wonderful it was to be there with her. When I left, we made a commitment to keep seeing each other. I was so happy. On the way home, I remembered what Uncle Cephus had told me. He had said there would be a girl out there for me, and I thought now for sure I had found her. I was in love!

I wanted to stay really cool about this, but it was so hard. I've decided that, when love comes, it just sticks out all over you. I did try, though. I told Mama I was dating a girl named Margaret Mason and gave her very few details. I held off from telling Uncle Cephus right away, but after a while I did talk to him about her. Still I tried to move slowly in letting everyone know how smitten I was with Margaret.

When it came time for Margaret to go back to school, she

told me she had decided not to go back until spring. I didn't press her for the reason, but I was concerned that it might be because she was low on funds. College can be expensive. John and James had hinted that her mother in California, who had been sending her money at times, had for some reason stopped doing so. They indicated that Margaret was going to work for a semester, and then go back to school in the spring.

I was sorely tempted to offer to help her out so she could go on to school. Uncle Cephus had given me a raise, and I had savings. I had second thoughts about that, though. It was highly likely that she would be offended. Back then it was disrespectful to offer money to your girlfriend. It was all right to give her gifts, but not money.

I had to admit that I considered how nice it would be for me that she was staying in Nelsonburg. We would have much more time together, time to deepen our relationship. That is exactly what happened. It was a very good time in my life. I was happier than I had ever been.

Fall came and Prairie View College, the school Margaret had attended, was having one of their fall football games. Margaret wanted to go, and I asked if I could take her. After getting consent from her grandparents, we made plans to go.

We had a frost the night before the game, but it melted early the next morning and the sun came out. The autumn leaves were at their peak of color. It was one of the most beautiful days of the year.

We had plenty of time to get where we were going. We decided not to go the quickest way, but to take some older roads and see some of the scenic areas of east Texas that we had heard about. We came upon a state park we had wanted to see, and Margaret asked to stop and take some pictures. We drove into the park. It was wonderfully quiet, and there seemed to be hardly any people there at that time. We got out of the car and walked until we found some benches to sit on where we could look at the beautiful trees and their reflection in the lake. Near our bench was a big concrete fountain built into the ground with water constantly bubbling up a pipe in the center and falling down into the fountain. The sound it made was peaceful and relaxing.

Margaret spotted a red bird sitting on a bare low limb. She

was so taken with the beauty of the picture it made. "Would you try to get a picture of me with that in the background," she asked me. "Maybe the bird will stay still long enough."

"Sure," I said, taking the camera and moving slowly to get up. But the bird flew away before we could get the picture. Margaret was so disappointed. "Maybe we'll see another one," I told her.

We sat back down on the bench and just waited in the quiet, taking in the whole scene of the lake and trees. The sun had risen above the trees and was shining down on us. The breeze was pleasantly cool. "Margaret, this makes me think about Adam and Eve being alone in the garden," I said.

"Yes, it is what you would imagine Paradise would be like."

"That is what I feel like, being here with you alone. I feel like I am in Paradise."

She didn't say anything, just sat quietly. Suddenly I found myself on my knees. "Margaret, will you marry me," I asked. She didn't respond at once. I repeated myself. "Will you marry me. I want you to be my bride."

"Randy, we've only known each other a few months, but I'm really glad you asked me. I truly believe I could spend the rest of my life with you. I think maybe I shouldn't say that so soon though."

"No, you should! I knew from the first time I met you that you were the girl for me. I don't think you have to wait a certain time to know something like this. I love you, Margaret. I'm saying it with all my heart."

"Thank you, Randy."

"Are you saying yes?"

"Yes!"

I got up from my knees and pulled her up against me."

"I just want to do something to show that you are mine," I said. I got some coins out of my pocket and threw them in the fountain there. "We can remember this day forever.

"Margaret, I had no idea I was going to get down on my knees and propose to you today. I didn't plan it or act out something I had thought up before. It just came out of me."

"You were pretty dramatic," she said smiling.

"Acting is something I do enjoy though. It was not that long ago I was in a play."

"Really?"

"Yes, It was a community theater effort. One of my teachers had some experience in directing, and we had a drama club. I was selected to be one of the characters."

"What was the play."

"It was an old one taken from an eighteenth century novel, It was called "East Lynne.""

"Oh, listen! That was one we did at my school too, and I had a part. What part did you play?"

"I was Richard Hare."

"I can hardly believe that! I played Richard's sister, Barbara. Isn't that something!"

"It sure is! It is another one of those things that connects us."

"Have you forgotten your part."

"I don't think so. Richard was such a memorable dramatic character, a fugitive from justice."

"I know that. Could we try doing some lines from it? Do you remember the part where Richard and Barbara met outside one night? He had slipped back home to talk to their mother while their father was gone and had motioned through a window for Barbara to come out."

"I certainly do."

"And Barbara goes out to meet him and then her father shows up and calls to her. Can we start there and say the lines?"

"OK. I'll start. I'll do both men's parts." I lowered my voice and bellowed out with the gruffness of the father. "Barbara! Barbara!"

Margaret melted into the meekness of Barbara and trembled convincingly. Her voice dropped to a terrified whisper. "Our father has returned. I dare not stay."

I lowered my voice too, but spoke with intense earnestness, "Barbara, I know our father has not believed my assertion of innocence, but I am telling you the truth. It was not I who committed the crime. As we stand here tonight, with the Lord above us, and I know that someday I have to meet Him

111

face to face. I swear to you I did not commit the crime. Goodnight, sister."

"Bravo," Margaret cried. "You were wonderful. We should go to Hollywood. You could give Clark Gable some real competition."

"Oh, come on, girl. But really, I'd like to think you could put Maxine Sullivan in the shade too, not just with your personality and acting ability, but with your beauty. I can never get enough of taking you in my arms and telling you how much I love you."

"How much we love each other," she corrected me.

We were totally absorbed with each other, and were startled when a car drove up and pulled in near us It was an old car with a small trailer hooked behind it. The people were strange looking. The intruders broke the romantic spell we were in and prompted us to get in our car and drive out of the park. "Listen," I told her as we got to the highway. "I cannot wait to put an engagement ring on your finger.

"That is so thoughtful of you."

"I am really serious. There's a song that comes to me at this moment that says what I'd like to say to you. It's in my heart and on my lips."

"What is the song, Honey?"

"The title is, "If I Had a Million Dollars." The first verse goes like this, "If I had a million dollars, I know just what I would do. I'd tie a string around the world, and bring it all to you."

"That is a beautiful thought, I want to hold on to the memory of every piece of this wonderful day. There is so much in front of us now. I can't wait for you to become better acquainted with my family and my friends. There will be a Halloween party tomorrow night in my neighborhood. I would like to take you and show you off."

"That sounds like fun."

"I need to tell you more about my family. You will meet my mother sometime. She is really more like my sister. She was very young when she had Randy and me. We have her maiden name because she was not married when we were born and never has been. Our grandparents have brought us up, and we look to them as our parents. They have been very good to us.

112

I can't wish that it had been any different. I had no control over the things that happened. I guess it was God's plan for my life."

"I do understand. I guess I think that way too. It was God's plan for me to meet John and Jimmy. They were His instruments to bring you and me together. I know I am destined to put a ring on your finger."

"Well, it can't happen today. We have a ball game to go to. We'll get around to that. We have agreed to be engaged. That is what is important. We don't have to let the whole world know yet. This year won't last much longer. The holidays are coming up. We'll have lots of occasions for each of us to learn and get closer to the other's family. Let's not overwhelm them with a ring yet."

"You are probably right. We don't want to shock them, do we? Now that you mention it, do you think your mother will come home for Thanksgiving or Christmas?"

"I think she probably will. I hope so. I truly do love her and don't blame her for our situation. I've been happy with my life and accept it as the life God planned for me. We don't talk about why it is different from most of my friends."

"I think that is a great attitude. We're still going to buy the ring."

"Oh, I know that, and I will be elated when the time comes. Right now we can think of spending time together during this holiday season. We'll both want to be with our families, but hopefully we can work out times that we can be together and spend time with each of our families. That is enough to fill our thoughts for the present."

"You'll find that my mother is a very understanding person. She will like you, and she will not be selfish about wanting me with her all the time. I love her dearly, and you will too. We'll get all these family things worked out. Do you have any thoughts about when you would like to walk down the aisle?"

"That is a good question. I have always thought I would like to be a June bride. How does that sound?"

"Are you talking about June of next year?"

"We have a lot of things to think about before we set a date. We'd need to have a place to live. I don't think we would want to live with one of our families. I would like to get married in church, and that will take some planning too. Let's not rush. We have made a promise to each other, and we are going to stick to it. That is what is important now."

"Sure, I can appreciate the need for planning, but I want you to know that I am solid on this, and I won't change. I'm like the song, 'My Love is Here to Stay.'"

"You sure are big on coming up with a song for every occasion, you know that?"

"I mean it, though, I really do."

We had come some way from the park by now and suddenly noticed a big sign that announced that St. Paul's Cathedral was one mile ahead. Margaret got excited on seeing it. "I've heard about that church," she told me. "Some of my Prairie View friends who live in this area have told me about it. It is over one hundred years old. They say many people come here to get married."

"I'm not familiar with it. I have never been on this road before."

"I'd like to stop and take some pictures here."

"Sure, we have time to do that."

It was a beautiful old building constructed of some kind of rock and surrounded by tall, old trees. There were parking places at the front and sides. I pulled into a space that faced the church and we got out and walked up the stone walkway. I took the camera, and Margaret posed herself standing on a big rock in front of the church for me to take her picture. Before I could, though, the door of the church opened and an elderly man walked out. He was dressed in a minister's robe. He spoke to us. We returned his greeting.

"Are you the minister here?" I asked him.

"Yes, I am."

"I hope it is all right for us to take pictures. We were passing through going to Prairie View and had heard what a beautiful, old church it is."

"You are quite welcome to take pictures. People come here most every day to do just that. It is nice for our church to be so well known. I'd be glad to take your camera so you could be together in the picture. Would you like me to do that?"

"That is very kind of you. We would appreciate it," I answered him.

He walked down the ten or twelve steps from the door of the church and took the camera. He had us to get posed in front of the church and took a couple of pictures to be sure we got a good one. "Where are you all from?" he asked when he was finished.

I told him I was from Nelsonburg and Margaret was from Mason, a smaller town a few miles from Nelsonburg.

"I've been in Nelsonburg not long ago," he commented. "You certainly are a nice looking young couple. Are you married?"

"Not married," I said. "I will tell you something though. Can I tell him, Margaret?"

"Sure, go ahead," she said, giving me a smile.

"Well, sir, we are engaged. The reason you don't see a ring is because it was just back a few miles at the state park that I proposed to her. You are the first person we have told."

"I am truly honored, and I congratulate you," he said, looking quite pleased. "Since I am the first to know, I would love to be able to perform the ceremony when you are ready. Would you like to go up and look inside the church?"

Margaret and I looked at each other. We both nodded that we would, and he led us up the steps to the door. He turned on the lights so we could see better. It was small and quaint. The pews and other furnishings were old but had been polished until they shone. It was unusual in those days, but there was actually carpet on the floor. Our movements didn't make a sound. The minister motioned for us to sit down and he sat there by us quietly letting us admire it and have our own thoughts. None of us spoke. Margaret and I finally got up and he followed us out the door.

"Thank you so much, Pastor," I said to him. "We will certainly consider your invitation."

"I'd like your name and mailing address," he said. "If you do decide to come back and marry here, whenever that may be, I will do the ceremony as a wedding gift to you."

"That is so kind of you!" Margaret exclaimed.

"We have no idea when we will have the ceremony," I told him. "I would like to come here, but I can't say for sure yet.

You have been so nice to us, though. Tomorrow is Sunday. I would like to leave a small donation for the collection plate."

He protested that a donation was not necessary, but I reached in my pocket and got out a five dollar bill and pressed it into his hand. "Please accept this as a token of our appreciation," I urged him. "Our visit here has been such a wonderful part of our day."

"Thank you. It was such an honor to have you here. God bless you, and may the rest of your day be just as special."

"We are headed to the Prairie View football game," I told him.

"Are you students there?"

"Well, yes and no," Margaret answered. I attended there for a year, and I am in my second year, but I have taken off for a semester."

"It has been really nice meeting you," the pastor told us. I hope you get to finish, and I hope your team wins today."

"Yes, sir. May the Prairie View Panthers win today. We will certainly remember you and this beautiful church," I told him as we walked away.

We headed toward my car, and to my amazement, that strange vehicle we had seen at the park had pulled up just a couple of parking places from where we were. This time I saw there was a sign on the side that said "Sister Shouting Nancy Will Tell Your Fortune for Only One Dollar."

The man who was driving got out and came toward us. He was a strange looking fellow, oddly dressed. "Good Morning," he said to us.

"Good Morning," we answered.

"Nice to see you again. We noticed you in the park back there. Wouldn't you like to have your fortune told? You are young, and you might like to know what the future holds for you."

"No, thank you," I said to him. "We were just leaving."

"Randy, why not?" Margaret whispered. "It would be fun. Let's do it."

"I don't think so." I whispered back. " I don't want mine told. I really don't believe in fortune tellers."

"Are you from Louisiana?" Margaret asked the man.

"Yes, we are."

"That makes it even more interesting," she whispered to me. "I've known others like them from there who were really good. Why not do it? It only costs a dollar. I'll even pay for it."

"It is OK with me if you want to do it. I will pay the dollar if it will make you happy, but it is not something I want to do for myself. I am skeptical about it."

Margaret nodded to the man and stepped toward him. He went to open the door of the car for the lady inside to get out. She had a colorful shawl around her head and shoulders. I noticed that she had a hard time getting out. There was something wrong with her foot. She had on a long dress with a coat over it. There was something about her that gave me a sense of fear, as if she were a witch of some kind. She hardly gave me a look. She went straight to Margaret and said, "Let me see your right hand."

Margaret extended her hand, and the lady looked it over. Then she asked to see the left hand. She held both Margaret's hands with hers looking at the palms. Then suddenly she let go of Margaret's right hand and mashed down hard on the left one with her free hand. I started to call out for her not to hurt Margaret, but before it was out of my mouth, she stopped. Then she took Margaret's right hand again and began to move her finger around, pointing to different spots. "I see you walking down a lovely path," she began. "Trees are budding, and flowers are blooming. It is a beautiful spring day, and you are walking among all the blooms. Then, suddenly clouds appear. A strong wind is pushing a very dark cloud toward you. It is a storm cloud. You need to run, run, run until you escape the danger of that storm.

"Here, I have something to give you, Margaret. She had a bag beside her that was held onto her shoulder with a strap. She reached into it and felt around. She pulled out something that looked like a marble, a large one of colored glass. "You take this and keep it," she told Margaret. "It will protect you from the storm."

Then the lady turned to me. I had the dollar bill in my hand that I was going to give her. All this had given me an uneasy feeling, and I just wanted to get away. As I handed it to her, she gave me a deeply searching look. "In days to come," she said. "You will wish you had let me tell your fortune too." With that, she turned around and walked back toward her truck.

"Let's go, Honey," I said to Margaret, and took her hand as we walked back to my car. I was very quiet. I couldn't think of anything I wanted to say.

Finally Margaret put her hand on my arm and asked, "Are you all right?"

"Yeah, why shouldn't I be?"

"You are being too quiet for you, and I guess I have known you long enough to know when you have something unsaid on your mind."

"Well, I have you on my mind, and the ball game we are going to see."

"No, it is something else. I feel like you are upset with me."

"Why should I be upset with you?"

"Because I had my fortune told."

"I told you that was all right with me for you to do that. I've got nothing to complain about that."

"Then I am through with it."

"Honestly, I am not upset with you, Honey."

She was quiet for a moment, and then she looked at me with tears in her eyes. "Margaret, I will turn around and go back and find those people and pay for them to tell you more, if you want. I'm not angry with you."

"Well, actions speak louder than words, and I just feel something is wrong between us."

With that I pulled off the road and stopped so I could take her hands and look into her eyes. "Honey, I just want you to be happy," I told her. "I would spend any amount of money or go to any lengths to make you happy. I love you that much."

"I'm sorry. I don't mean to make you feel like you are making me unhappy. "Here, let me show you something," she said as she reached in her purse and pulled out that marble. "I want to show you something that says more than words." She took that marble, and threw it all the way across the road. "That is to let you know how much your love means to me and that it is only your protection that I need. I just want to depend on you no matter what comes. Is that clear?"

"Thank you, yes, it is very clear and you are making me

very happy," I said with a smile that could banish any storm clouds that might arise. "Now, let's get on to that ball game." The heaviness I had felt melted and we drove on to the ball game with our spirits lifted.

We arrived there early, well before the game. We had time to walk around the campus. Margaret showed me the dormitory where she had lived. I was surprised at how many people knew her and seemed so delighted to see her, complimenting her and making a fuss over her. She seemed to be a very popular student. She showed me a small café, where we had lunch, and she was greeted by many people there. I felt very proud to be in her company.

We got in the crowd going to the stadium, and there too, everyone seemed to know her. We got seated, and a gentleman came up to us. "Margaret Mason!" he exclaimed. "How nice to see you again. How are you?"

"I'm quite well."

"We've missed you here at school."

"I've been out this semester, but I will come back."

"Oh, I hope so. Is this your friend."

"Yes, this is Randy Carter from Nelsonville."

I'm glad to meet you, Mr. Carter. I am Blaine Weaver. Are you a student here?"

"No, I attend a business college in Houston."

"What are you planning to do when you get through."

"He is already in business with his uncle," Margaret told him.

"Do you all happen to be planning a future together?"

"Yes, we are," I told him proudly. "As a matter of fact, I proposed to her today."

"Well, I certainly congratulate you! Do you mind if I sit here beside you?"

"Go ahead. We'll be happy to have your company," I told him. Margaret was sitting on the outside, so he sat down beside her. He took a package of chewing gum from his pocket. He offered us both a piece, and I took one. Margaret declined. I thanked him. He and I were unwrapping our gum, and Margaret asked for half of mine. "Sure," I said, and handed her half.

Mr. Wheeler's expression changed suddenly and he got up

and walked on up the bleachers without saying goodbye. I was somewhat puzzled, but I didn't say anything.

The ball game had started, and that held our attention. It was an exciting, close game, and Prairie View won. We walked out of the stadium feeling good. Margaret was saying goodbye to lots of people, but we finally got to the car and headed home.

After we got started, Margaret said, "Randy, I have something to tell you."

"What is it?"

"That Mr. Wheeler who stopped to talk to us before the game started was one of my instructors. He was always very friendly with me, and I accepted it for just that. Then later he let me know he was single, and indicated he wanted to go out with me. I wasn't interested, and I told him so. He asked me more than once, and I refused. Then a movie came to campus that everyone wanted to see, and he asked me to go with him. He promised that he would get me home in plenty of time and all that. As I said, he had always been very polite and nice. I hated to keep turning him down, so I finally agreed to go with him.

"After the movie, he took me to a campus café to eat. Then he asked me to go and visit him at his home. I said no, that it was late. He urged me some more, saying he just wanted me to see his nice apartment and promising to get me home before midnight. I said no again, that I had some work to do before bedtime.

"He finally insisted that I go with him, and I was angry and threatened to get out and walk. Then he was profusely apologetic and took me home. I immediately got out of the car and told him goodbye, as I was still upset.

"Another day, I ran into him on campus and he apologized again. He told me he knew he was out of line, that the movie and being with me had caused him to lose his head. I accepted his apology and told him he had surprised me with his forwardness.

"Then he told me he had not slept for thinking of me and that he would wait till I was ready, but he wanted me to be his bride. I was astonished. I told him I was not ready to be anybody's bride or to have a serious relationship at all. I told him he was wasting his time and mine. I told him I could not be more than friends with him and that I would see him in class. Then I walked away from him.

"I wanted you to know that was why he left so abruptly without saying anything back there. I want you to know that there was never anyone I wanted to date or make my life companion until I met you."

"Thank you, Margaret. I feel like the luckiest man in the world. Do you remember the words in that East Lynne play when the character, Archibald Carlysle spoke to his bride, Lady Isabelle?"

"I think so,"

"Would you sing them to me?"

She smiled and began to sing in a beautiful contralto voice," I love you truly, truly dear." What a moment! It is stamped permanently into my memory as one of the highest peak of joy in my life.

As we drove on, it suddenly hit me like a slap in the face that I was a married man and not divorced. I had conveniently forgotten that fact and had not told Margaret. I realized that it would be a mistake to keep something of that magnitude from her. I took a deep breath and began, "Margaret, there is something in my past that I have failed to tell you. I must tell you now."

"Randy, I don't care what it is. I know what kind of person you are. You have dignity and character. Your past doesn't matter. It doesn't matter if there was someone before me. We love each other. This has been a happy day. Let's keep it that way."

"I agree on that, but I really think I need to be open with you."

At that moment I heard a siren I looked into the rear view mirror and saw a police car behind me signaling me to pull over. I obeyed, and he pulled over and got out and walked toward us. He greeted us politely and asked if we had come from the game.

"Yes, sir," I answered him.

"Your car seemed to be weaving some. I thought that perhaps you had been drinking."

"Honestly, I have not had anything stronger than a soda

pop, sir," I told him. I guess I was being careless. There is no traffic, and we were talking." He asked me to get out and walk a few steps and I did.

"I guess you are OK to go on," he said amiably. "Just be careful."

We thanked him and drove away. I guess that interruption, along with the fact that she had expressed disinterest in my past, gave me a chance to let that confession go for the moment. Instead, I said to her, "I'd like to stop when we get to your house and tell your grandparents of my intentions and ask them for your hand."

"That surprises me."

"Why do you say that?"

"Well, even though parents are usually accepting of that, men usually find that a pretty scary thing to do. I thought you would put it off a little longer."

"No, I would like them to know how we feel about each other. I would really like to go ahead and do it if you are agreeable."

"Sure, that is fine with me."

They seemed glad to see us when we got there and even had dinner cooked for us. After we had eaten, Margaret told her grandmother that she would take care of the dishes later because I had something to say to them. Mr. Mason suggested that we all go into the living room. After we were seated, he invited me to say what was on my mind. Margaret and I looked at each other and her smile gave me courage.

"On the way to the ball game, I proposed to Margaret," I said. "I asked her to be my bride. I wanted to ask you and Mrs. Mason for your blessing and your consent for our marriage."

"Well, mama, what do you think about that," Mr. Mason said.

"I have a few concerns. Margaret has more school in front of her and she is not twenty yet. It seems like a pretty big step for her to take. Randy, I know you are a very nice young man and I have great confidence in you, but I hope you all will not jump into this so quickly. There is a lot more to marriage than love. You just need to think things through well. Papa, what do you say?"

122

"Mama, I agree with what you have said. Marriage is an honorable thing. It gives you many responsibilities that you haven't had before. You all are very young. I am not opposed to your getting married; I just hope you will take some time and make some concrete plans about making a home together. I do want Margaret to have the opportunity to finish her schooling."

"I want that, too." I told him. "We think we are able to face the future together."

"That sounds good. Have you talked about when you want to get married."

"No. We haven't decided on a time yet. I am in school too, you know. We do plan to wait a while, but not a long time."

"That sounds like you are going to take a little time and do it right," Mrs Mason declared. "Plan a nice wedding. It doesn't have to be big, but I would like to see you have a beautiful church wedding. We will start a hope chest."

"That sounds like a blessing," I said happily.

"Yes, you have my blessing and consent."

"And mine too," Mr. Mason chimed in. "We will be proud to have you in our family."

I left there on top of the world. I felt like I had made the greatest accomplishment of my life. Still that other marriage loomed over me as I drove home. I knew I had to get that straightened out. I was anxious to talk with mama about all this.

At first Mama was pleased about my feelings for Margaret. "She's a lovely, intelligent girl," she said. "I would be so proud to have her for my daughter-in-law. Then I have to think that I already have a daughter-in-law, Sylvia. Have you told Margaret about Sylvia."

"Actually not yet. I wish I had gotten that divorce before now. It was stupid of me to wait. Now I have to get it done. I want to talk to Uncle Cephus about it. He'll give me good advice. It is not that Margaret and I are going to get married right away, but I feel like I am hiding something from her and her family."

"I understand that, son, but it seems to me like you should have let her know about it from the beginning."

"Yes, I know that, but I was afraid she would not have

anything to do with me if I told her. I started to tell her today, but something happened and I didn't get a chance. When I started to tell her, she told me my past didn't matter, then something startled us and we didn't get back to it."

"I see, and I do understand. Do talk to your uncle and let him advise you."

"I'll do that first thing tomorrow."

Uncle Cephus was not surprised that I had completely turned around from the last time we had talked about a divorce for me. "I hate to say I told you so," he said. "I knew there was some girl out there who would change your mind."

"I remember, and I admit you were right."

"I told you when it happened to come tell me, so I'm glad you did. I do have a lawyer. I will call him today and see where we go from here. I also have some news for you. It is a bit of a mixture of good and bad news. Your Aunt Bessie heard at choir practice the other night that Sylvia had a miscarriage and lost that baby. It is sad about the baby's life, but it means you won't have to pay any child support. Have you had any conversations with Sylvia since that wedding."

"No, I sure haven't. I have not said one word to her since the day we got married."

"Well, I'll just get to work on getting something done. I'll keep you informed as I go on with it."

I felt a little guilty at the relief I felt at the news about the baby, and in somewhat of a daze at the ease at which Uncle Cephus was tackling the problem. I just had to wait, and that was going to be hard.

Meanwhile, Thanksgiving was coming up and Margaret and I were making plans. Margaret's grandmother had decided to have a big breakfast feast at her house on Thanksgiving and invite all their family. She suggested that Margaret plan to have dinner with my family. It was a great holiday for us because it gave Margaret and me both time to mix with the larger families we would be joining.

124

CHAPTER 8

Merry Christmas and an Unhappy New Year

Next we were talking about Christmas. I asked Margaret if her mother would be coming home, and she said that indeed she would. I was looking forward to meeting her.

"My mother may be a surprise to you," Margaret told me. "She is a fancy dresser and acts very much like a city girl. I don't know why I feel I have to tell you this. I guess I feel like you need to be a little prepared for her. Her lifestyle is quite different from ours."

"I think I can deal with that. Hey, why don't we go Christmas shopping together. I am not a great shopper, and I could use some help picking out gifts for my family. I know what to buy Bobby, but I'm at a loss when it comes to presents for Mama and Rose."

"That sounds like fun. I can get presents for my family at the same time."

Our shopping day was great. The shops were decorated and bells were ringing. It really got us in a Christmas mood. We planned to make a day of it, eat lunch together and learn new things about each other. We put a lot of thought into our gifts, found something for everyone and bought everything we needed to wrap them. I couldn't have done it in that kind of time without Margaret.

It seemed like Christmas came so quickly. I did get to meet the other Miss Mason, Margaret's mother, Charlotte. Most people come home for Christmas to see their family and friends. My impression of her was that she came home so everyone could see her. She had really gone all out to dress up for dinner. She had on high heels and a lot of jewelry and her hair was done in a fancy up-do. She was very nice to me though and asked me questions about my family and about school.

The dinner was very nice and we had a good time exchanging gifts. After that we were sitting around talking, and Charlotte wanted to know what we had planned for the rest of the evening.

"We really hadn't planned anything," I told her.

"It's Christmas night," she said, as if thoroughly exasperated. "If I were back in California, I would be going to a party or a movie or dancing or something. The night is young, and it is a time to celebrate."

"There is not much going on around here," I told her. "Most people stay home with their families on Christmas night."

"I guess that is what I get for coming to east Texas," she grumbled. "I guess I can put up with it until New Year's Eve. I will find something to do for sure on that night!"

"Dear me," I thought. "I had not expected to feel responsible for entertaining Margaret's mother. But after thinking about what kind of possibilities there were for New Year's Eve in east Texas, I remembered that a cousin of mine who lived in the city had told me about a dance her sorority was having on the Friday night before New Year's Eve. She had invited me to come as her guest and bring a date. Margaret and I had already discussed going. "Do you think your mother would like to go with us to that dance?" I asked her. "It is mostly for the sorority members who are out of school. There would be people her age there. Does she belong to a sorority?"

"No, she didn't go to college, but she might like to go."

"There will be a live band, and it will be about as fancy as it gets in these parts. Let's ask her."

When we asked her, however, she hesitated and said she hadn't really brought formal clothes. Margaret assured her that the dance wouldn't be all that formal, that after-five clothes would be quite acceptable. "We'd be honored to have you go with us," I told her. I think you would really enjoy it, and you would meet lots of people."

126

"I think I can find something to wear," she said finally. "Margaret, I have sent you a few dresses that had gotten too small for me. You should wear one of those."

"I have some things of my own too," Margaret declared. "I will look and see what I think looks best on me."

"And what will you wear?" Margaret's mother asked me.

"I have a brand new tux I wore to my high school prom just a few months ago, " I told her, and she looked quite surprised and pleased about that.

So the three of us went to the party, and it was lovely. It was a very sophisticated party. Alcoholic drinks were served, but there was nothing wild or loud going on. There was a great band, and I danced with both Margaret and Charlotte. There were a few unattached men there who also asked Charlotte to dance.

The people there were quite friendly and tastefully dressed. We introduced Charlotte to many people. Some of Margaret's teachers were there, and I knew some of the people because they had connections with my family.

"I really enjoyed that," Charlotte told us on the way home. "I appreciate so much that you invited me. It was really something quite different from what I am used to. That was a once-a-year event, and everyone was so reserved. In Los Angeles, I am used to parties every weekend, and they are anything but reserved. It was so sweet of you to take me, though."

The next day I was taking Margaret to a movie. When I went to pick her up, I had some time alone with her grandparents. They told me that Randy was out somewhere, and Charlotte was resting in her room.

"Does Charlotte know that Margaret and I are engaged?" I asked them. I had thought that Margaret or her family would have told her when she first arrived. I didn't think it was my place to do it. I was surprised and a little uncomfortable that Charlotte had never mentioned it.

"No," Papa Mason. replied. "We don't need to tell her that. She would probably react badly. She'll think she has to take over the wedding plans and decide everything for you. Don't tell her till right before she leaves. You agree with me on that, don't you Mama?"

"I do indeed! She is a good girl, but she is so willful. She just has to have her way about things."

"I do feel I need to ask for her consent," I told them. I hope she will be happy to give it. I want everyone to share our joy."

They assured me that all would be well.

The next day was Sunday. I saw Uncle Cephus there and had a chance to ask him how things were going with the divorce. "We're getting there," he told me. "These things do take some time though."

I always visited Margaret on Sunday, and that afternoon was no exception. I was with Margaret and her grandparents in the living room. Charlotte was again in her room. I brought up the subject of getting Charlotte's consent again. I really wanted to get this chore behind me.

"Well, if you really want to, I guess it is time," Mama Mason sighed.

"I'll go get her," Papa M. spoke up.

Charlotte entered the room in her elegant housecoat like a queen. "Papa says you have a surprise for me," she said expectantly. "You have all given me so many beautiful presents. What more can there be?"

I stood up and went over to her. "You will soon be leaving, and we didn't want you to go without knowing about our happiness. I have asked Margaret to marry me, and she has consented to do so. We have talked with Mr. and Mrs. Mason, and they have given us their consent and their blessing. We want you to be as happy as we are and to give us your blessing, too."

She just stood there for a moment looking blank. "Are you surprised?" her mother asked.

"Yes, I really am. Margaret is in school. How is she going to get married and go to school?"

"They didn't say they are going to get married tomorrow," her mother said gently. "They are in love and making a commitment to marry in the future."

"Well when?"

"They haven't set a date yet."

"Well, they can't live on love. Margaret, speak up girl! You are just standing there. Tell me what you are thinking."

128

"Grandma has said most of what needs to be said. Randy and I have lots in common and feel so connected. Each time we are together, the bond between us strengthens. We feel we are old enough to make this decision, and it is what we want to do."

"Where do you think you will live?" Charlotte asked with an anxious look.

"Randy works at the mortuary in town. I guess we'll live in Nelsonburg."

"In that hick town?" There is nothing going on in east Texas. I just can't imagine that you would want to spend your life in this place. You really need to think more about it. Take some more time."

Mr. Mason spoke up then. "They may not be like you. You can't choose what somebody else should do. They are grown-ups. They need to decide on their own. All they are doing is asking you to give them your consent."

"I'm going to tell you something. I had kept it to myself till now. I brought enough money to buy a ticket for Margaret to go back with me to California. She has never been out of Texas. I want her to see what it is like in my world, to have some new experiences. I just can't see her staying here all her life!"

"Mother, it is like this!" Margaret interrupted her. "Randy and I are in love. We have promised ourselves to each other. What you are planning just isn't going to take place. It is really our decision to make. We just want your blessing. As for going to California with you, how were you expecting me to get ready to do that in just two days. I'm not prepared to do that, nor do I want to. I'll stay here with Mama and Papa."

"Why, they're doing fine. They don't need you. Mama is still able to do all the cooking and cleaning."

"It's not because they need me. I just prefer to stay here. It is home to me."

At that Charlotte turned to me. "Randy, do you feel comfortable asking my daughter to live in Nelsonburg? What kind of job or business would you have?"

"Like Margaret said, I work with my uncle in the mortuary."

"You mean you pick up dead folks and that kind of thing?

129

That doesn't seem like the kind of life I want for my daughter."

"No, that is not my job. We have other people who pick up the bodies and do the embalming and all. I am in the business part of it. I take care of the bills and insurance and contracts."

"Well, it still feels wrong to me. It is not what I want for Margaret."

About that time it started to thunder.

Mr. Mason interrupted, "Look how dark it is out there. I heard there was a cold front coming in and possibly even some snow."

"I might better get on home. I don't want to be driving on a slick road. Please excuse me. We had better talk about this another time." I said, feeling relieved to have an excuse to get away from this conversation.

They all walked with me out on the porch and it was obvious that the weather was changing rapidly. "I hate to see you go," Margaret declared giving me a hug. "You'd better get on, though."

I started to walk down the steps, and just then a car drove up and pulled in right behind my car. I didn't recognize the car, but a lady got out with some papers in her hand. As she came to the gate, the car drove away. To my surprise, it was Sylvia. She walked right up where we all were. "I came to tell you all something I think you need to know," she began.

"I am Mrs. Carter, Mrs. Randy Carter. I am married to that man right there, and I have a copy of the marriage licence here to prove it. He's come up here to see this girl, and he is already married to me, and there has been no divorce."

"Let me see that paper," Charlotte demanded. She looked at it, and she looked at me. "Of all things! You should be ashamed of yourself, Randy Carter. Mama, did you know anything about this?"

"No, I surely didn't."

Charlotte asked Papa too, and of course he had not known a thing about it. Like everyone else, he looked stunned. "How could you be here asking for my daughter's hand in marriage, when you are already married? Is what this girl says true?"

I was in shock. I managed to stammer out, "Well, yes, but . . .

130

"But what!" She demanded stridently.

I could see that Margaret was crying. Mama Mason had her arms around her. "Please, let me explain! I really can explain all this."

"What the devil do you mean?" Charlotte demanded. How are you going to explain a wife who is here right now? I want you off this property, away from here, right now!"

I looked beseechingly at Papa Mason. "I would like to explain myself. Please!"

At that point Margaret's brother, Randy stepped between us and shouted at me. "No, man! Don't say another word. Get off this porch right now! If you have a problem with that, I will help you. You had better leave at once!"

Margaret was crying harder than ever, and her grandmother was urging her inside the house. I could think of nothing else I could do at the moment except leave. I walked toward my car with my head bent. Sylvia followed me and started to get in on the passenger side.

"Don't you touch my car!" I commanded her furiously.

"It's raining! You've got to take me somewhere."

"I'm not taking you anywhere. Who brought you here?"

"That doesn't matter." She started to open the door again, and again I dared her to do it. "Help, help! Police!" she called loudly.

Besides the Masons who were still on the porch, neighbors were coming out and gaping at us. I walked around the car to confront her, but she had gotten in and shut and locked the door. I was furious. About that time, the sky opened up and the rain began to pour down. There was nothing I could do but go back around and get in and drive away. I didn't speak to her; I just started the car and drove off. I cut a corner so fast the car swerved hard toward the ditch.

"You're going to kill us," she screeched.

"I don't care," I shouted back. I drove on furiously until I got to the edge of Nelsonville. I came to a café there and saw a car that looked like the one she had come to the Mason's in. I didn't know for sure, but I didn't care. I know there would be a phone inside and she could call someone. I pulled in by the car. "Get out," I told her. "If you don't, I'll come over there and pull you out."

She hesitated. People were looking out of the windows of the café. It was still raining, but not as heavily. "Get out," I demanded again, and finally she did.

There was nowhere to go now but home. The anger I had felt had given me strength. Now that the source of it was out of sight, I suddenly was overcome with despondency. I felt like my life was over. So much had gone badly for me this year, and, now, just when I had found someone who seemed so perfect for me, the ill wind had blown over me again. I could not have imagined such a terrible turn of events. I was sick at heart, and thought I would never recover.

Everyone was in bed when I got home. I was glad, because I wasn't up to talking about it. I went to bed and slept fitfully. When I woke up, it was very cold and ice covered the ground. Nevertheless, I felt stronger. "I'm not giving up," I thought. "I'm going to fight to get Margaret back."

I waited till about nine o'clock that morning, and then called the Mason house. Randy answered the phone. "Is this the Mason house," I asked.

"Yes, and you are the other Randy. We don't want to talk to you." He hung up the phone.

That didn't deter me. I had to think of something else to do. I remembered a neighbor of Margaret's I had met recently, a girl close to her age. Maybe she would talk to me and get Margaret to listen to a message from me. It was a long shot, but I had to try. Her name was Sarah Mayberry, and I found what I thought was her number in the phone book.

I was relieved when it was Sarah herself who answered the phone. "Sarah, my name is Randy Carter. Remember me, I'm Margaret's friend."

"Yes, I remember you. Is something wrong?"

"There was a misunderstanding between Margaret and me and, actually, her whole family."

"Well, it has been awfully quiet over there this morning, but then it is so cold and icy that no one is getting out.

"I need so badly to talk to her and try to straighten things out. She hasn't answered the phone when I call, and nobody else over there will talk to me. Do you think you could get her to come over to your house and call me."

"Well, maybe later. It is just too icy to get out right now. The sun is out. Maybe this afternoon I could do something."

"Well, OK. I will try you again later. I really do need to talk to her badly."

It was torture, but I waited. After lunch it was still cold, but it was clear. I tried Sarah's number again.

"I'm afraid they are gone," Sarah told me. Miss Charlotte told me they were going to California. They have been gone an hour or so. She said they were going to catch a train."

I knew that train. It didn't come through until around two. I thought perhaps I could catch her before she left. I dressed hurriedly and got in the car and headed toward Houston, where the train came in. There was some ice on the roads, but I was careful. I wanted so to have her thinking a little better of me before she left.

I knew the way to the train station. When I got there, I could see that the train was already there. I parked and jumped out and ran. Sure enough, they had not boarded the train yet. Margaret and her mother and Randy were all there in a huddle talking.

Before I got to them, Randy picked up their luggage and headed toward a door on the train, and they were following him. I got there just as they were getting on. "Margaret!" I called to her. She turned around and looked at me somberly and barely raised her hand. The train was starting to move. Randy stepped in front of Margaret and off the train. He looked at me angrily, like he wanted to kill me. Then slowly, the train pulled away I watched it pick up speed and take Margaret away from me. I watched till it was out of sight.

I'll never forget that day. I just stood there, and my pain must have been pretty obvious. A white man was standing there close by me. "Kind of tough, ain't , brother," he said sympathetically.

"It sure is," I admitted.

"I've been in your shoes," he declared. "I know what it feels like."

I looked him in the eye and knew he was speaking the truth. I felt slightly comforted. "Thanks, brother," I said softly.

"I wish you better luck," he replied.

I walked back to my car and got in. I just couldn't go home yet. I drove aimlessly around the city. I drove and drove, looking at shop windows, but not really seeing what was in them. I finally had to stop at a filling station for gas. I noticed a sign there that said FIREWORKS.

I thought I would buy some of those fireworks for Rose and Bobby for tomorrow. It would be New Year's Day. The attendant pumped my gas, but before I went into the station to pay and get the fireworks, I noticed across the street that same strange vehicle that Margaret and I had seen on our trip to the football game, Sister Shouting Nancy's truck. The curtain of the trailer was open, and she was sitting there looking out.

I remembered what she had last said to me, that I would regret not having my fortune told. I wondered if perhaps I should seek her advice. But just as that thought had entered my mind, a handsome black car drove by and the people inside must have noticed her sign because they turned around and came back to turn in right beside Nancy's truck. They got out and went into the trailer, and Sister Nancy closed the curtain. Those people would be taking up her time for a while, and since I was still reluctant to believe what Sister Nancy would tell me anyway, it seemed enough of a sign to me that I should go on and leave my future to the Lord. I got in my car and drove on home.

I could think of nothing but Margaret. I had no way of getting in touch with her. I felt I had lost her forever. It was the hardest, saddest, coming of a New Year I had ever experienced. I had to think about Sylvia. Why would she want to cause me so much pain. I had done nothing to her that should warrant her behavior toward me.

CHAPTER 9

Was It Suicide or Murder?

THE FOLLOWING WEEK I had a huge surprise. Someone called the office at the mortuary and told the receptionist there that Mrs. Malvo had been found dead. She had not gone to Mr. Levy's house to work that day, and when Mr. Levy sent the yard man to look for her at her house, she was lying across the bed dead.

Apparently there were some pills poured out on her dresser, and suicide was suspected. The Justice of the Peace had been called to determine if that was a fact. Sylvia had been out somewhere with Buster and Gertrude, and no one had found her to tell her about her mother.

The Justice of the Peace declared it a suicide, and even though Sylvia had not yet been found, Mr. Levy took responsibility for having the body picked up and promised to get Sylvia to the funeral home to make arrangements as soon as possible. Uncle Cephus came into my office shortly after we had been called. "I have some news for you," he began.

"What's happening?"

"They found Mrs. Malvo dead this morning. They are saying it is a suicide."

"Wow! That is a surprise. I'm sorry, but I don't think there is anything I can do."

"Well, you are really her son-in-law you know. Mr. Levy might expect you to help make decisions. Sylvia was not there and hasn't come in yet."

"Why? Sylvia hates me, and I'm trying to get a divorce. I certainly don't want to see her. I'm sorry the lady died, but I don't want to have anything to do with it unless I am forced.

I have a feeling that Sylvia may try to force me to be involved in some way. I don't know why she does any of the things she does. I'll stay out of it as much as I can."

"I do have to send somebody to get the body."

"Sure, I understand that. Go ahead."

It was really hard to work after Uncle Cephus left my office. I couldn't concentrate on anything. I kept thinking about Mrs. Malvo and how little I knew about her. I wondered if Sylvia would ship the body back somewhere they had lived before. I went out to the drink machine and sat down to drink a Coke. I wanted to go home, but I felt like Uncle Cephus might need me to witness something about Mrs. Malvo. I went back in my office to sweat it out.

The next thing I knew, Uncle Cephus was back, knocking on my door again. "Come out here! I am going to tell you something that will floor you!"

"What in the world?"

"We've been working on Mrs. Malvo's body, and you are not going to believe what I'm about to tell you."

"Well, tell me!"

"She's a man!"

His statement didn't quite get through to me. I felt befuddled. I thought there must be a mistake. "Have you somehow gotten the wrong body?"

"No, no. It is the same person. Come out here and see for yourself. She has all the things that make her look like a woman, make up and feminine underclothes, and she was wearing a wig. She still looks like a woman, but she is a man! Come on! You have to look."

I saw with my own eyes that Uncle Cephus was right. I could hardly believe it, but it was true. "Maybe when they find Sylvia, she will tell what this is all about," I said. "Have you talked to Mr. Levy about it?"

"No, we haven't told anybody," Uncle Cephus replied. "I feel like we should talk to the girl first. I'm still waiting to hear from her. And, by the way, Randy, the divorce papers have come. All you have to do is get her to sign them."

"I have to wonder if she will. She is anything but cooperative, and this is certainly not the time to ask. I am so tired of all this. I don't know what I have done to her to make her treat me so badly. She has made a mess of my life, and I feel like I've lost the only person who could make it bearable, all because of her. I know it is partly my own fault for not telling Margaret the truth from the start, but Sylvia's behavior has made me think there is really a demon in her. She has the power to ruin me. I just need to go home and try to get some peace. I certainly don't want to see Sylvia today!"

"I understand, and I hate to do this to you, but I have to ask you to stay. I need you to be here with me when she comes to help me determine the truth of what she will say. We have to get to the bottom of this man's deception. We may need to call in the Sheriff. You are involved and you need to be here. Take courage, I will be right here with you. Surely we can face down this devil together and, with God's help, the truth will come out, and things will get better."

"Yes, sir," I sighed, and there was no conviction in my voice that I believed any of his encouraging words.

Just then the phone rang and I answered it. "This is Carter Mortuary. Randy Carter speaking."

"Has someone in the community recently died?" the voice on the other end asked.

"I think we have gotten a body just now, but I can't give out any information on it yet."

"We live in the neighborhood and saw the ambulance go by. We were just wondering."

"Call back sometime later, and we may be able to tell you something. We have to talk to the family first." Uncle Cephus was listening and nodding his head that I was saying all the right things.

After that the receptionist came to the door and told us that Sylvia was here with Buster and Gertrude. "Come on," Uncle Cephus said. "Let's go and get this over with. I have certainly never had an experience like this, but it is just something we are going to have to deal with. You know, your Aunt Bessie is really good when it comes to dealing with difficult people. I think I'll call her and get her to come down and be with us."

Aunt Bessie was in the house that adjoined the funeral home. Uncle Cephus gave her quick briefing over the phone, and she came right over. Then we all walked down to Uncle

Cephus' office where Sylvia was waiting with Buster and Gertrude. Uncle Cephus asked them to wait in the reception hall while we spoke with Sylvia privately.

Uncle Cephus explained to Sylvia how Mr. Levy had given us permission to pick up the body and begin preparing it, and that part of that preparation included undressing it. "And I guess you know what we found," he finished.

Sylvia's expression changed to one of horror and she looked like she was going to jump up and bolt. Aunt Bessie went to her, and began to talk to her soothingly. "Look, honey," she said, "we're not here to make trouble for you. We just want to help you"

Sylvia dropped her head and let her tense body go limp. "I'm sure you know that the truth has to come out in this situation," Aunt Bessie continued. "We're here to help you get through this. You need to tell us who this person really is. There is no one here but you and the Carters. It is possible that no one else will need to know."

"Sylvia sat there twisting her hands in her lap. "It is a very long story," she began. "For starters, I have lied about my age. I am almost nineteen. My real mother gave birth to me, and I guess she didn't want me. She gave me to an old lady who died when I was about ten. Every one in the community just sort of shared me after that. I went to school and after school went from one house to another for my meals and a place to sleep. I didn't know enough about my birth mother to try to find her. When I was fourteen, I ran away from the small Kansas community I grew up in and went to Kansas City. I had saved enough money working for farmers and caring for children to rent a room and buy some food. I thought I could get a job and take care of myself.

"I lied about my age then, too. I said I was sixteen. I got a job in a hamburger stand, and that is where I met the person you knew as Mrs. Malvo. His real name was Eddie Walker. He came to eat at the stand regularly and we got to know each other. He asked me to be his girlfriend and said he would take care of me. He seemed to have plenty of money and he gave me money for different things I needed. I was easily persuaded that he was a good person and that I would have a better life with him.

138

"He told me he worked as a cook in a fine hotel. I assumed that was why he had money. He had a new car, too. He started coming to my room and spending the night. He acted very jealous. He said he didn't want any other man fooling with me. He wanted me to stay in my room when I was not working. He told me he would get me anything I needed. I could have my hair fixed and my nails done. I loved that.

"Then one night he came in late and told me to pack just what I would need for a few days, that we were going to leave town at once. I had been asleep, and I was flabbergasted, but he ordered me to get everything I had together and that we had to be gone very quickly. I was terrified, but I did what he said.

"As we left, he had me lock the door. We got in his car and drove. I was still not familiar with Kansas City. It was dark, and I had no idea even which direction we were going. After we had gone about fifty miles, he stopped for gas and he gave me the money and made me go in and pay for it. We drove all night. I began to notice signs that made me realize we were going south. I woke up often enough to know we drove through Oklahoma and into Texas. When dawn came we turned off the main highway and drove to a big lake and stopped. He made me get out and get my things out, too. I thought he might be going to leave me there or throw me in the lake. Instead, he told me to stay still and be calm. He got in the car and started it, then jumped out and let the car go into the lake. I watched it disappear.

"Eddie had a small bag and a briefcase. He had me carry the briefcase, and he took the two bags. We walked about a half mile back to the highway. There was a gas station in sight, and we walked there. He looked up a number and called a cab that came and took us to a motel. The sun was coming up as we got there. I have no idea what town we were in but it was a fair size and at this time of day pretty quiet, people weren't out yet.

"Instead of going right into the motel and finding a room, Eddie found a corner to put our bags out of sight, and got me to walk with him all around the area as if he were checking out the other motels. I had no idea what he was doing, but later I realized that he was planning to have a place to move if he got wind that someone was looking for him.

"When Eddie was satisfied, we went back to the motel where we had started and got a room on the second floor. It wasn't a fine motel, but it was nice enough. We were both exhausted and went to bed. He was restless, and his tossing and turning kept me awake, but I guess we both dozed off and on. We got up around noon and we were hungry. At first he was going to get me to go to get us something to eat, but he changed his mind. He said we were going to go together because we had some shopping to do.

"Before we left, though, he carefully wrapped his briefcase in some big bath towels and got some bills out of his bag and then put some in his pocket and some under the mattress next to the springs. He told me we would go shopping after lunch.

"We found a small café and had lunch. He asked our waiter if there was a used car lot near by, and the waiter gave him directions to one. We went straight there after lunch, and he bought a car without even driving it. The salesman tried to get him to drive it, but Eddie acted like a big shot and told the man that, if the car gave him trouble, he had a lawyer who would make sure he got his money back. He paid the man cash, and we drove out of there.

"The car salesman had given him directions to a department store. That is where we went next. He bought new clothes for me, and started picking out some larger sized women's clothing. I gave him an astonished look. That is when he told me he was going to disguise himself. He told me he had made some enemies, and they wouldn't be looking for two women.

"He was not a big man, and he was not muscular. He was slender and had small feet. He easily found women's shoes he could wear. He had me try on wigs, and we bought two. At another store we bought makeup, razor blades, shaving cream and tweezers.

"I had sense enough to know he had been involved in crime, and I should have gotten away from him right then, but I didn't even know where I was. I had money from my last paycheck, but I had no confidence that I could get myself back to Kansas City or survive in a new place. Eddie had made my life easier and he was good to me. I was just sixteen then, and I'd never had anyone who made me feel cared for like he did.

"We went back to the motel and spent the night there. We left before dawn with Eddie in his new disguise. We drove all day, and again I had no idea where we were going. I didn't ask questions, and I slept most of the time.

"I hope you all aren't getting weary of this story. I have never told anyone any of this before. I hope you will try to understand my part in it." At that point she looked directly at me with pleading eyes and said. "Especially you, Randy, I hope and pray you can understand. I am truly sorry for all you have suffered because of me."

"You poor, poor child!" Aunt Bessie said gently. "You have been through a lot. We are not tired of hearing your story. You are not responsible for the things he made you do." She looked at me, expecting me to say something.

"All I wanted was to understand why you were treating me so badly when I had not done anything to hurt you," I said. "I'm beginning to now, I guess, so please go on with your story."

"Well, this is the town where we stopped. We stayed in the hotel here the first night. The next day we heard that Mr. Levy had lost some of his workers, and that one was his cook. Eddie had learned to cook from his mother, and then had worked as a cook in a hotel. He thought a farm would be a peaceful and safe place for him to stay hidden from the people who were hunting him. Eddie was smart. He had already pitched his voice higher, and the clothes he had chosen were plain and drab, just perfect for applying for a cook's job. He could have fooled anyone.

"He went to Mr. Levy and introduced himself as Edith Malvo who had come from Louisiana. Edith boasted about all the fancy French and other foreign food she knew how to make. She said we had been through some changes in our life and just needed to get away to some small place where we could live quietly. Mr. Levy was impressed with her and gladly hired us. Her job was to do the cooking and housekeeping in the main house, and I was to share in the chores. I was given a small salary, too.

"We were pleased with the house Mr. Levy put us in. It

only had one bedroom, but it had running water, and all the things we needed to make it a home. We met the other people who worked for Mr. Levy. Buster and Gertrude became good friends. Edith told everyone I was her daughter. She would send me to town with Buster and Gertrude, and I bought all the groceries. She avoided going into town.

"She still had the bag full of money and kept it well hidden. I had seen her fooling with it and knew it was full of bills. I never asked her about it though. She made me call her Edith even when we were alone, and made me dress like a high school girl in bobby socks and low heeled shoes and skirts like the girls wore to school.

"I was loyal to Edith and did everything she told me to do. I was fairly satisfied with our situation. Life for me was far better than it had been before. I had a feeling of security. Eddie or Edith was both my parent and my mate.

"But then I got pregnant. We had taken precautions, but somehow it had happened anyway. Eddie was furious and tried to blame me for it. He talked about an abortion, and that was something I knew nothing about. He carried on about how people would talk and wonder how I could have gotten that way since I'd had no boyfriends, and I was always on the farm or with Buster and Gertrude.

"Eddie began to talk about going to Mexico. He said he had enough money that we could buy a house there and live well. I wanted to stay here. I felt safe and liked all the people on the farm. I reminded him of how the farm was fenced and remote from anyone who would want to do him harm. Mr. Levy kept the gate locked at night and was on personal terms with the Sheriff and other important people around.

"Eddie told me he would think about it, but something had to be done about the baby. I could not imagine what, and I was afraid. Shortly after that was when he decided to get Buster to teach me to drive the car. It was on one of those first driving lessons that I almost ran over you, Randy. When we came home, Buster was telling Edith about how nice you had been about it and talked about your family and all the property they owned.

"A few days later, Edith cooked that barbeque for you and suggested to Buster that, when he delivered it, to ask you to go to a movie with all of us. When that didn't work out, he thought up the fishing trip and how to get me alone with you and manage to get Buster and Gertrude sidetracked long enough that something could happen between us. He coached me to seduce you. Then when that storm came up unexpectedly, it worked into our plans perfectly.

"I was desperate when I insisted we go on down to the river and not wait for them. I was playing the role Eddie had told me I had to. Then when we got down there and started catching fish, I really got excited about that. It was true that I had never caught a fish, and I almost forgot what I had to do, partly because I really didn't want to trick Randy.

"Honestly, whatever Randy has told you is the truth. He did everything he could to get us out of there, and he treated me with every consideration. He tried so hard to make me feel comfortable and acted like a perfect gentleman. He was so kind and good looking and talked to me like I was a person who was worth something. In that isolated piece of time, it was as if we were the only two people in the world, and I fell under a spell of passion for him. I wanted the comfort of his arms. I did everything in my power to get him to make love to me, and it crushed me that he would not.

"I hope you understand me telling you all this. The trouble I have caused Randy has been weighing heavy on me. Now that I can tell it, I have to tell it all.

"I was angry with him because it seemed to me that he thought he was better than me. I thought I was desirable and I couldn't understand him rejecting me after he had been so kind to me. I'm sorry, Randy. But that made it easier to lie and say that you were responsible for my pregnancy and force you to become my husband.

"Randy, I truly want to make that up to you somehow. I want to take away this cloud I have brought into your life."

My emotions were in such a turmoil, I hardly knew what I was feeling. I did feel some sympathy and understanding for Sylvia, but my heart still felt hard. I was relieved that Uncle Cephus and Aunt Bessie finally heard those words from the only person who could verify my truthfulness, but I believed my injuries where Margaret and her family were concerned were irreversible. "What could you possibly do to make all this right? I feel like my life is always going to be tainted by this marriage."

"Randy, and Mr. and Mrs. Carter, here is what I want to do. First I would like to bury this body, and then I want to go away from here. I have no kinfolks to go back to. I don't know where I'll go, but I need a new start.

"I have enough money to pay for the funeral and go somewhere. I was at my house at Mr. Levy's before I came here. I feel sure that some people who had it in for him finally found him. There were some things gone from the house that Eddie had guarded that I know were there when I left. They thought they got everything, but they didn't. And as for those pills, I think they just spilled them to make it look like he took them. I think they poisoned him with something else. They wrote a note to make it look like he killed himself, but I know his handwriting. That was not his.

"I have no idea who they were or how they managed to find him. I believe they were in some kind of big racket and that, for some reason, he had run away with all their money. He kept most of it in a certain bag that he kept well hidden, and they found that. He had also taken part of it out and put it in other places. There is enough they didn't find to get me a start somewhere.

"Everyone here has always known Eddie as Edith. They would be so shocked by all this. I really don't want to have to explain it all. It is so unbelievable. Is it possible for us to just bury him as Edith Malvo and keep his true identity a secret? I doubt that Eddie Walker really is his name. Everything about him was made up. We have no friends but those we have made here. He never told me about any family he had. He talked about a mother, but he never told me her name."

Uncle Cephus didn't answer at once. "Let me think about it," he finally replied. "For the time being, we won't say anything about it to anyone. We'll just go ahead and plan the funeral for Edith."

"I just want to take a few of my things and leave here." Sylvia said anxiously. "I will give the Edith clothes away or throw them away if no one wants them. There is a lot of meat in the freezer. I will give some to Buster and Gertrude and

144

some to you all. I can't take it with me, and it will keep well for a long time in the freezer."

Uncle Cephus was uneasy about burying a man as a woman, but he went to see the Sheriff and asked to see pictures of people who were wanted by the law. He told the Sheriff the he had some suspicions about somebody, but he didn't let on who he was talking about. He looked and looked for a long time, but he never found one that looked like Eddie or Edith, so he decided that we could go ahead and bury Edith as she was known here. Sylvia wanted it done as quickly as possible, and we managed to bury her the next afternoon.

Later she did bring us some packages of meat and two of them had my name on them. I didn't want to take anything from her. I suggested to Uncle Cephus that we just use it all for one big barbeque. When we opened them, however, one of the packages with my name was full of money, bills that had been wrapped just like meat. It was a lot of money, more than I had ever seen at one time. The other package was T-bone steaks, a favorite of mine. I realized how hard Sylvia was trying to make up to me for all the problems she had caused me.

I had to get her to sign the divorce papers, so I had to meet with her again. I thanked her for the gifts and told her I understood the terrible position she had been in and forgave her.

"Randy, do you think you could take this car that Eddie bought?" she asked me. "I am afraid to drive it. I am afraid those people who killed him know the car and might try to do something to me if I take it. Your family could use it as a second car and those people will think I sold it to you. I will give it to you, if you will take it. I am planning to leave here by bus, and go out west somewhere. I have enough money to get myself started somewhere in a city. "

"Sylvia, you have done enough for me. I don't really need a car."

"It is worth something. I just don't have time to stay here and sell it, and I would like you to benefit from it. Please take it. Let somebody in your family drive it or you sell it."

"Well, my brother and sister will both be old enough to drive soon. I guess we could use it."

"Thank you," she said. "And before I leave here, I have some other things in mind to make up for the harm I've done you. Your forgiveness means everything to me. I can leave here now with my conscience at rest."

"Sylvia, I know now that you have suffered from all this as much as I have. I am sorry your life has been so difficult. I hope and pray you find some true happiness in your new life. You will truly be in my prayers." I spoke those words from the bottom of my heart. Then we said goodbye, and I never saw her again.

CHAPTER 10

Reconciliation

THE VERY NEXT DAY I had a shock. I got a call from Margaret. I knew her voice the moment she said my name. "Margaret, I am so thankful you called. I didn't know how to get in touch with you."

"I just had to call you," she said.

"Is anything wrong?" I asked.

"No, nothing's wrong. I just couldn't not talk to you again."

"Thank goodness. I am so happy to hear your voice."

"I am glad to hear yours, too. Randy, that girl called me, Sylvia, the one who came to the house that day. She had been to see my grandparents and gotten my phone number. She told me about what really happened and how she had tricked you. She explained to me about what had happened and how you had been so kind to her and then she had lied and said that you raped her. She said she wanted to clear it all up with me so that you and I could get back together. I should have known that you couldn't have been guilty of all that. I should have been patient and given you a chance to explain. I am so sorry. I beg you to forgive me."

"Of course I forgive you. Forgive me for not telling you the story before I asked you to marry me. I got so carried away that day, and I was going to tell you, but after that police car stopped us, I lost my nerve. I don't blame you for your reactions that day. I blame myself more than you."

"Oh Randy, do you still love me?"

"I have always loved you and always will. I just have one question for you."

"What it that?"

"Will you marry me?"

"You already asked me that, but yes, I truly want to be Mrs. Randall Carter even more than ever."

"Will you be my June bride."

"Yes I will, and June can't come soon enough."

"I will count the days."

"Mama and I will be home at Easter, and then it will be no time till June."

"I'm glad. I was afraid you would like California and want to stay. I was in agony not knowing how to get in touch with you, but I couldn't go ask your grandparents."

"I know. Sylvia went to see them too, you know. She apologized to them and made them understand how innocent you were in spite of how it looked. Please go see them. They will welcome you."

"You don't know what a burden this news takes from me. I will go see them soon. It will be hard to wait till Easter to see you."

"Yes, that sounds great, and we can talk on the phone and write letters."

"I feel like a new man. I am going to be dancing and leaping with joy everywhere I go. I can't wait to tell my family the good news!"

And that is just what I did as soon as we finished our conversation. I was so elated, and everyone I told was just as happy for me. It was like we had all been living under a heavy rock since the year began, and now it had been lifted off.

I didn't waste much time about going to see the Masons, and apologize for my part in the deception. They were welcoming and apologized to me for their lack of faith, that they didn't give me a chance to tell my part of the story. I told them I never blamed them, that I should have been straight forward with them from the beginning. They restored their blessings on me and my engagement to Margaret. Even Randy Mason apologized profusely for the way he had shunned me and kept me away from Margaret.

The good news was traveling fast, and when Mama told Aunt Molly, she told Mama that she was going to move in with her daughter within the next month, and she would like for

Margaret and me to live in her house and use its furnishings. She didn't want to rent it to just anybody. She wanted someone she knew to live there. I was overwhelmed, because Aunt Molly had beautiful antique furniture. She was quite elderly, but she had been to school in the east and was very refined. She prized the nice things she had, and had spent years collecting them.

I started right away going over there to work on the yard and flower beds and see what I might want to paint and fix up. It pleased Aunt Molly so. She told me to do whatever I wanted to do to the house to make it like Margaret and I would want it to be.

When Margaret came home for Easter we were together constantly and so happy. Everyone we met seemed to enjoy being around us. Everywhere we went it seemed like people were celebrating our love with us.

We had a beautiful week together. Our families had dinners for us, and I took Margaret to see the house we were going to live in. Aunt Molly had moved out by then. We spent one day painting the bedroom that would be ours. We took a picnic out to the farm. We spent some time with John and James. They were still so happy that they were the ones who had gotten us together. Everyone believed we had a wonderful life in front of us.

Margaret's mama was another story. She and Margaret had come back from California together, and she did not come out of her room much when I was there. When she did, her conversations with me were brief, and she still seemed angry with me. "I still don't feel right about this engagement," she would say pointedly. "I don't like the idea that you have been married before."

"There was nothing I could do about that at the time or now, ma'am," I would answer as politely as I could. "I was not intimate with that girl, and she is gone now. The divorce is final, and she is out of my life."

Charlotte still kept a scowl on her face when I was around and looked at me suspiciously. I did my best to stay out of her way, and did not try to argue with her.

I begged Margaret not to go back to Los Angeles, but she insisted that she had to. "I have a job, you know," she told me. "I need to keep it a little longer, and mama needs me. She has these awful migraine headaches lately. That is part of the reason she is so cross. I think I can bring her around to being happy about you and me if I give her a little more of my time. I've never spent much time with her, you know. There will not be a better opportunity for me to let her know I love her and convince her that you and I should be together. When June comes, it will be time for you and me, and that is a promise.

CHAPTER 11

Eventide and One Last Call

I GOT A SURPRISE CALL from Margaret one day. It had been a little while since we had talked. "I'm so glad to hear from you," I told her. "Is everything OK?"

"Well, just fair."

I could tell by the sound of her voice that she was less than fair. "What's wrong?" I asked her.

"I've decided to come home."

"I'm expecting you to come in June."

"No, I mean right away."

"Is something wrong?"

"Yes, Mama has been giving me a hard time. She is trying to push this other man on me. He has been over here a few times. I don't like him at all, but he is wealthy, and I think she owes him some money. She likes to play the horses, you know."

"No, I didn't know that, but somehow that doesn't surprise me."

"Well, this man is really coming on to me, he has even proposed to me. She is trying to talk me into it because he has money and a good job. He is thirty-nine years old, for goodness sake! She acts like she doesn't even hear me when I remind her I'm already engaged. She says things like I've never done anything for her, as if I owed her something. I've told her I'll do most anything for her but that.

"Then when I talk about coming home to marry you, she gets upset and won't talk to me. She is constantly putting you down to me and saying she is not going to let me marry you.

"I tell her I love you and you only, and I have a right to marry who I want to and choose the life I want to live. I tell

151

her I want her to join in my happiness in marrying you. She is saying she is never coming back to east Texas, and if I'm going to marry you, she doesn't want me in her house. She has told me to pack my things and leave."

"I'm so sorry about this. I hate to come between you and your mother, but my heart is still with you, and all I want is to marry you in June."

Then I heard her mother yelling at her to get off the phone, that she had no business calling long distance on her phone.

"I give you money to pay for my calls," Margaret yelled back.

"You don't give me enough," Charlotte retorted.

"Go ahead and hang up, and let me call you back," I said to Margaret.

"Wait a minute," she pleaded, but her mother had jerked the phone from her hand.

"Randy Carter," Charlotte barked. "Is that you?"

"Yes, ma'am."

"I wish you would leave my daughter alone! Don't you know it will ruin her life to come back down there in that no man's land. East Texas! I don't want her stuck down there for the rest of her life. She should be where she has opportunity to be somebody."

"I'm sorry you feel that way."

"You should be sorry."

"Excuse me, Miss Mason. I love Margaret, and she loves me. East Texas is not the worst place she could be. I have plans for our life, and Margaret will be happy and so will I if you will just accept our decision."

"I refuse to give you that acceptance."

Just then Margaret picked up a phone in another room and interrupted. She quickly gave me another phone number and told me to call her at that number later. Charlotte ranted and raved about how she was not going to let Margaret talk to me, but I ignored Charlotte and told Margaret I had the number she gave me. Then I hung up.

The call depressed me for a while. I couldn't understand Charlotte's attitude toward me. I didn't stay depressed for long though, because I knew that Margaret still loved me, and somehow we were going to get married.

152

I waited for several hours because I had gathered that Margaret was going to have to leave her mother, and that might take a little time. It was that night when I called the number she had given me. I was surprised when a man answered.

"This is Randy Carter," I finally said. "I'm calling from Texas. Miss Margaret Mason asked me to call this number."

"Yes," he answered. "I'll get her for you."

"Randy," Margaret sounded so relieved. "Finally we can talk."

"Oh, Margaret, I am so sorry about how things are. I surely don't want to come between you and your mother, but I want us to get married. I want you to do whatever you think you need to do. I will do anything you ask me that you think will help."

"I am going to come home. I came to stay with some cousins of mine that live here. They are going to come to Texas the day after tomorrow and bring me with them."

"Are you sure that is what you want?"

"I'm very sure. This is an interesting place to be for a while, but I miss my grandparents and the lifestyle I lived there. I miss you. Mama kept trying to control everything I was doing, what I wore, the people I spent time with, everything. She wants me to be like her, and I am not. My mind is definitely made up. I am coming home."

"I can't wait to see you. I would gladly send you a bus or train ticket. Are you sure your cousins were planning to come anyway?"

"Yes, they had been planning to visit relatives there."

"Will you call me from a pay phone when you get to El Paso?"

"Yes, I'll do that. I'll be so glad to get home."

"I can't wait either, darling. I love you so much."

"I love you too. Goodbye until then."

I was beside myself with excitement. When the day came, I could hardly keep my mind on my work. I got her call that she was in El Paso while I was still at the office. When I went home, I hurried to get bathed and dressed. It was a school night, and I was the one who was driving. I went out to get my car cleaned up and was about to head to the gas station to get it filled up, but I had not yet started the car when Mama called me in to the phone.

"Who is it?" I asked. It was not time yet for Margaret to be home.

"It's Margaret's brother," she said, and her voice sounded distressed. I thought it was because she wasn't sure how good my relationship with him was at this point. It did occur to me that his mother may have called him and tried to influence him in some way to cause Margaret and me trouble. I gave Mama a reassuring smile as I came in to get the phone. Whatever it was, I thought I could handle it.

"Hey, Randy Mason," I said easily.

"I didn't want to call you, but Mama and Papa just couldn't."

"What in the world is wrong?" I exclaimed. I could tell by his voice that he was very upset.

"There was an accident!" he blurted out.

"Was it Margaret? Was Margaret in an accident? I just talked to her two hours ago when they stopped in El Paso."

"Yes. They were already in east Texas. There was a sandstorm. Another car got in the wrong lane and hit them. She was riding in the back seat."

"Is she in the hospital? Tell me where to go. I will go there at once."

"Randy, she didn't make it!"

"What do you mean?"

"She died on the way to the hospital, Randy. We're all going to have to get through this somehow. I am so sorry you have to hear it from me."

"Oh, no!" I cried out. "Mama!"

Mama was right there beside me. "I know, son," she said. He told me."

"What am I going to do?" I cried in despair.

Mama took the phone. "I'm sorry, Randy," she said to Margaret's brother. "He is in shock. Give us some time to take this in, and we will be with you after while. I am so sorry. I know this is such a hard thing for you and Mr. and Mrs. Mason. I will go now and see after my Randy."

In a moment she hung up the phone and held me in her arms. We didn't speak for a little bit. We just stood there and cried. Then, between sobs, she said, "Randy said to tell you that you and Margaret may not have had a chance to get married, but you are family to them anyway." Of course that brought a new gush of sobs from me.

Rose came in and found us that way. "What is wrong?" she cried out. Mama somehow managed to tell her what had happened. She started crying, too. "Oh, poor Randy, poor Randy," she sobbed as she embraced me. "My poor brother."

"Your Uncle Cephus needs to know about this right away," Mama said. "I'll call him."

Uncle Cephus came at once. He came straight to me and embraced me. "I don't know what to say," he whispered to me. "This is such a terrible blow, more than anyone should have to endure. We can't change it. We have to take it and do the best we can. You are young and strong. We will all help you endure this. I will be with you all the time." Then to all of us he said, "Maybe I should call the Masons and find out what has been done about bringing her back here."

But just then John and James came to the door. "No, none of us will go to school tonight," John said sadly. "We just came to be here with you and do anything we can to help."

"Maybe you can tell me someone to call to see if any plans have been made," Uncle Cephus suggested to John.

"Yes," John said. "Some of the neighbors have come in to be with Mama and Papa Mason and Randy. Call and ask for Mr. Perkins."

Uncle Cephus made the call. He wanted the Masons to know that he would take care of the funeral himself as if Margaret were a member of his family, but he knew they might have reasons to make use of another mortuary that was closer. He wanted to make sure they knew what their options were.

John and James were as full of grief as I was. "In a way we feel bad that we introduced you to Margaret," John said. "We feel like we have brought you this terrible sadness."

"Don't feel that way," I told them. "I can't be sorry for knowing Margaret, for loving her and having her love me. None of us could have dreamed that something like this would happen."

"But we can't help feeling like we caused you some of this pain," James spoke with tears in his eyes. "We should maybe be at her house right now, but we feel like we need to be here with you. We were so happy about you and Margaret, and we think of you as our family, too!"

"I am thankful you brought Margaret and me together, and you will always be dear to me because of that. I've been wondering about your other cousins that were in the car wreck. How did they come out?"

"They didn't get a scratch."

A couple of days passed before I felt up to going to see Margaret's family. It was the day before the funeral. Mama went with me. We pulled into the driveway and walked arm and arm up the walk. It was Charlotte who came to the door even before we got there to ring the bell. "Don't you come in this house," she hissed. How dare you come here after all the trouble you have caused my family."

I opened my mouth to speak, but she didn't give me a chance. "I don't want to hear anything you have to say," she went on in a loud voice. "You are the cause of my daughter being dead. I don't want you here, and I never want to see you again."

Papa Mason came up behind her. "What is going on?" he asked.

"This man has the audacity to come here after causing my daughter's death. He has no business here, and you, too, Madame."

"She is Randy's mother," Mr. Mason told Charlotte firmly. "They have come to pay their respects and they are welcome."

"I don't care who she is. I won't have them here!" Charlotte kept on ranting in her strident voice.

"It is not for you to say," he corrected her. "Now calm down and hush. Go back in the house." He stepped out on the porch and took Mama's hand. "You will have to excuse my daughter," he said apologetically. "She is upset, but she is not behaving well. I am sorry. I thank you both for coming."

"We are so sorry," Mama told him "It is such a hard time for all of us."

"I do appreciate your coming," Mr. Mason said. "I would love to have you come in, but you see how things are with her. She has just gotten here and she is very upset. It will take some time for us to reason with her. I will get back in touch with you when things are calmer here. I know that you are suffering as we are, and we should have time to grieve together. Just give us some time."

Mother and I both shook his hand and told him we understood. We walked back to the car. "I'm sorry Mama," I said.

"That is all right, son. Mr. Mason seems like such a nice man, and I know he was sincere in his welcome. I hope he has good luck with that daughter of his."

It was a big funeral. It was held in the largest white church in the community. The Masons were respected people in the community and the people of that church invited them to use it to accommodate the large crowd that would surely be there. The church was full of people, black and white from miles around. Students and teachers came from Prairie View. I was there, of course. I didn't sit with Margaret's family as I had not been invited to do so. All my family was with me, including Uncle Cephus and Aunt Bessie.

I did my best to find my strength and accept this cruel loss life had dealt me, but I just was not able to do so. The minister's words, and the huge choir's beautiful music could not console me.

"We are here to celebrate the life of a beautiful young person," the minister began. "We don't want to be sad today. It is a day to be joyful."

"I looked at him through my tears, and wondered how I was supposed to be happy, when the source of my happiness had been taken from me forever."

The minister went on. "In the Bible Job says, 'The Lord giveth and the Lord taketh away. Blessed be the name of the Lord.' We have to understand that God did this, and whatever God does is for the better. We are all going to miss Margaret, but we have to realize that she has gone home. She is away from the world's misery and temptations and burdens. That is behind her now. She is free from it all. We will remember what a blessing she was to us. She leaves a glorious legacy to this church and this community. She has been taken from us, and we can't have her back. All I am saying, children, is let us celebrate this lovely, bright, kind girl who God gave us, celebrate the time she spent with and brightened our lives. Let us give thanks for her."

Many people said "Amen" or "God bless you, Preacher." I

157

could hear crying too. At least there were some people there who might understand how I was feeling. Maybe I was wrong, but I couldn't feel joy. The only thing that kept me from dissolving in my grief was that I was angry. There was no way a preacher was going to make me feel any different.

Mama asked me if I wanted to go down and see Margaret's body. My feelings about that were so mixed, but I let her lead me down there. There was my Margaret in a fine, expensive casket. She looked like she was just asleep. She was as beautiful as ever. I lingered there, holding up the crowd, thinking how she would never speak to me again. I would never feel her warm hand in mine. When that casket was closed, I would never see her again. Tears streamed down my face. I heard other people behind me weeping loudly. Some were even screaming and groaning out loud. I did not make a sound, but, when I finally walked away, I was saying goodbye to Margaret in my heart.

I had brought a bright red rose surrounded by white carnations to lay on her grave. The rose reminded me of the bright red bird she had so admired and wanted me to capture in a photo with her. I still had the flowers in my hand after the service at the cemetery. I saw grandmother and grandfather Mason, and went to speak to them.

Mr. Mason shook my hand with his strong grip. "We are proud of you, son," he said to me. This is so painful for you and for us. Somehow we are going to have to live with it. Be as strong as you can. We want you to stay in touch with us."

"I will do that," I assured him.

I turned then to Mama Mason, and she put her arms around me "Oh, Randy, Randy," she sobbed. "To think she was coming home to us! She was almost home! I can't believe she is gone." She clung to me and we stood there a long time holding each other.

Finally Papa Mason said, "Let's go on home, dear. This has been a long, hard day."

She turned to go with him, but as they started to walk away, she looked back and said, "Whatever happens in the future, Randy, I want to think of your children as my great-grandchildren."

"That will be an honor," I told her, but my heart was

breaking to think that any children I had would not be Margaret's.

Charlotte was talking to someone nearby. I turned toward her as if to speak, but she turned her back and walked away.

In the days that followed, grief weighed heavily on me, and I burned with the question, *Why?* When Sunday came, I didn't really want to go to church. It was only because I appreciated my pastor and church family so much that I made myself go. A huge flower spray at the funeral had come from my church and another smaller one from Pastor Ike's family. Pastor Ike had spent much time with me, and I had received many notes of consolation and visits from my church family. I wanted to thank them all, so, in spite of the negative feelings I was having, I went on to church. I didn't go early enough to get to Sunday School, but I got there in time for church.

Everyone I met in the vestibule and sitting in the pews spoke words of sympathy and encouragement to me, "Bless your heart." "Be strong." "We love you." "God loves you." "You are a young man, and you must look to the future." I heard those words many times as I went to my seat.

When church was over, I told Pastor Ike I needed to talk to him. "Sure," he agreed. "Do you want to talk today?"

"If you can."

"Why don't you just stay now? Your mother and Rose and Bobby can ride home with Ella Mae. We can go and talk in my office."

Ella Mae was glad to take my family home. In no time I was sitting in Pastor Ike's office. I had never had a problem talking to him. He was a good listener and not judgmental. I quickly put what was bothering me on the table. "I just don't understand that pastor who did Margaret's service. How could he talk about celebrating and being joyful? She was going to be my bride in June. My whole idea of the future was about the life we would have together. How can I be happy? I just can't digest what he was saying, and I couldn't believe that people were saying 'Amen' and 'Tell it like it is.' It was so hard for me in church today. Everyone was trying to encourage me, telling me to be strong, and that I am young and will recover and all. I just don't want to hear any of that. I know they mean well, but it doesn't help. I want to be left alone."

159

"I really understand how you feel, Randy," Pastor Ike said gently. "It is something most of us humans have trouble with. When the Lord does something, however, it is final, it can't be undone. We have to come to accept it."

"I know that. But all I am saying, is why should I rejoice? I remember a sermon you gave out by the river about when Moses died. The people mourned. You said it, and I read it. They mourned! Then there was Job. When his children died, he shaved his head and sat in the ashes. He mourned! How is it that I am not supposed to mourn but rejoice?

"Mary and Martha cried for their brother, Lazarus, and Jesus brought him back. When Jesus died on the cross, people cried. Why am I supposed to be happy?

"Pastor, we are friends. I've talked to you about many things. I trust you to give me good advice. I have to tell you that this is the hardest thing I have ever experienced. I can't be happy. There have been times, as you know, when I have been deeply involved and interested in the church, that I thought I was called to be a preacher, but, after all this, I just don't think that can be."

"I don't think you can really make that decision now. It is true that we have free will, but when God chooses you, He finds ways to break down your resistance."

"God really hasn't spoken to me. It was just what people were saying. Because I have been so active in the church. I don't want to do it because people want me to do it. After all this, I absolutely don't want to do it."

"Why are you saying that?"

"Because I can't stand up in front of people and tell them something I don't believe. I can't tell them to be happy about something that I can't myself. I can't tell them not to cry, not to mourn. For that reason, I can't be the person people have anticipated that I would. I want no part of it!"

"Randy, there are many things that we don't understand. I am not saying that you should not cry and mourn. I was looking so forward to being the one to marry you and Margaret. I am so sad that it is not to be. What I am saying is that this is in God's divine plan. He had you in mind before you were ever born. He said that to Jeremiah. He told him that, before he was conceived in his mother's womb, God knew him. He has

160

a plan for your life, and you have to believe that. I can't explain it, but He tells us that His ways are not our ways, and His thoughts are not ours. I'm not telling you not to cry, but you have to accept God's will. Pray to the Lord for help with that."

"Thank you, Pastor, but I still have to say that I don't want to be a preacher. I don't want to have to tell people those kind of things."

"That is your decision?"

"Yes, that is my decision."

"Let's pray," he said and grabbed my hand. He prayed and I listened, yet when he was finished I told him to tell the secretary to put my name on the inactive roll of the church. I thanked him again. I knew he was trying his best for me, but I just couldn't be moved. He didn't try to keep me with him or change my mind. He just told me he would be praying for me.

To Hell and Back

AFTER LEAVING HIS OFFICE, I had some thoughts. I remembered when I was a child in school reading *Aesop's Fables*. They could be so frightening sometimes that I couldn't sleep at night. Yet they always ended well. Someone lived happily ever after. Real life is not like that.

I thought about what good friends Pastor Ike and Uncle Cephus were to me, and that made me think about my father and the good relationship we had, the good times fishing, hunting and working together. I felt right then that had he still been here, he could tell me what to do. He wasn't though, and I drifted from week to week. I didn't change my mind about not going to church. After a few weeks passed, I discovered a rodeo that took place on Saturdays and Sundays on the edge of town. I started going and became involved with it. I felt like doing something daring would somehow help me get back my peace of mind.

I got rather good at riding the horses and bulls. One day there was a new bull. He had a reputation and there was speculation about who would ride him. I volunteered. I was excited about the challenge. Some people were discouraging me, saying what a mean hard ride he was, but I was not dissuaded. I insisted on riding him.

I could feel the heat and excitement in him as I sat on him in the chute. When they opened the gate, he went wild. Oh, how he pitched and bucked. People in the stands were cheering for me. He made a rapid turn and I fell off. He turned around and came toward me. I don't remember what happened then. When I came to, I was in bed in the hospital and

Mama was sitting near me. When she saw I had opened my eyes, she started talking to me. "How are you feeling, son."

"I don't know. Everything hurts."

Can I get anything for you?"

"No, I don't think so." I felt dazed, not at all like myself. I'm sure I was not entirely conscious. Later as I stayed in that semiconscious state, I heard Mama talking to doctors and nurses and visitors. The bits of conversations I picked up told me that I only had a chance to live, and that they did not expect me to walk again. I knew then that I wanted to die. I could not imagine spending my life in a wheelchair.

Though I was not able to move or speak much, pain overwhelmed me. I thought of my father and wanted to go to the comfort he had given me when I had gone to him with my hurts as a child. I believed he would be in Heaven, and I wanted to go to him there.

I thought of Hell, and knew it would be worse than what I was feeling now. I did not want to go there for sure. I drifted back into unconsciousness and dreamed I was in a desert. People were chasing me on horses. I was running to try to get away from them. Somehow I managed to hide from them behind a bush, and after they passed by me I ran into a house that suddenly appeared. There was an old man in the house who pulled me in and shut the door and locked it. Looking out the window, I could see no sign of those terrifying people. The old man just told me not to worry. "Thank you! Thank you!" I said in relief.

"Can you read?" the old man asked.

"Yes, I can read."

"Well here, read this for me." He handed me a Bible and asked me to read the third chapter of Lamentations.

I turned to that text. I didn't remember ever in my life reading it before, but I began to read it aloud:

> I am the man that hath seen affliction by the rod of his wrath. He hath led me, and brought me into darkness, but not into light. Surely against me he is turned; he turneth his hand against me all the day. My flesh and my skin he hath made old; he hath broken my bones. He hath builded against me, and compassed me with gall and travail. He hath set me

in dark places, as they that be dead of old. He hath hedged me about, that I cannot get out; he hath made my chain heavy. Also when I cry and shout, he shutteth out my prayer. He hath enclosed my ways with hewn stone, he hath made my path crooked. He was unto me as a bear lying in wait, and as a lion in secret places. He has turned aside my ways, and pulled me in pieces; he hath made me desolate.

He hath bent his bow and set me as a mark for the arrow. He hath caused the arrow of his quiver to enter into my veins. I was a derision to all my people; and their song all the day. He hath filled me with bitterness, he hath made me drunken with wormwood. He hath also broken my teeth with gravel stones, he hath covered me with ashes.

And thou hast removed my soul far off from peace; I forgat my prosperity. And I said, my strength and my hope is perished from the Lord: Remembering mine affliction and my misery, the wormwood and the gall. My soul hath them still in remembrance, and is humbled in me.

This I recall to my mind, therefore I have hope. It is of the Lord's mercies that we are not consumed, because his compassion fails not. They are new every morning; great is thy faithfulness. The Lord is my portion, saith my soul; therefore will I hope in him. The Lord is good unto them that wait for him, to the soul that seeketh him. It is good that a man must both hope and quietly wait on the salvation of the Lord. It is good for a man that he bear the yolk in his youth He sitteth alone and keepeth silence, because he hath borne it upon him. He putteth his mouth in the dust; if so be there may be hope. He giveth his cheek to him that smiteth him; he is felled full with reproach.

For the Lord will not cast off forever. But though he cause grief, yet will he have compassion according to the multitude of his mercies. For he doth not afflict willingly nor grieve the children of men. To crush under his feet all the prisoners of the earth, to turn aside the right of a man before the face of the most High, to subvert a man in his cause, the Lord approveth not.

Who is he that saith, and it cometh to pass, when the Lord commandeth it not? Out of the mouth of the most High proceedeth not evil and good? Wherefore doth a living man complain, a man for the punishment of his sin? Let us search and try our ways, and turn again to the Lord. Let us lift up our hearts with our hands unto God in the heavens.

We have transgressed and have rebelled; thou hast not

pardoned. Thou hast covered with anger, and persecuted us; thou hast slain, thou hast not pitied. Thou hast covered thyself with a cloud, that our prayer should not pass through. Thou hast made us as the offscouring and refuse in the midst of the people. All our enemies have opened their mouths against us. Fear and a snare has come upon us, desolation and destruction.

Mine eye runneth down with rivers of water for the destruction of the daughter of my people. Mine eye trickleth down, and ceaseth not, without any intermission, til the Lord look down and behold from heaven. Mine eye affecteth mine heart because of all the daughters of my city. Mine enemies chased me sore, like a bird without cause. They have cut off my life in the dungeon, and cast a stone upon me. Waters flowed over mine head; then I said, I am cut off. I called upon thy name, O Lord, out of the low dungeon. Thou hast heard my voice; hide not thine ear at my breathing, at my cry. Thou drawest near in the day that I called upon thee; thou saidst, fear not. O Lord, thou hast pleaded the causes of my soul; thou hast redeemed my life. O Lord thou hast seen my wrong; judge thou my cause.

Thou hast seen all their vengeance and all their imaginations against me. Thou hast heard their reproach, O Lord and all their imaginations against me; the lips of those who rose up against me, and their device against me all the day. Behold their sitting down and their rising up; I am their musick. Render unto them a recompense, O Lord, according to the work of their hands. Give them sorrow at heart, thy curse unto them. Persecute and destroy them in anger from under the heavens of the Lord.

I had read every word of it, and I handed the Bible back to the man. That was the end of the dream. I'm not sure how long after that I came to myself, but when I did, I remembered the dream vividly. It troubled me greatly. When Mama came I told her I wanted to talk to Pastor Ike. "Well, he's been coming to see you every day and praying for you," she told me.

"I guess I haven't been aware that he was here."

"I'll surely let him know you want to talk to him. He will be glad you are back with us."

Soon after that Pastor Ike came to my room. I told him all about my dream and how I had been fretting about what it meant. He had his Bible, and he got it out and turned to that chapter. He read the whole chapter out loud.

"I know that is Jeremiah speaking, Pastor, but what is he talking about?" I asked him.

"Jeremiah was called the "weeping prophet," Pastor Ike began. "The word Lamentations means something like weeping. You must remember that in the Book of Jeremiah, he had many bad experiences. He got badly injured and his enemies put him in a dungeon. He decided he couldn't possibly preach any more.

"I know what you are going through. You are in pain; you have broken bones. I thank God that you are healing. Jeremiah was suffering with pain, too. He was going through the same thing. You see, the spiritual man didn't have any bones, but the physical man did. Both were hurting. His enemies had put him in a hole and left him to die. But God was not ready for him to die; God had a job for him to do. When God has something for you to do, Son, you've got to do it. God won't call anybody who can't do the job assigned them. In that experience you had last night, I would dare to say that God was talking to you. I believe he has sanctified you, set you apart. You might not understand it, but I think you will in time. This is my conviction. God waits for you to be a messenger of his word."

"Reverend, you know how things are with me. The doctors say I may never walk again. How can I be a preacher if I can't walk. I can't see it. Would God call a person in my condition?"

"Nothing is too hard for God. Besides, the doctor said you may not walk, not that you would not. God has the power to do whatever is needed. You've got to believe that, if God assigns you something, he is going to make it possible for you to do it. You'll do it if you trust him."

"Thank you, Pastor. I'll admit that I do have a yearning to go back to church. I want to get up and leave this hospital, and even if I have to go in a wheelchair, I'm going to go back to church. There was a change in me even before I had this strange dream. I have been feeling the need to go back. If the Lord will let me walk, if it is no more than three steps, I will preach. Is it wrong to bargain with God like that? Didn't Gideon do it?"

"I don't think it's wrong. Just ask the Lord to show you that he is with you. Let's pray together that it will happen."

It was Pastor Ike who prayed out loud, but I prayed silently with him with all my heart. He left after that. My thoughts were in a turmoil for the rest of the day, and I was troubled. I wasn't afraid of making the effort to become a preacher, but I had to wonder how I would be accepted after I had stayed away from the church for so long. I mulled that over a great deal.

By the time Pastor Ike came back the next day, my resolve was stronger. "I've made up my mind," I told him. If I walk again, even just a few steps, I am going to preach."

"That makes me very happy," he said, beaming at me. "God bless you. I'm not a prophet, but I discerned something in you ever since I've known you. I am so thankful that it has come about, and I believe that God is going to let you walk."

From that day on, I began to get better. They finally dismissed me from the hospital. My ribs still hurt, as some of them had been broken. My foot was still in a cast, and I had a brace on my neck. I was something to look at. I went home in a wheelchair, and Mama treated me just like a baby. The neighbors came in and checked on me often, and when Rose and her friend Peaches came home from their collages for the summer, they fussed over me and waited on me hand and foot. They were great nurses, and I kept getting better.

Vernon Stewart called me almost every day or so to check on my progress and visited me often. He was both encouraging and apologetic. He still couldn't shake the feeling of being somehow responsible for my bad luck because he had wished for me to stay in Nelsonburg. He brought me things to read and did everything he could to keep my spirits up. His steadfast loyalty was an anchor for me.

The doctors had me coming in fairly often to check my progress. Finally I was able to have some crutches and managed to hobble from the bed to the bathroom. After a while the brace was taken off my neck, and I could touch my foot to the floor sometimes when I was standing still on my crutches.

I was still an invalid and unable to drive or go out. I had time on my hands. I began to read incessantly. I ordered Bible commentaries and books by theologians. I became very interested in the Word. I took notes on my reading, and worked on retaining all that I could. I had never realized how little I did know. I had taught Sunday School with so little real knowledge.

My recovery was slow, but I continued to make progress. Finally the cast came off my foot. It was very tender, and no one was sure whether it would ever be able to hold my weight. Soon after that I told Mama that I was ready to try to put on my Sunday clothes and go to church. Mama was pleased. Uncle Cephus and I will see that you get there, and if you wear out before it is over, we will get you back home," she assured me. My brother Bobby, at that time, was away at CCC camp, so he would not be able to help us.

Sunday came, and we had decided to start slowly. They were going to get me there for the morning service only. I would come home before Sunday School. I had shed my neck brace and my foot cast, as I said. Only my ribs were still bound.

Mama had a barber come out and cut my hair. She went to great lengths to make sure I looked as good as I could. Uncle Cephus came to get us in his big car, and we took my wheelchair along. They fussed over me, gave me more help than I really needed and got me into the church. When Uncle Cephus rolled me down the aisle, many people voiced amens and applauded. That support and attention filled me with gladness and humbled me, too.

We went to a pew, and I sat in the aisle next to Mama, I remembered that the last time I had come to church, I had felt angry. That attitude had changed.. This day the service seemed marvelous to me. Rev. Ike delivered a beautiful sermon. As always, his message was deeply rooted in the Bible and had a powerful finish. I rejoiced in it.

Then he gave the Invitation, and the choir started singing "Just As I Am." I told Mama I wanted to go up to the altar. We unlocked the wheelchair and she rolled me down the aisle. I told her to turn me around to face the congregation. Two other people had come first. One came to ask for Baptism and another to transfer membership. Reverend Foster came first to them, giving them welcome and introducing them to the congregation. The choir continued to sing softly. Then my Pastor and dear friend came to me. "Welcome back, Brother Carter," he said to me. "Is there something you have to say to the congregation?"

"Indeed, I do." I said softly to him. Then I addressed the congregation. "I've come back. I've been through a lot of bad times, and I've thought God had deserted me, but I'm back, and I'm back to stay." The walls reverberated with a chorus of loud Amens.

"I'm not well yet, " I continued, when the voices quieted. "It will be a while before I am fully healed, but I'm here like that song they are singing. I'm here 'Just As I Am.' I've strayed away and maybe I've disappointed many of you. I ask your forgiveness. I wasn't thinking straight. I let my faith waver, but you continued to have faith and prayed for me. I can't thank you enough for that. It is your faith and Pastor Ike Foster's faith that has brought me back here. I intend to be back next Sunday and the Sundays that follow." The Amens rang out again.

"God came to me in a dream," I told them. "I know now that he was telling me that he wants something from me. I made a decision to believe he can give me back the faith I need to do what he wants. I promised him that if I could walk again, I would preach for him."

"Praise the Lord. Have mercy, Lord," came the multitude of voices. The voices hushed quickly. They knew I was going to say more.

"I've promised, and I'm ready to step out in the faith he has brought back to me, not just mentally, but physically. I'm ready to try my faith right now. I want to get out of this wheelchair and stand up by myself!"

My crutches were in my lap. I laid them down on the floor. Mama and Uncle Cephus got on either side of me to help, but I told them, "Let me do it myself. I am going to try out my faith."

I could hear the piano still softly playing the hymn. I put my hands on the arm rests of the chair and slowly stood up. Mama and Uncle Cephus both reached out again, as if to steady me. "Let me alone," I told them. "I am trusting in the Lord."

I steadied myself and let my weak foot hold its share of my

weight. I took a step with my good left foot and followed it with a step on the injured right one. Then I took one more step. "Thank you Lord," I shouted. "Now I am ready to preach."

Then the congregation went wild. Mama was shouting, "Thank you Lord." People were standing up and singing and shouting and laughing. I thought it must be something like Pentecost in the Upper Room in Jerusalem.

After a while, Pastor Ike began to try to get things quieted down. When he finally succeeded, he spoke, "I am so happy. This is the answer to my prayer." There followed another uproar of praises.

"We're going to accept your promise," Pastor Ike went on. "You think you have done the church wrong. The Lord forgives you, and we forgive you. You are still one of us. You go home and study and pray about this calling, and when the day comes that you feel ready to preach, you come tell me. I'll see that you will preach in this pulpit right here. Until then, we'll look for you to be here every Sunday sitting in the congregation."

Oh, what an outstanding experience that was for me. Mama and Uncle Cephus got me back in the wheelchair and that is how I left the church that day, but not before I heard words of encouragement and thanksgiving from every person who had been present with me. I went home on fire with determination to give my best to the Lord.

I studied the Bible fervently and I ordered more books. Pastor Ike came to see me, and we had hearty discussions, and I asked him many questions. I was hungry for every piece of information I could get hold of. My greatest concentration was on the New Testament. I finally determined what I was going to talk about in my first sermon.

My walking improved slowly—by now I was wearing shoes and walking more each day. I told Pastor Ike I was ready, and we set a date. Pastor Ike announced it the following Sunday. I was to preach at an evening service. When the time came, the church was packed. The ushers had to put chairs in the aisle.

Pastor Ike had me sit down with the deacons. When it was time for me to preach, he came down and escorted me up to the pulpit. We stood there together and he spoke first. "I want to present to you a young man I am so proud of tonight," he told the congregation. "I have prayed with him and studied with him, and I believe the Lord has ordained him to preach. I want to present to you for the first time, a son in ministry of mine. I want everyone who can stand to do so, to receive and welcome Randall Carter." The crowd stood up and amens filled the sanctuary. I was astounded. I looked into that sea of faces and recognized almost all of them. Then I saw some I had not expected to be there. I saw my uncle and auntie from Austin. Maggie Brown was there with her husband. John and James were there with Grandfather and Grandmother Mason. Buster and Gertrude were there, and, as always, my dear friends Vernon and Cindy Stewart. I was overwhelmed with gratitude, and the first thing I did was to thank everyone for coming.

After I prayed, I read the text I had chosen:

> The steps of a good man are ordered by the Lord; and he delighteth in his way.
> Though he fall, he shall not be utterly cast down; for the Lord upholdeth him with his hand. PSALMS 37:23-24

"The title of my sermon is 'From the Pit to the Pulpit,'" I told the congregation. Pastor Ike had coached me in the proper protocol, and I was careful to follow his instructions. I kept my sermon concise and to the point. When I finished every one stood up and shouted amens of approval. Pastor Ike got up and complimented me, then faced the congregation and asked, "Did he do a good job?" There was another chorus of amens.

When he gave the Invitation, several young people came up and joined the church. This was the true sign to me that I was doing the work God had assigned me. It made this first step of mine so very fulfilling.

After Pastor Ike had welcomed these new members, he addressed the congregation again. "Now we are going to show Brother Carter our appreciation," he said. "He is going to need some things to begin his career as a preacher. He will need books, and I think he wants to go to school. Let's give him a love offering to help him get the right start. This is the only offering we will take tonight." The choir stood up to sing, and the ushers came down and got the plates and started passing them. I could see that everyone was putting money in the plates. When they were finished, Pastor Ike asked me to come give the Benediction.

Before I gave it, I again expressed my thankfulness for all those who had come, and told them how humbled I was at their generosity. Then I spoke those final words of blessing and peace, and felt them deeply within myself.

Pastor Ike and I walked up to the front door where the people greeted us as they went out of the church. Everyone was shaking my hand and giving me compliments and encouragement. I don't think I have ever before had such a wonderful feeling of being appreciated.

Suddenly I noticed that Aunt Molly was in line. She was quietly waiting her turn to speak to me. When she finally reached me she grabbed my hands and spoke my name. "I'm calling you Randy tonight," she said. "I'll have to get used to calling you Reverend Carter."

"Oh, Aunt Molly, it was so kind of you to come to hear me." I probably should have called her Sister Smith, but I'd never called her anything but Aunt Molly.

"I put some money in the plate, but I'm going to give you a check, too. I want you to go to school, and I want to help you all I can."

CHAPTER 13

The Road to Recovery

I TOOK THE MONEY the people at church had given me that night. I took Aunt Molly's check and her advice. I talked with Uncle Cephus about how I might go to school and keep on working some for him. There was a private college in a town not too far from Nelsonburg. It was in a town called Conroe, Texas. I knew it was academically good and also that it had some good courses in theology, ministry, and religious education. I knew preachers who had gone to that school and were preaching in cities like Dallas, Kansas City, and Chicago. I knew it put out some good preachers. I could drive the distance there every day, take mostly evening classes and still live at home.

I burned the "midnight oil," a phrase my grandmother had often used. I studied hard and I graduated. I learned so many things I had not known about preaching, and I made many new friends who brought me new blessings. They were from many surrounding towns and quite a few were from Houston. One of those friends got me an invitation to preach at a church in Houston. The pastor there had moved away, and the church needed someone to fill in.

I was somewhat hesitant about going. It was a big church in a big city. I talked anxiously about it with Pastor Ike and Uncle Cephus. They both kept encouraging me to go on, that I could do it. Finally I decided I would give it a try.

I admired the looks of the church when I got there. It was not one of the biggest churches in the city, but it was definitely "up town." I preached at both the morning and evening services that Sunday and received many compliments on my sermons. They asked me to submit a resume and told me they wanted to consider me, among a few others, as a candidate for their pastorate.

"I'm not sure I am ready yet," I told them. "I am not even ordained yet."

"Is that a problem?" someone asked.

"That's for you to say, I think."

"Do you expect to be ordained soon?" another asked.

"Yes I do."

"Just let us know as soon as it happens," the head deacon told me. "We really want to wait and consider you. We like your preaching."

I felt really encouraged. I wasn't sure what to do next, but I went immediately to talk to Pastor Ike. "This is not a problem," he told me. "Usually, when a young man considers himself ready to preach, and a church is wanting to have him for their preacher, it is my duty to ordain him. We will certainly get that done. I will start working on it right now."

I had to study hard again because there was a difficult test I had to take. It was an oral exam with a number of preachers there to question me. They asked me all kinds of questions about scripture and its meaning and the doctrines of the church. After the questioning, they excused me and had me wait in another room. In time they came and told me I had passed the test. I was elated.

I didn't send a resume to the church in Houston, though. I still just didn't feel like I was ready. I felt like I needed some training. I had not had enough experience.

As it happened, Pastor Foster became infirm. He was getting older, and arthritis and other problems were making it hard for him to get around. He talked to his deacons and he talked to me about becoming his assistant.

"This is a big church," I said, feeling again my meager experience. "Do you really think I'm ready for this."

"I'm not about to die, boy!" he said loudly, and then chuckled. "I'm not asking you to pastor the church. I need some help. This will give you the experience you need. There are days my feet swell, and I just don't feel like coming to preach. You live right here, and have your degree and are ordained. You are the perfect choice to be my assistant. The dea-

174

cons are pleased to have you do it, thrilled in fact, and the church will go along with whatever the deacons have decided. Just say yes, please say yes."

"I really feel honored that you are asking me and that the deacons approved. I will be your assistant and do the best I can for you."

CHAPTER 14

And Who Was Cousin Elberta?

I BECAME A VERY BUSY MAN. I still worked for Uncle Cephus during the week. His business had been growing and had to move to larger quarters in a new building out on the highway next to a dentist's office. Uncle Cephus was getting older. He was depending on me more and more.

I had a great helper by this time, my wife, Elberta. She also worked as a school teacher and played the organ and piano at church.

"Let me interrupt you here, Cousin Randy," my young cousin Antony asked me. Antony was writing this story down as I told it to him. "Where did Cousin Elberta come from?"

"Why right here in Nelsonburg," I answered him.

"She did? Who was she, then?"

"You remember Rose's friend, Peaches?"

"Peaches! You mean Rose's friend and Bobby's girlfriend."

"I thought she was Bobby's girlfriend, too, but I found out later that was never true. She was our neighbor and a buddy to both Rose and Bobby. From the time Bobby started liking girls, Peaches was always the one who carried his notes to the ones he liked best. You know, she was named for the Elberta Peach. When she was born, her parents thought she was just the color of a ripe peach. That is why they gave her that nickname. When she went away to college, she went by her real name. I still slip and call her "Peaches" sometimes, but she thinks the nickname is inappropriate for her image as a teacher and musician and, most of all, as a preacher's wife."

"Well, how was it that she became your wife?"

"When I came home from the hospital after that terrible accident with the bull, she and Rose were home from college for the summer. They took care of me just like they would have cared for a baby. They pampered me and read to me. When I got able to feed myself, I had to insist they let me do it. They were a godsend to me. Mama would have taken care of me well enough, but she didn't have the time or the strength to do all that the two of them did. They kept me comfortable and kept my mind occupied. They probably had a lot to do with my recovery.

"When the summer was over, she went back to school in Louisiana. Soon after that, she wrote me a letter that really surprised me. She told me that she had admired me since she was twelve years old, and that by the time she was sixteen, she knew she was in love with me. She told me she knew I had thought of her as Bobby's girlfriend, but all the time it was me she had her heart set on. She reminded me that I had not even given her an encouraging look.

"After Maggie broke up with me, she confessed to me that it occurred to her she might have a chance with me. Then when I fell so madly in love with Margaret, Elberta said her hopes were dashed to pieces.

"She said she grieved so when Margaret was killed. She said she could not bear to see me so hurt. After that terrible time when she saw me so depressed and withdrawn, she thought that, if she could draw me out and make me smile sometimes, that she would have a chance with me. She told me it was such a joy to get to nurse me and see how I began to recover.

"She even went so far as to tell me that she didn't think she could ever marry anyone else but me. Then she apologized for being so bold as to say these things.

"She said she had told Rose and Bobby how she felt about me, and made them promise not to tell me. Mama even knew how she felt about me, and hadn't said a thing.

"The letter went on to tell me she wanted me to call her after I had received the letter and tell her just how I felt about it. She was putting aside her pride, she said, because she needed to decide what she was going to do with her life if I couldn't be as big a part of it as she wanted.

"I was totally in shock. I had thought of her as almost a

part of my family, and I had assumed that she would probably become my sister-in-law. She was pretty and talented and smart. I had certainly noticed those things. I guess because she had been around me so much since she was a pre-teenager, I still thought of her as my sister's cute little girlfriend."

"Weren't you flattered, Cousin?" Antony asked. "I mean, after all she had seen you go through. I would think it would be a much needed ego boost for you."

"Oh, yes. I couldn't imagine that I could have been attractive to her when I was so helpless. She had seen me at my very worst."

"Well, you must have called her."

"I did. I protested that I was certainly no catch in my condition, but she would hear none of that. She told me I was going to continue to recover and be as fit as any man. She even said she was going to see to it that I did. I have never heard anyone so determined about anything in my life. 'Talk to Rose; talk to Bobby,' she insisted. 'They will tell you how much I love you.'"

"Did you still hesitate? I know that you didn't turn her down, but did you make her wait some more?"

"I don't know why. I guess it just all seemed too good to be true. I called Bobby, and he laughed at me. He said he just couldn't believe a man as smart as me wouldn't have recognized Elberta's adoration. He would have told me, he said, but he had been sworn to secrecy.

"Bobby told me about a girl he was going to bring home to meet all of us. He obviously had matrimony on his own mind, and before we hung up he had told me that he would be thrilled to have Elberta join our family as my wife. 'Give yourself a chance,' he had encouraged. 'You'd be a fool to pass that up.'

"Rose was every bit as pleased and positive. 'Oh, that girl,' she had laughed. 'She had it written on her heart that she was going to wind up with you. She is one headstrong lady. Don't underestimate her when it comes to will power. You'll never be sorry, brother. She'll make you happy.'

"And so she did. We didn't get married right away, but we started seeing each other. She read my sermons and made wonderful suggestions about them, and praised me when I delivered them. She became my right hand, and my body and spirit healed in the presence of her nurture. I fell in love with her with each day that passed. She was so good for me.

"My family was elated when we got married. It was a beautiful wedding that was held one Sunday right after church. The church was filled to capacity with all my friends and family. Rose was the maid of honor, and Bobby came home on leave to be my best man. Elberta was a vision as she came down the aisle on the arm of her father. I don't think I have ever felt so blessed and at peace as that moment when I saw her coming to me and felt the joy of all those who had come to celebrate our union. My past sorrow and shame had been like a heavy block of ice I thought I would always have to carry with me. At this moment I realized it had gradually been melting, leaving me free to look into the future with renewed faith. Pastor Ike beamed as he pronounced us man and wife. As I looked into Elberta's eyes and kissed her, I knew I could face anything life could bring with her by my side.

CHAPTER 15

The Death and Eulogy of Pastor Ike

AFTER WE CAME BACK from our honeymoon in Key West, things really took off.

So much time was taken up with our work, and our social life blossomed too. There were all kinds of church affairs, and many people invited us into their homes for dinners. Sometimes we cooked and had people over. We loved our life and time flew for us.

Soon after we married, Vernon and Cindy Stewart invited us to go to Houston and eat out with them in a very fine restaurant. Vernon told me he was so happy things had finally turned out well for me and he wanted to celebrate with us in a big way. We had a wonderful time together. "I can remind you now of that advice I gave you the night you graduated from high school and not feel guilty about it," he told me. "Many times I thought maybe I had been so wrong, but today I feel good about that advice."

"Yes," I agreed. I think I had to go through all that mess to find out who I really am. It wasn't your fault I didn't go to live in California, Vernon. It was just the way things happened. When I look back, it seems like there was some kind of divine plan in all that happened."

As time went on, Pastor Ike needed me to take over more and more at church. He was declining in health. He was still a wonderful mentor, however, and I loved spending time with him. We often went fishing together out at Uncle Cephus' place on the river. I took him with me when I had to go out to our farm and check on things. Sometimes we took walks or drove together to visit our church members who were ill at home or in the hospital. We had many great talks about theology and books that we were reading. He was such an intelligent and thoughtful man. I felt I learned something new each time I was with him.

Pastor Ike's wife, Ella Mae, had lots in common with Elberta, too. They worked together on Bible School projects and activities for the church women. Often they would plan and cook our evening meals at our house or theirs, and it would be waiting when Pastor Ike and I came back from one of our adventures. We all enjoyed the fellowship these combined meals provided us.

"This is where you came in, Cousin Antony. During these wonderful years, Elberta and I had two little girls we named Maybelle and Rose Ann. We named them after my mother and sister. Rose Ann was just a baby when your mother died and you came to live with us. You made our family complete, and the three of you were just like more grandchildren to Ike and Ella Mae. You grew up spending as much time in their house as ours."

"I remember those times so well, Cousin Randy. I was so sad to lose my mother, but I had such a wonderful big family to comfort me and take my mind away from my grief. Pastor Ike and Sister Ella Mae were a big part of that. I was just out of high school when he died. I was already a deacon in the church, remember?"

"I sure do remember. I was so proud that you had that kind of respect in our church. That was such a hard time for me. I wasn't prepared for losing Pastor Ike. That was really a dark time in my life. It was you who comforted me then. But I will go on with the story"

ONE DAY ELLA MAE CALLED ME and urgently asked me to come to the hospital. Ike had collapsed and been taken there by ambulance. She feared it was his heart. He was conscious, she told me, and asking for me. I went at once.

Ella Mae was standing on one side of his bead and a doctor on the other, listening to his heart. When I came in, the doctor looked at me grimly and shook his head. "I'll leave you

181

folks alone for a moment," he said at once. "Reverend Foster seems to have important things to say to you."

I looked at Ike's pale face and across into Ella Mae's teary one. Fear clutched at my heart. His eyes were bright, though, and looked knowingly into mine. "Now don't panic," he said weakly. "I'm not afraid, and I'm not hurting. You are my dearest friend. I want you to know that it is you I want to do my eulogy, and I want you to sing that song you sang at your graduation. You know the one I mean, "I've Done My Work.""

"You know I'll do whatever you want me to, but don't give up yet."

"I hear the Lord calling me," he said decidedly. "You are my assistant. I want you to stay at our church and take my place. You are a fine pastor. You have been like one of my sons, and I am so proud of you. You and Elberta help my children look after my Ella Mae."

I promised him we would, and that seemed to satisfy him. He didn't speak any more, and he seemed to drift back into unconsciousness. I called Elberta. School had just ended for the day. We stayed with Ella Mae until Ike breathed his last.

It was nearing dark when we left the hospital and took Sister Ella Mae back home. People had already heard the news and, as soon as we got there, some neighbors were watching for us and brought food over for our supper. We were all tired and still in shock, but the warm food was comforting, and it was a relief to be away from the hospital in a familiar home.

While we were eating, the chairman of the deacons come over to visit. He sat down with us at the table. "I know this will not be easy, but you are the one who knows how Reverend Foster would have wanted his funeral, Sister Ella Mae. I need you to tell me so I can call a meeting of the deacons in the morning and get it planned."

"I understand, Brother Amos," she said. Ike wrote out some things he wanted some time ago. I'll go find the paper." She rose and went out of the room.

While she was gone I spoke with Brother Amos. "Reverend Foster asked me to preach his eulogy," I told him. "I feel very honored that he asked me but a little uncomfortable about it. He was so well known all over the state. Maybe you and the other deacons would like to ask the State President of our

Convention to do that. He knew our pastor very well. I went with Ike to many of those state meetings and got to know the president myself. I know he was fond of Ike, and would willingly come."

"We'll talk about that in the morning with all the deacons," Brother Amos said.

Ella Mae came in with the paper she had gone to get. "Here it is, Brother Amos. We'll have to wait a few days for the funeral so that all our children can get here. You'll find he had some really specific ideas about what he wanted. I heard him ask Brother Randy to do his eulogy right before he died, and he wanted him to sing a special song."

"Thank you, Sister Ella Mae. We will keep all that in mind at our meeting tomorrow. Pastor Randy, could you get away for a short meeting around lunch time tomorrow?"

"Yes, I'll be there at noon."

After he had gone, I told Ella Mae what I had said to Brother Amos about calling the president to come here and do a eulogy. "It was you he wanted, Randy. You were closest to him. I think it should be only you."

I had to go to the funeral home early the next morning and took Ella Mae with me so she could choose a casket and bring the clothes she wanted us to put on Ike. I was amazed at how calm she was. She had called all her children, and they would be arriving the next day. Elberta took the day off from school and stayed at Ella Mae's house to receive callers. People would be bringing food all day long.

I took Sister Ella Mae home, and later that morning we had delivered Pastor Ike in his casket to their home. It was customary then for the body to stay in the home until time for the funeral. Church members and friends would come by the house to visit and view the body. A few close friends would sit up all night so the body was never left alone.

When noon came I was at the church to meet with the deacons. "I have just talked with Sister Ella Mae," I told them. "She wants to have the funeral in two days. That will be on Thursday. She wants to have it at ten in the morning. Then she would like to have a lunch at the church. So many people are coming and wanting to bring food. It needs to be here at the church to accommodate so many people."

183

The deacons all nodded. Having lunch at the church was something we often did after a funeral.

"Elberta and the girls would prefer to sit with Sister Ella Mae and the family. Would it be acceptable with you all if Deacon Antony plays the organ in her place?"

They were all agreeable to that. They understood that Elberta and I felt like we were family to Ike and Ella Mae. We talked some more and had everything arranged except the eulogy.

Brother Amos spoke up then. "Randy, as you have said, our pastor was well known and recognized all over the state in our denomination. I have talked to the president, and he is coming and will say a few words. There will be others from around the state who will be here. We all talked this over before you got here. Pastor Ike wanted you to preach his eulogy. Ella Mae wants you to preach his eulogy. We are all agreed that you should be the one to do it. You knew him better than anyone. We are unanimous in this decision. It has to be you."

"I appreciate your confidence, and I am honored and humbled to have this task. I will do my best to be worthy of it. I'd better get busy on it right away. I just hope I can give him half the praise he deserved. He was truly a saint of a man and such a friend to all of us."

The men all shook my hand and patted me on the back. They let me know they believed I would make them proud. I was certainly going to put my whole heart into this sermon. It would be one of my life's greatest challenges.

It was a labor of love. The fact that I would be preaching before state-wide church officers didn't make me anxious. I just thought about Ike and all he had been to me and many others. The words came to me easily, and I wrote without much hesitation.

Indeed it was a funeral I will always remember. Not only did state church officers come, but the whole community came out to pay tribute to Reverend Ike Foster. The deacons were setting up chairs as fast as they could, and finally there were people standing in the vestibule. The Sheriff and the Mayor came and many other prominent people as well, both black and white.

Sister Ella Mae was surrounded by her eleven children and

many grandchildren, and Elberta and our girls were right there with them

"Then, Deacon Antony Williams, you began your prelude. I was so proud of you. What a good musician you are. Your father was a good teacher, and Elberta continued to teach you music after you came to live with us."

I called the state president to come up and say a few words. He briefly told how Pastor Ike had been such a faithful participant in the affairs of the denomination in the state and how wise and thoughtful he was in being a part of the decision-making process.

The choir sang a fine arrangement of "Amazing Grace," and it was time for me to speak. I felt very confident as I got up and walked to the podium. I felt as if Jesus was standing beside me.

After I spoke, we sang a hymn, and I gave the benediction and invited all who were there to go to the cemetery and come back to the church for lunch. Many of our church women would stay and have a fine meal waiting for us downstairs when we returned.

So many people came up to me at the cemetery and at lunch to compliment my sermon. The old Sheriff, now retired, who had insisted I marry Sylvia, was one of them. He had long ago apologized to me for judging me so wrongly in the situation with Sylvia. Word had gotten around that she had confessed to making false accusations against me. "Reverend Foster was a good man," he told me. "Over the years, when I had dealings with him, I learned he was trustworthy and wise. I am learning the same thing about you. I hope you will continue in his footsteps."

"That is quite a compliment," I said. "The deacons will have to decide what happens with the church now. I will definitely keep preaching as long as they want me here."

Vernon and Cindy Stewart were among those who sought me out. They both hugged me and told me how proud they were of me. "Tell me you are glad you stayed here in Nelsonburg." Vernon looked at me as if he already knew.

"I am. I am glad because of people like Pastor Ike and you and my family. I am not even sorry about all the bad things that happened to me. The love and support I had from all of you helped me get through all that. What I've learned will help me minister to others. Yes, I'm very glad I stayed. Thank you for encouraging me to do that. Although, the fact that I did stay was all due to things beyond my control. I think God was keeping me here."

Pastor Ike had told me he wanted me to take his place as pastor, but I wasn't assuming that would happen. The church was in mourning. I did my best to be considerate of that and give the members a time to adjust. I preached every Sunday as the assistant pastor. I would be happy to remain the assistant pastor if the deacons determined that was in the best interest of the church. After all, my income was mainly from the funeral home, and that business and my farm kept me very busy.

It was three months before Brother Amos asked me to call a church meeting about calling a pastor. He told me I was being considered and asked if I would accept if chosen. It was not a surprise; I had thought about what I would say if they asked. "Yes," I had said. "I will accept."

At the meeting, I was asked to go into a separate room and wait till they voted. It was a formality I was accustomed to. When I came back they told me they had decided unanimously to have me be their preacher. I felt very honored and I thanked the deacons and the congregation for having confidence in me. I had a new sense of fulfillment. I thanked the Lord for helping me arrive at this destination of my life's journey.

I met regularly with the deacons, and we worked together very well. We talked about their expectations and mine. We set goals and worked to help our congregation thrive and grow. In one year we had met our goals so well, I recommended we build a new church. I gave the first thousand dollars toward it. Uncle Cephus gave the second thousand dollars. The third person to donate a thousand was my good friend, Vernon Stewart. He wasn't even a member of the church. That is the kind of friend he had always been to me, supporting my every endeavor.

The people of the church pledged generously and paid regularly on those pledges. The church was built and paid for in a short time. It was something for me to feel very proud to see accomplished.

Less than two years after Pastor Ike's death, we lost Mama. That was one of the trying times of my life. I tried to be as strong as I could, but those who have lost mothers will surely understand how I was feeling. My brother, Bobby, was still in the service, and my sister, Rose, was married and living in Phoenix, Arizona. They came home with their families. We worked together going through her things, but they had to go home, and I was left with deciding what to do with most of it. It was just things, china, silver, linens and all that, but it was full of memories for me. It was difficult. I'd never gotten over failing her in finding daddy's watch. She stopped asking me about it when she realized how painful it was for me that I never found it. I could never tell her the whole story, and she didn't press me. I was thankful for that, but I always felt something was lost between us because of it. It added to my grief at losing her.

Not long after Mama's death Uncle Cephus passed away. As you know, he was like a father to me. I had so depended on him. His girls came back for the funeral, of course, and stayed for a while with their mother, but they too lived other places. In the long run, it was me who Aunt Bessie depended on. I was glad of that because I owed so much to her and Uncle Cephus.

I suffered greatly after these two important people were gone from my life. But for my church members, who surrounded me with support and comforting words and deeds, I might have gone into a deep depression. What a blessing it was to have such wonderful people to uphold me.

I was vividly remembering the day of that funeral and Cousin Randy's eulogy. I had listened to every word of it, and even today, I could tell you basically what he had said. That is how much of an impression his words had made on me.

"Cousin Randy," I interrupted him. "Do you know that I had my friend tape the eulogy you gave for Pastor Ike."

"Why no, Antony, I had no idea you did that. It was so long ago, I hardly remember what I said."

"Well I did, and I have kept it all these years. I remember that it was even better than I expected it to be. I looked up to you so much. I thought you were the best."

"I don't know what to say. At the time I was so afraid it was not good enough."

"I want you to hear it like I did then. Can I go get it and play it for you. You need to hear it. You were so passionate and unselfconscious when you gave it. I was so proud of you. You wait right here. I am going to get it and you are going to listen."

"All right, I guess I would like to hear it."

I knew right where I had put the tape. I returned with it and my tape player, and we sat there and listened. These are the words Cousin Randy spoke that day.

Ike Foster was pastor of this, the Antioch Missionary Baptist Church. He truly knew what the word *pastor* meant, and he did what it meant. He went by the prescribed book of rules, the Holy Bible. He was my mentor. He was a wise guide in my years serving as his assistant. His encouragement was much of the reason I had the courage to become a pastor and serve the church. I am deeply honored by his request that I give his eulogy. I am both humble and proud to be able to stand here and speak about this great man, your pastor.

Pastor Ike, as we sentimentally called him, on several occasions said to me, "Son, when I pass off the scene, before they take my body and plant it out in Rose Hill Cemetery, I want you to sing the song you sang the night you graduated from high school. You remember it, don't you?" As always I would reply, "Yes sir, Rev." Then in unison we would say, "'I've Done My Work,' Carrie Bond and George Caldwell, published 1920."

My lovely wife, Sister Carter, our music director here at this church, has chosen to sit with Reverend Foster's family. That is how close we feel to that family. I have asked my cousin, Deacon Anthony Williams, to play for the service and accompany me on the piano when I sing at the end of my message.

Hear the scripture from the book of Isaiah, chapter 28, verses 24 through 26:

Doth the plowman plow all day to sow? Doth he open and break the clods of his ground? When he hath made plain the face thereof doth he not cast abroad the ditches and scatter the cumin and cast in the principal wheat and the appointed barley and the rye in their place? For his God doth instruct him to discretion and doth teach him.

With your indulgence, I will read a companion scripture, Ecclesiastes 3, verse 1: *To Everything there is a season, and a time to every purpose under the Heaven."*

My subject today is, "Time, the Most Unique God Given Utility to Humanity." Time is a creation under the third Heaven. It is defined as a period between two events. It is unique because the human body with its five senses cannot relate to time. It is too abstract. You can't hear, see, touch, taste, or smell it. The only thing you can do is use it for the period of your life. John 1:1-3 tells us that Jesus created everything, and that includes time. He came out of eternity into time and gave respect to what he designed and created. He said in John 9:4, *I must work the works of him that sent me while it is day: the night cometh, when no man can work.* Jesus tells us that our time is given to us that we might accomplish God's work.

Someone has said, "Time is of the essence." We cannot measure our lifetime or eternity because we cannot know when it ends, and strangely enough, time is not matter. We are matter, but wind is not, neither are noise, heat, nor spirit. We can measure the velocity of wind, the distance sound can be heard, and the degrees of heat or cold. We measure time in hours, minutes and seconds, but we can never know how many we have. Yes, it is a utensil, and God gave it for us to use. How are you using your time, my brother and my sister?

Now, Jesus had a physical body while the church is his spiritual body. In the human body, the eyes have lids. The body has no choice but to raise those lids so that the eyes can see. The ear has no choice, it must hear sounds. Only the nose can smell and only the tongue can taste, and the heart has no choice but to beat and the blood must flow as long as we live. So, if the church is Christ's body, the members have no choice but to work because He worked.

189

Solomon, through the inspiration of the spirit world, has us to know that even seasons have a time to perform. I would like to suggest that time is the third greatest God-given gift in the universe. Jesus was number one; life itself was number two. You see, the Holy Ghost was given exclusively to the church, but God gave time to everything under Heaven. Allow me to call to your attention Revelation 10, when John says he saw an angel standing with his right foot on the sea and left foot on the earth and cried out saying that time would be no more. But brethren, let us not postpone our work in view of this untimely event. Our time is out when this life is over.

In Isaiah, chapter 28, the writer presents the scenario of a dedicated farmer. We see him going to the field early in the morning to plow his land as he prepares the ground to sow his seed, but notice he does not plow all day. He ceases from plowing and begins breaking the clods up to make the ground more accessible for accepting the seed he sows. Once he has prepared the ground and secured the seed, he sows with great expectation.

Now as I remember, Reverend Foster had forty acres of land which he worked hard to pay for. He had four mules and a riding horse. It is remarkable that he and Sister Foster reared and educated eleven children on those forty acres. There were times when one of the boys would visit us and stay all night, and I would reciprocate by going and spending a night in the Foster house. No matter what time we went to bed, we had to get up early in the morning. If that smell of bacon or ham Mother Foster had gotten out of the smokehouse and was cooking or the aroma of that perking coffee didn't get us out of bed, then the voice of Reverend Foster would. He didn't have to tell us a second time. We knew that next thing might be the razor strap. There was always a place for a visitor to sleep in his house and always a place at his table to eat. Everyone ate at the same time. No one took their plate to the other room to watch television. As a matter of fact, there was no television to watch at his house.

During the summer when school was out, he was out preparing his mules to plow right after the sun rose. Like the plowman Isaiah talked about, he had a plow called a middle buster. It plowed so deep, he needed four mules to pull it. He also had another plow called a turning plow that turned the clods upside down. He had another tool called a harrow which was a composition of steel bars, and when the mules pulled it, the steel would break those clods to pieces. Then he was ready to sow his seeds.

Reverend Ike was never all for himself; he shared his bounty at harvest time with his members or friends. When his corn was ripe for eating, you could always come by and get a mess of roasting ears. Mother Foster would pick her turnip and mustard greens and share with neighbors. When Reverend Ike plowed up the sweet potatoes, the widows and their children would get a half or more bushel free. How well do I remember in the summer time when he would load his wagon with watermelons he had raised and take them to town to sell at the city market. On his way, he would stop and give some to unfortunate people who could not afford to pay twenty five cents for a watermelon or ten cents for a cantaloupe. Back in the thirties and forties money was tight. He took pleasure in his giving.

On the spiritual side, he asserted that same process in his ministry. On Wednesday nights he plowed the ground of the hearts of men with the word of God. Sometimes the ground of men's hearts were like clods, but like that harrow, he had a way of breaking it down for us to understand. He never refused to carry his Bible when he would visit the sick or to share it with a bereaved family. Because of his compassionate spirit and his benevolence, God blessed him with a tractor to farm with and a brand new pickup to haul his products to the market.

On Sunday morning in Sunday School, he was breaking and harrowing clods with the word of God. At eleven o'clock on Sunday, he took the chemistry of Mother Foster's Sunday dinner to get his message across to the people. You see, Mother Foster's menu consisted of meat, vegetables, and starch foods. Most of the time there were two meats, red meat and chicken with dressing or dumplings. If that red meat was tough, she had an instrument she used to beat it until it was tenderized. She always had dessert, but you could not have any until you ate the main course. That peach cobbler or dewberry pie would look so good. It was hard to wait to get that sweet desert and tasty juice. As I have said, Pastor Ike used the same chemistry in his sermons. He served God's word like a meal to the congregation. He first gave us the meat of the word and kept breaking it down until we got the message. Before he closed it down, however, like Mother Foster's dessert she made from those peaches he grew on his trees in his little peach orchard, or her delicious dewberry pie, or the potato pie she made from the summer crop and put in a potato keel, or the pumpkin pie she made from the pumpkin vine in the peach orchard, Pastor Foster also served dessert.

He put gravy to the meat of the Word, and he topped the sermon off with dessert. Like the juice from those wonderful pies, his words drew exclamations of pleasure and joy. There was shouting in the pews. Pastor Ike had a passion for excellence whether in the field or in the church.

When Antioch built a parsonage in town for Pastor Ike and imposed on his humility, he with gratitude and mixed emotions moved in that he might effectively serve his parishioners as well as the general community. He kept his farm, however, the land that for so many years he had induced and compelled to bear his bounty. Like Isaiah's plowman, at the close of the day as the sun neared its setting, he prepared to go home. Better still, on the spiritual side, he was preparing his soul for a better home.

I am reminded of a story I heard about our forefathers who were slaves. I thank God for our freedom. The story goes like this: Some men came from across the Mason Dixon Line on a tour of the southern plantations. One evening at sundown they watched the slaves as they started to their cabins at the close of the day. I understand that during that time the plantation owners had a bell that they would ring in the morning at daybreak signaling that it was time to go to work in the fields. In the evening, at the going down of the sun, the bell would ring to signal that the day was over. As the slaves trudged along the road, tired and weary and bruised by the hoe and the plow, they were silent. Their heads hung down and their shoulders were bent. As the visitors watched, they noticed one young man walking with his shoulders square and his head high. His walk was proud. One of the visitors asked, "What about the young slave I see walking with pride and grace? Would he be some kind of boss over the others?"

"No," the guide answered. "He was brought over here when he was a small child. His people told him that his father was a tribal king. Because he believes he has royal blood, he expects that one day his father will come and take him home."

That is what I would like to say about Reverend Foster. Tuesday morning the bell rang and the King of Kings said, "Isaac, the day is over. Come on home." I know he was tired from a long day's journey. He laid aside his utensils, his working tools. He had used them well and also that wonderful utility God gave him, time. With a heart stained with the blood of Jesus, he went on home to an eternal home to give an account of his stewardship. He has escaped from time. He used it well, but time too has an end somewhere and some day. Eternity has no end. I like to think I can hear him saying, "Goodbye time; welcome eternity." I hear a voice calling to him, "Servant Ike, welcome home."

Then Cousin Randy, you nodded to me that you were ready to start his song. I gave you an e flat, and you sang these words in your powerful voice.

> I've done my work; I've sung my song.
> I've done some good; I've done some wrong, and I
>   shall go where I belong. The Lord has willed it so.
> He knows my heart and every thought;
> He know what pain and joy have brought,
> And by His love I shall be taught; the way to Him I know.
> He knows my soul so weak and blind, so full of fears
>   of mortal mind.
> And He will lead, and I shall find the way to Him I know.
> He guides my steps, and He knows best; He will not harm
>   where He is blessed.
> And so goodnight; I'll take my rest where sweet wild roses
>   grow.

The tape ended and once again I was in awe. Uncle Randy was as quiet as I. I think he was surprised at the power of his own voice and words.

I said, "Cousin Randy, you were so wonderful and inspired that day. Did you hear Uncle Tobe Small saying "That's deep water, boy?" And Aunt Lou Dean was shouting, "Preach Pastor Carter!" You could hear them above all the amens in the building.

"Thank you for playing that, Antony. I think God must have put the words in my mouth. I had forgotten much of what I said, but Pastor Ike was certainly deserving of them. What a friend to me he was!"

CHAPTER 16

Nana Ella's Revelation

BUT WE HAVE PUT OFF TELLING YOU *the whole story of how I,*
Tony, came into Cousin Randy's life and how we became so im-
portant to each other. I've been trying to get him to talk about
this, but he's kept saying I've lived it with him and already
know. I keep telling him that much of it is vague to me.

I was just nine years old when my father died, and my
mother brought me to Nelsonburg where she had grown up with
her brothers, Cephus and Joe Nathan, who was Cousin Randy's
father. This was well before Cousin Randy became pastor of the
church. A few years later Mama died, and I went to live with
Cousin Randy and his family. I was like a big brother to his
daughters, Maybelle and Rose Ann.

We've had a relationship much like he and our Uncle
Cephus had. I have worked with him in all his businesses and
continue to be a deacon at our church. He put me through
school, and I've continued working with him. We like working
together. Now that I am married and have a family, I live just
around the block from him. We often have our meals together.

After I came to live with him, he told me that Mama had left
me some property and money. When I turned twenty-one, he
gave me the money and the deeds to the property, and then he
told me the most astonishing thing. He told me that I was not
my father and mother's biological son, that a stranger had left
me on their doorstep and they had adopted me. I couldn't be-
lieve it. People were always telling me how much I look like my
mother's family. How could I not be their natural child. I was
in shock over that for a while. I knew, however, that Cousin

Randy wouldn't lie to me. I trusted him completely. I finally had to accept it for the truth.

I've kept pressing him to tell me everything he remembers about the time before I came to live with him and what he learned from my parents about how I became their son. He has told me some of it before, but I convinced him to sit down with me and let me get it all written down. We were alone in the living room while Aunt Elberta was finishing up dinner. Maybelle and Rose Ann were away at school at that time. My wife, Anna, and our sons, Joe and Sam were at home icing cookies to bring for our dessert. The sun was going down that evening, and the light was still coming through the window, resting on him as he told me this part of the story:

My brother and sister and I always called your mother Nanna Ella. Even after she married your father and moved to Baltimore, our families stayed in close contact. We were so sad for her when Uncle Tony died so young, but we were very happy that she brought you and came back to Nelsonburg to live after he died. She had lived in Boston all of her married life.

Uncle Cephus helped you and your mother just like he had always helped us. He saw that she always had housing and a job, and that you were well cared for. He was always so proud of your musical abilities and Nana Ella insisted that you keep up the music studies your father had begun with you. As young as you were when you came to Nelsonburg, you were already playing the piano and the saxophone. Elberta said you were a prodigy. She continued to teach you piano.

I loved your mother and we became even closer because she was working at the mortuary and you came there after school to stay until you both went home. You would have dinner after church with Elberta and me or we would all have dinner at your house or at Uncle Cephus and Aunt Bessie's. We were family.

A few years after you moved here, Nanna Ella got sick. I just couldn't believe how fast she went down. It was cancer. I went to see her daily when she was in the hospital, and you were staying at our house. I took you with me to visit her until she got so sick I feared it would upset you. Then I took you less often, and was often with her by myself.

On one of these hospital visits, as I was leaving, she told me she had something important to tell me sometime.

"I'm here every day, Nanna Ella, I told her. I can stay a little longer, if you want to tell me now."

"No, you come tomorrow, and I will tell you."

"Sure, I'll be here just like always."

I was most curious about what she was going to tell me and a little troubled, too. I wondered all the next day about it until it was time to go back to see her.

"Here I am," I announced cheerfully when I arrived at her bedside. I was trying to act like I hadn't been anxious all day about what she was going to say.

"Come right on in here and pull up that chair over there so you can sit close beside me. I have something to tell you that is just between me and you. I don't want people out in the hall to hear us."

I put the chair on the side of her bed that was farthest from the door and leaned my head close to hers.

"As you know, I was quite a bit younger than my brothers. I used to stay with you and your brother and sister when your mama needed help. You were a pretty big boy when I went away to college."

"Yes, I remember. You took us to movies and ball games sometimes when you were still in high school."

"I went to Atlanta, Georgia, and went to Morris Brown College there," she began. While I was there, I met my husband, Antony. He was going to Moorehouse College. The two colleges were close together. We spent time together as friends and our relationship grew into more than a friendship. We were finishing our studies the same year.

"Before we graduated, Antony proposed to me. He was from Baltimore. Moving up north was something I had never considered. I told him I would marry him if he would marry me in Texas.

"My father and brother, Cephus, came to my graduation. My mother was sick at the time. While my father was there with us, Antony asked him for my hand in marriage. My father consented.

"After graduation, I went home with daddy and Cephus. Soon after that, Antony and some of his friends came to Texas, and we got married. I became Mrs. Antony Williams, and we went back to Baltimore to live. We lived in an apartment there.

"Tony was smart, and he could play the saxophone like nobody else. He had played in school bands and small independent groups for many years. He got a job right away playing in a twelve piece band. It was a good and popular band. It competed with some of the bigger bands in town. They got offers to play in Washington, D.C., and places as far away as New Jersey. I traveled with him when I could.

"We always needed more money, though. My first job was working in a home for unwed mothers. I taught the girls and young women there things like hygiene and nutrition and how to care for their babies after they were born. That was something I really enjoyed doing, but it didn't pay much. After I started to work, I couldn't travel with Tony much, but I went when he played in town at night.

"Antony was a good ball player, too. He played on a semi-pro team during the season, and still had time to play in his band at night. He brought home extra money during those months, and we began to feel very secure.

"We wanted a child so much. Tony wanted a boy. We really tried, but I just didn't conceive. I saw doctors, but nothing seemed to help. Finally I did get pregnant, and we were elated. Then five months later, I lost the baby. Of course we were distraught. We grieved, but Tony was very good and loving to me. He comforted me and said we had time to have a child, but time passed and we didn't. Tony told me not to worry about it, but I did.

"After a while I got a job in the field I had prepared for, teaching in an elementary school. I really enjoyed working with the children, and my salary increased. We moved into a bigger apartment. I still volunteered some at the home where I had worked before. Since children weren't coming to us, it helped keep my mind and heart busy and fulfilled. I was really considering adopting a baby, and I thought there might be an opportunity there, but we still had hope of conceiving our own baby. I put off taking that first step toward adopting.

"It was winter, and Baltimore is pretty cold in the winter. One morning quite early when we were still in bed, we heard someone knocking at the downstairs entrance. Antony put on his house shoes and robe, and went down to see what it was. I stayed in the warm bed. It was not time for us to get up. In minutes, however, Tony was calling me to come down.

"I was overcome with curiosity, and hurried into my robe and house shoes to find out what could be going on at such an hour. Randy, are you guessing what I'm about to tell you."

"No, Nana, I have no idea, but I think it must be something important."

"You are right there. Well, there was a basket on the couch and in it was a whimpering baby. I heard and saw, but it just didn't sink in. 'What is that, Tony?' I asked stupidly.

"'Why, don't you see, it's a baby?' he said gently.

"'Where in the world did it come from?

'When I unlocked the door and looked out, there was a car pulling away. Then I looked down, and there it was. I couldn't just leave it there. So I brought it in. What should we do? I guess I need to call the police and report it.'

"I picked the baby up and held it. The baby was wrapped in a nice blue blanket. I wondered if that meant it was a boy. It had a tiny gold ring on its finger. When I held it close to me, I could feel that it was wet. Tony was looking in the basket. The first thing he pulled out was some dry diapers. There was also some powdered formula, bottles with nipples and extra clothes, and a note."

"What did the note say?" I asked Nana Ella eagerly.

"It said, 'Please take care of my baby.'"

"Is that all it said?"

"That's all. There was no name, nothing we could see to indicate where the baby had come from.

"I had Tony to bring me a warm, wet washcloth and towel, and I took off the wet diaper and cleaned him up. The baby was a boy. He wasn't more than a few days old, and he was a pretty little thing. I had Tony to hold him while I fixed the formula. I knew how to do all that. I had learned that helping with all you young nephews and nieces.

"The baby drank all the formula, and went right to sleep. We put him back in his basket, and things were so quiet. We decided to call the police. Perhaps someone was looking for this little fellow. The police, however, had no reports of a missing baby. They suggested we call the hospitals, but they didn't seem to be missing a child either.

"We called the police back and they sent two men out. They asked us to come to the police station and bring the baby to make a report, but we were not dressed yet, and we both were planning to go to work. They suggested that we might keep the baby for a few days and go the station one afternoon after work. By that time, someone might show up to claim the baby.

"I decided to call into my school and tell them I had an emergency. I had not taken any days off recently. The principal was most accommodating. He would find a substitute for me. It was Friday, and I would have the weekend off.

"I kept the baby that day, and went into the police station that afternoon to make the report. They told me no one had called, and they were glad I was keeping the baby. The weekend went by, and Tony and I were becoming more and more attached to the baby. I went to the store to buy some more diapers and a few more clothes.

"When Sunday came and there were no inquiries about the baby, we were thinking about how we could continue to keep him. I thought of a retired nurse who lived close by, and when I approached her about keeping the baby during our working hours, she was delighted at the prospect. Tony was nearing the end of his baseball season and would be spending some of his daytime hours at home with the baby, too.

"We continued to keep the little boy, and Tony adored him. He would come in at night after playing in the band and just look at him for a long time. I even began to wonder it it could be Tony's baby. Tony was very handsome and he had so many fans who loved his music and his prowess on the baseball field. Could he have been seduced by some young admirer who brought this baby to our doorstep? I couldn't help but ponder on that, but I never asked. I searched the baby's face for resemblance to him, but I did not see it. I counted back the months to about when I thought the baby would have been conceived. I remembered that Tony had been ill about that time. He had suffered terribly from asthma. He had stayed at home or in the hospital for more than a month. I decided it couldn't be Tony's baby, and put my mind to rest about that, but, as I fell more and more in love with the baby, I worried every day that someone might show up and claim him. It was a terrifying thought."

"Oh, Auntie Ella. I think I am beginning to see things more clearly. You adopted that baby, didn't you. It's Antony. I'd always thought he was your natural child."

"Yes, you are right. People didn't talk about being with child back then. Nobody here had seen me, and no one was surprised when we announced we had a baby. We went through the process of legally adopting him and named him Antony, after his father. You are surprised that he was adopted, and there are more surprises yet to come."

"What are you telling me?"

"One day, when he was about five, I got a phone call. I almost fainted when the person on the phone told me she was my little Antony's mother. I had been afraid of this all his life, but she said she was only calling to thank me. She told me she had been driving by the house all these years and noticing that Antony was well cared for. She wouldn't give me her name, she just kept thanking me and then hung up. It shook me up a bit.

"When I told Tony, he reassured me that we were Antony's adoptive parents. She could not claim him after all this time. I was still worried."

"Bless your heart, Auntie. I never knew how much you suffered to be Antony's mother. He is a fine boy now. I know he is surely worth all you went through."

"That is the truth, but keep listening. There is more to this story. After two more years, the lady called me again. She said she was sick in the hospital and she wanted Tony and me to come see her. She said she had something important to tell us about our Antony. Her voice sounded weak, and I could hardly understand her when she was telling me where to come. I thought I heard 'City Hospital, room 434.' She hung up again without telling me her name.

"I told Tony as soon as he came home. He decided that we

must go and try to find her, that we needed to know all we could about little Antony.

"Tony set to work trying to find her. Fortunately there are only a few hospitals in town, and only two of them had a fourth floor. The patient in the first hospital we called was a man. Tony found out a lady patient was in the other hospital room. We went to that floor and Tony asked the nurse if the lady in 434 was expecting a Mr. and Mrs. Williams to visit. The nurse seemed to be expecting us and showed us to her room and left us alone with her. I recognized her at once. I had known her at the home where I had worked as Julia Trotter. She was not a teenager, but older than most of the girls, maybe even a little older than me. She had been so appreciative of everything I had done for her there. We had discovered after talking a little that we were both from Texas, and after talking some more, that we had both lived part of our lives in Nelsonburg."

"Julia!" I exclaimed. "I had no idea it would be you.

"'I am so glad you came,' she said softly. Her voice was still weak. 'I am very sick. The doctor tells me I have a terminal illness and only a short time to live. I cannot thank you enough for taking in my child. I was not in any position to care for him. Mrs. Williams, you were always so nice to me at the home, and I knew you hadn't had a child of your own and wanted one. I knew you would be good to my baby and learn to love him like your own. I knew you could give him a better life than I could. And now I know I have done the right thing. There is one more thing I hope you will do for me. I have no relatives left, and I hope for the boy's sake, you will see to my burial."

"She went on to tell us about a briefcase she had and said she would give us the key to it. She said there was a one hundred dollar bill in the briefcase as well as things she wanted her son to have. It was all she had left of her savings. She said she wanted to be buried in a white dress, but not to spend all the money on that. It could be inexpensive, she told us. With the rest of the money, she wanted us to buy a stone marker for her grave. She wasn't concerned about where we buried her, just that the grave be marked so her son could know about her and visit the grave. She told us there was another locked bag

202

inside the first one, and she would give us a key to each of them.

"Tony and I agreed to take care of all the arrangements. It seemed little enough to do for the woman who had given us her child.

"She told us she had been changing her life in the last seven months. She had been going to church and felt she had experienced a major change of heart. She had not officially joined a church here, but she had felt a part of the fellowship in one. She had felt God's grace and acceptance and wanted her son to know about that. 'Could I please see the boy,' she had asked us.

"I stayed with her while Tony went to get Antony. I talked to her about Antony, telling her about his personality and how well he was doing in school and that his father was teaching him to play the piano and saxophone. She listened intently and expressed joy at all I told her.

"Antony came into the room quietly and respectfully. He was such a good and thoughtful child. She asked him to shake her hand, and he did, looking directly into her eyes. She commented on his how nice his glasses looked on him and told him that he was a handsome boy.

"She told him that he was lucky to have such loving parents, and that he must always love and respect us. His head moved up and down in assent, and he told her he would surely do that. I had no idea at the time what Tony had told him about her, but his behavior for the situation couldn't have been better.

"She soon seemed tired, and was quite willing to let us leave. She thanked us for coming and putting her mind at ease. She made sure we had the briefcase and keys. 'There is a letter I wrote to you and the boy in the briefcase I want you to read right away.' she told us. 'It will tell you some things I want you to know about me and your son.' Just two days later that the hospital called to tell us she had died.

"Tony had bought me a beautiful white dress for Mother's Day. I thought it would be just the right thing in which to bury her. Tony agreed. He said we could buy me another one when Easter came again.

"We buried her and had the stone put on her grave as we

had promised. It took her money and a good part of our savings, but we felt good about it."

"That was hardly any time before Uncle Tony died, was it, Aunt Ella?"

"You are right. Antony was only seven when his birth mother died, and then he was almost nine when Tony had that heart attack. You all came up to his funeral, and Antony and I came back home with you. There was no reason for us to stay up there. I wanted to be back near my family. Cephus was my older brother. He was so supportive and helpful to me, and your mama was, too.

"You are my oldest nephew, and you live here. I want you to be the one to look after Antony when I am gone. I want you to be the one to raise him for me. You are a good man. I would like him to be like you."

"Of course I will do that. Tony has always been a good boy. For a teenager, he is exceptionally good. You and Uncle Tony were good parents to him. I would be pleased to have him with me. Elberta and the girls already love him. He has been in our house so much since you and he moved back here. He is already like a big brother to the girls."

"I still have that briefcase Antony's birth mother gave me and inside it is a bag of things she wanted him to have. They are in the bottom of my wardrobe, that antique wardrobe I got from my mother's house, and the keys are in the bottom drawer. I want you go to my house and get those. Since Tony died, no one knows about those things but me. It will be yours now."

"Yes, ma'am, if that is what you want."

"I know Antony will do well with you. You have prospered. You continue to do well with the funeral home, and you have added to your farmland and have a fine herd of cattle. Besides all that, you have done such a wonderful job as pastor of the church. I am so proud of you. Elberta is a wonderful wife to you and is such a good mother to your girls. She will be good for Antony, too. And how about you getting appointed to be trustee of that big bank!"

"Well, you know, Vernon put me in that position. He is vice president of that bank."

"Yes, I know; he is a fine man, that Vernon Stewart. I'm

proud of him, too. You know he couldn't have recommended you to that board if you hadn't had money. You are prominent in this town."

"I am grateful for what I have. I've had a lot of help from my family and friends."

"Yes, and that is what I want for my Antony. I want him to have good people to keep him turned in the right direction. You know, I've never told him that Tony and I aren't his real parents. He'll need to know that sometime. You tell him when you think the time is right."

"I'll do that, Aunt Ella."

"You make me happy, Randall. I feel like I can rest now. I've done the right thing for Antony. You go on back home now. I want you to get that briefcase as soon as you can. It is important that you read the letter Antony's mother wrote to Tony and me. What you will learn will surprise you. It is easier for me to let you read the letter than for me to tell you. It is a long and difficult story, and I am tired."

"I'll see you tomorrow, Nana Ella. We'll talk some more." Each time I visited Nana Ella after that, however, she seemed weaker and didn't want to talk. It was only a week after our conversation that she died.

After her funeral was over, I locked myself in a room and cried my heart out. That helped, but I still felt on the edge of depression. I had help once again from all the out-of-town family members, but as always, the time they spent here was short. Once again, there were things to deal with that only I could do. Elberta helped and comforted me a great deal. And Antony was growing up and such a serious youngster. He and I became great companions, doing many of the things that my dad and I used to do together. I began to call him Tony, like his dad had always been called.

"I had not heard about that black bag before, Cousin Randy. Did it tell anything about who my mother was? You've always told me you didn't know anything about my parents."

"I'll get to that soon, Antony. Just be patient and let me go on with the story. You were such a joy to Elberta and me, a really good boy. You were young, and your mother wanted you to think of her and Tony as your real parents. I did as she told me and told you about the adoption when you were twenty-one. That's when I gave you the money and deeds to your property. That was part of what was in the bag. Be patient, and let me get to the rest in my own time."

"All right, but I can't help being so curious. This is about me!"

"Aunt Ella had talked about my holdings and my status in the community, but I wanted to give you more. I wanted you to know all the things I had learned from my experiences and all the wonderful people who had guided, nurtured and supported me throughout my life. I was constantly telling you stories of my past and the good advice I had gotten from my family and people like Pastor Ike and Vernon Stewart.

"Aunt Ella and Uncle Tony had taught you to be respectful, and maybe you were just naturally so. You always listened to me with something near reverence and you were good at following instructions. Like my father did for me, I gave you and the girls tasks to complete and made sure you kept at them until they were done. I gave all of you Uncle Cephus' best advice over and over: 'Always pay your debts and always be honest with people. It will be to your own advantage in the end.' I told you, too, how Vernon Stewart had urged me to stay in Nelsonburg. At the time that had made no sense to me at all, but now I knew it had been the right thing to do.

He had just finished telling me all this when Cousin Elberta called us to dinner. Anna and my boys had just come in. It was to be just the six of us at dinner this night, Cousin Randy and Elberta, and my little family. We sat down and held hands around the table and said a blessing together. As we started eating the wonderful food Cousin Elberta had made for us, Cousin Randy excitedly began telling us about something that had happened in town that day. He was always telling us stories at the table, sometimes about family and friends of the past and some-times about the happenings of the day. Listening to those stories had always made me think of more questions to ask him and to start writing about all I learned of him. Tonight's story brought past and present together:

"I could hardly wait for my work day to end so I could come home and tell all of you who I ran into today. I was at the bank on business, and someone called my name. I looked up, but didn't see anyone I recognized. A women came up to me and spoke, 'You *are* Randall Carter aren't you?'

"Then I was amazed when she told me she was Doris Smith, my neighbor when we had lived at the farm. We were delighted to see each other, and she asked me all about my family. You all remember who Doris was, don't you? She was my neighbor at the farm. The one who was the cause of my family moving to town. I've told you all that story before.

"I told her all about Rose and Bobby and how I had married Rose's best friend. I had to tell her that Mama had died, but she, too, reported that her parents had died. We talked for a long time there and had such a nice conversation.

"Doris had married a trucker and moved to Colorado not long after we left the farm. She was back here in Nelsonburg visiting some of her family who still lived here. We talked about how things had changed since those high school days, and about that fateful day when we had walked home from school together and set tongues wagging about us. Today we could laugh about it. 'Now all the children, black, white and Hispanic, are riding the same buses and going to the same schools,' she remarked. 'It took a while, but it happened. You and I knew it was the right thing all along, didn't we?'

"I agreed with her, and then we laughed and talked about how nice it was that we could stand there and talk and not worry that we would be gossiped about. I asked her if she knew that I was a preacher now. She said she had and other good things about me, too. She told me she always knew I would become an important person in my community and was so proud I did.

"I thanked her and we talked on about how good life was back then and how our parents had been such good neighbors and worked to help each other and shared the good things we had. We didn't have to have integration laws to make us treat each other with respect. Doris and I agreed that life had been good for us back then. I was so glad I bumped into her. She seemed happy with her life too. That is good to know."

Joe and Sam were full of questions. They loved hearing Cousin Randy's stories, and he had to tell them again about why Uncle Cephus had come that long ago Sunday to get his family to move away from the farm.

CHAPTER 17

Jukebox Nick's Confession

AFTER DINNER WE ALL SAT in the livingroom for a while and played some games with Joe and Sam. After a while Anna took them to our house to get ready for bed, and Cousin Elberta went upstairs to read a while. She had been giving us time to be alone together since I had started writing down Cousin Randy's stories. We had begun doing this seriously in the early part of the fall as darkness began to come sooner and sooner. Now it was winter, and it had been dark for several hours.

We had put on a pot of coffee to get ready for another storytelling session and had just settled in to begin, when suddenly there came a soft knock at the door.

I looked at Cousin Randy. "Who could that be?" he asked me.

I was puzzled. "It is Christmas time. Maybe it is just somebody needing a handout."

"Well, just go to the door and see. Be careful though."

I went to the door and turned on the porch light. I opened the wooden door. The screen door was fastened. I looked out at a well-dressed, middle-aged white man. "Good evening, sir," I addressed him. "Can I help you?"

"I'm sorry to be calling so late, but I was hoping to see Mr. Randall Carter. I saw his name on the mailbox. I saw the light was still on, and I knew Mr. Carter long ago. I would really like to speak to him, if I could. Are you his son?"

"No, but I am a family member."

"You look like him."

"Who is it, Tony?" Cousin Randy called from his seat in the front room.

"Tell him my name is Nick Navarre. Randy knew me as Nick, the jukebox man."

Cousin Randy must have heard him because he jumped up and hurried to the door. "Why, Nick, what in the world are you doing here this time of night? Come in, man, I am glad to see you. Where have you been, and how did you happen to find me?"

"Those are good questions. I haven't been around here since the thirties."

"That's right. I haven't seen you since my high school days when you came in to service the jukeboxes in the cafés where my crowd went for Cokes after school."

"That's right, I came to Nelsonburg often during those days. You still look like you did back then, and this young man looks so much like you did. Is he your son?"

"We're first cousins, but he is like my son. His mother died when he was young, and I raised him after that. Come on in here and sit with us a while. I have just been telling Tony about some of those old days."

I could see that this conversation was going to be very interesting. This was going to be some new material for my story about Cousin Randy. I wasn't about to leave. I went to the kitchen and got us all coffee. Then I sat down quietly with them. They were so engrossed in each other, they seemed to have forgotten I was there.

Mr. Navarre continued, "Well, I saw your name on the mailbox, and saw that *Reverend* in front of your name. I knew it had to be you. I saw your light was still on, and I just had to try to see you. I'm so glad I did. You sure have a nice house."

"Thank you. We like it. I would like to introduce you to my wife, Elberta. You might remember her, too. She was Rose's best friend. She went up to bed early though. Where have you been all this time?"

"I live in Chicago now. You know, I had a sister who lived here. She moved to Brooklyn, New York, back then. She stayed up there till she retired, and then she wanted to come back to Texas. She lives here now, and I just came down to visit her.

She always goes to bed early, too. I am not used to her

210

hours. I read all the newspapers and watched the news, and I still wasn't sleepy. I just had to get out her car and come out to see what was here that I remembered. I passed your church and saw your name on the sign there, and then I passed by this house. I just knew it had to be you.

"I have thought of you so often. You were such a respectful young man. You always called me Mr. Navarre when all the other boys called me Nick. I remembered that always. When I saw your name, I just had to stop and try to see you. I have owed you thanks for a long time."

"What did I ever do for you?"

"You saved my life!"

"I did?" Cousin Randy seemed totally taken by surprise at that statement.

"It was back when I was on my route, installing the jukeboxes and changing the records. There was a café I used to come to there on Ninth Street."

"Oh yes, that was on Ninth and Chestnut. It was called Dan and Dora's Inn."

"You are exactly right. I remember now. That Dora could really cook. That is where I always ate lunch when I came to town. Dora worked so hard. She did everything. She cooked and served and washed the dishes. Old Dan just seemed to stand around and smoke a cigar. I would feel so sorry for her. One day I just flat told him that he ought to hire someone to give that woman some help. I kept after him about it, and finally, he took my advice.

"He hired that cute little colored woman that everybody called "Miss Tiny." I recommended her for the job. I knew her from another place that was going out of business. You have to remember her because you were there a lot during that time."

"Of course I remember her."

"I remember you so well, too, Randy. You were such a quiet boy. You would dance with some of the girls, and you were always such a gentleman. I was impressed with you. You were respectful to everyone.

"That Miss Tiny, now she was a worker. She really moved around in that place, and she was nice looking, too. She loved music, and was always interested in the new records I was bringing in. There was nothing shy about her. She talked to me all the time. I would give her the old records that I was not going to use anymore.

"Then one day she ran up to me as soon as I came in and told me her phonograph player at home had broken. She was so upset about that. I figured I could fix it, so I took her home that evening and got it playing again for her.

"She was so energetic and fun to be around. We talked often when I came in the café, I'd wait around after I'd had my dinner and take her home when she got off from work. We became great friends. I was lonely. My wife and I had separated and she had taken our two children and moved to Houston.

"Soon Tiny and I were more than just friends. I would stay late and visit with her after I took her home, and our relationship became intimate. I bought her a newer console record player, and she was thrilled to death about that. Dan paid her more than the other place did, but it was still not as much as he should have. I had enough money from my commissions that I could help her some with her bills.

"Before long she got me a key made to her house so I could come and go as I pleased.

I was kind of a cocky hothead in those days. I carried a pistol, and I was jealous of Tiny. She was outgoing and flirtatious. I thought Dan had eyes for her even though he never raised her salary as he should have.

"I found out another customer of mine on the other side of town was needing a waitress and got her to leave Dan and Dora's and go to this better restaurant that was owned by a white family. They were willing to pay her more, and I didn't have to worry about Dan making passes at her.

"That didn't end my jealousy. I could see that she turned the white men's heads in the new place. Then there were times, when I was going into her house or looking out one of her windows, I would see old Dan drive slowly by. I didn't trust that man at all, and I thought obsessively about what he might do if I weren't there.

"One night I got into town very late to work there the next day. She wasn't expecting me, but I decided I would go spend the rest of the night with her. I parked in my usual inconspicuous place in the alley and went to the back door. I meant to use my key, but the screen door was latched. I knocked, and there was no response, so I knocked louder. Tiny heard me and asked loudly who was there.

"It's me," I told her. "Let me in, I came to spend the night. I could hardly believe my ears when she opened the door just a crack and told me I shouldn't have come that late and that I couldn't come in. She told me she had company.

"Who is it? I wanted to know. I was at once suspicious it was a man. She told me it was a relative of hers. She told me I'd have to go somewhere else. I threatened to cut the screen. She had never before not let me in.

"I was furious. I threatened to get my gun and cause trouble. She stood firm and shut the door and locked it. I paced outside and walked by her bedroom window. I could hear someone snoring. I thought surely it was that Dan who I had seen driving by before. I walked back to the alley and decided to stay there and watch the house. If he came out, I was going to shoot him. I confess I had been drinking some before I had gotten there, but I wasn't drunk. I was determined to stay awake and watch till someone came out.

"I managed to do it, and around dawn I saw someone come out. It didn't look like Dan. He was a big man, and this man was very slender. I got my pistol and started out of the car. It was not fully light, and I couldn't easily see who it was. I followed him. When he turned to open the gate and go out in the alley, a light from the side of the house shone on him. I recognized him. Randy, it was you!"

"Me!" Cousin Randy said in a loud shocked voice.

"Was I surprised," Mr. Navarre went on. "I was horrified that I might have shot you. I thought perhaps you were really her relative. Knowing you, I was sure there was some reason I hadn't thought of about why you were there. Maybe you were there to protect her from someone, someone like Dan maybe.

"I put my gun down at my side and walked away, back to my car. I was ashamed of myself. It really hit me how I would have felt if I had shot a nice kid like you. It shocked me enough to make me know I needed to make a change in my attitude and my life. I got in my car and went straight home. I

213

swore that when I came back to Nelsonburg, I would go and apologize to Tiny and tell her she didn't have to worry about me any more because I was going to have better thoughts and live a better life.

"Before I had a chance to get back to Nelsonburg, I had a sick spell. I even had to go to the doctor. It was several days before I had a chance to go back and see Tiny. When I did, I couldn't find her. She was not at the café, and when I went to the house and got out my key to open the door, I was surprised by a padlock that I could not open. At the back the screen was fastened and the inside door locked. I assumed the padlock was for me, that she didn't want to see me any more. I never saw her again after that.

"The whole incident made such an impression on me, that I did a complete turnaround. I asked for a transfer and didn't come back to Nelsonburg. I got back with my wife and children and I became a born-again Christian. I gave my life to the Lord, and many years after that, he called me to preach. Would you believe that I am a pastor now, too? My church is in Chicago. It is not a big church like yours. It is one of those store front churches. I don't have a big congregation, but I love what I have. I could not be happier in my work."

Cousin Randy had a joyful look on his face. "That is wonderful, and what a testimony. I am deeply moved and proud of you."

"I'm proud of you, too." Mr. Navarre said emphatically. "I want to come to hear you preach. I have promised my sister I will take her to her church this Sunday, and I am supposed to leave on Wednesday. But I swear, if I can get my ticket changed, I am going to stay and go to church with you next Sunday. Would that be all right with you?"

"You really flatter me. I am honored that you want to do that." Cousin Randy declared.

"You really had something to do with the change I made in my life, and I am so grateful as well as just plain interested in hearing you preach. I really hope to see you next Sunday."

"I'll be proud to see you there," Cousin Randy exclaimed. Like I say, it is an honor."

"I'll go on now. I apologize for coming this late and keeping you up. I'm glad to meet you, too, young man," he said to me. "You are definitely a Carter."

"I'm glad to have met you, too. Your story was wonderful. I have been writing stories that Cousin Randy has told me. Yours will go in my book."

"That is great. I am glad to be in a book about your cousin. By the way, Randy, what was Tiny's real name?"

"Why it was Lizzie Belle, Lizzie Belle Bell."

"Sure, that's right. I do remember that. Do you know where she is now."

"I heard she died," Cousin Randy told him. "She left here and went to work up north, and we heard she had died."

"Is that so? I am really sorry. She was a good person. Well, I'll say goodnight, and have a Merry Christmas. I hope I'll see you again before I leave."

"Merry Christmas to you and your sister, too," Uncle Randy and I said in unison.

CHAPTER 18

It's in the Bag

AFTER MR. NAVARRE LEFT, Cousin Randy sat down with me again. "That was some kind of story," he mused.

"It sure was." I agreed.

"It's late. Do you want to call it a night and start again another time?"

"I don't think I could sleep after that story. You have told me the part of the story Mr. Navarre never knew. That incident that started all your bad luck and did so much to change his life in a good way. When you really think about it, all that trouble you had then and after that, made you a stronger and better person, too. That really puts my mind in a tailspin. It seems like God had a hand in all of it."

"It does seem like that. You know, I'm not at all sleepy either. If I went to bed now, all these memories would just be boiling in my head. I would toss and turn. I feel like we need to do something. As you know, I've had a lot to grieve about lately. So many people have died or gone away. It is only you and your family and Elberta who keep me from being lonely. I miss those people who supported and helped me through my life. Your mother, my Nana Ella, was one of them. She was a blessing to me and our whole family. I want you to know that.

"I know what we need to do right now. Elberta has been after me for years for not trusting your love enough to tell you everything. This thing that has happened tonight has given me courage. Your mother gave me something for you before she died, things she wanted you to have and know about when you got older. I gave you part of it and part of the truth when you were twenty-one. There is more. I've been afraid you would be shamed by it. I've put it off long enough.

"You are a man now and have been for longer than I've given you credit for. There are more things in that bag that had her will and deeds that I gave you when you turned twenty-one. Your mama told me when she gave me that black bag, that there were many things that would come clear for me when I looked in it. She told me first that all the property that was in her name would go to you. The information and other things she left up to me when I should give them to you. I'm going to get that bag now. There are some things in it that I've never even looked at because I thought they were meant for you. The bag has been locked in a file drawer in my desk upstairs all this time."

Cousin Randy went to get the bag. I was surprised when he brought it in the room. It was not very big at all, just a small satchel. He unlocked the satchel and opened it up. From it he took a pouch about the size of two books and began to pull things out and lay them on the table. There were envelopes of various sizes and some small packages. When it seemed empty, he felt around in it and pulled out a small gold ring. It was so tiny, it looked like it would have been for a doll. Except for that tiny ring, I couldn't tell what anything was. It was all wrapped or in some kind package or envelope.

Cousin Randy sighed and shook his head as if he wasn't sure where to begin. "Are you sure you are ready for this?" he asked, as if now he wasn't so sure himself.

"I'm ready," I assured him. "I am wide awake and ready for whatever you are going to lay on me. It is too late to stop now!"

"You're right, I guess I have to be ready also." He picked up a composition book first. It was tied all around with string. He took the string off. "This is the first thing you need to know. This book contains the life story of the woman who gave your mother this bag. She was the mother who gave birth to you."

"Cousin Randy! I asked you who my real mother was the day you told me I was adopted. Why have you kept this from me?"

"Forgive me, son. I just couldn't bring myself to do it. I was afraid you would be shamed by it. I was afraid it would change how you feel about me."

"I don't understand."

"You will. Just bear with me a little longer. Here is the book she wrote in. Just go on and read it."

My hands were shaking as I took the book and opened it. It was handwritten, and the writing was difficult to read. "I feel really nervous, Cousin Randy," I said hesitantly. "My eyes just don't seem to focus well, or this handwriting is too difficult to read. You said you have read it before. Will you please just read it to me?"

"I am sure I feel as anxious as you do about going through this once again, but here goes. This is the story of how you came to be:

Dear Mrs. Williams,

I was born in Fort Worth, Texas. I was told that my name in the beginning was Julia Trotter. When I was only two years old, my father went to west Texas with a group of men to pick cotton. He got into some kind of fracas out there and was shot and killed. I don't remember him. My mother had been born somewhere around Nelsonburg, Texas, and her only family was an aunt who still lived there. She decided to go back there and live with that unmarried aunt. The auntie and my mother agreed that they could help each other. My mother went back to her maiden name, Bell, the same as her auntie's. I don't know why, but they started calling me Lizzie Belle Bell. I guess they thought I was like some other member of the family who had passed on. Then my mother died when I was only five years old. They said it was consumption. It was my great aunt who took care of me after Mama died. She bought a house up in Nelsonburg and we moved up there. She was really good to me. She kept me fed and clothed and sent me to school.

It took a few minutes for my brain to register what my ears were hearing. "Cousin Randy!" I interrupted. "Are we talking about the same woman that you and Mr. Navarre were talking about tonight? *That* Lizzie Belle! Surely she was not my mother. That is too much of a coincidence!"

"One and the same, Tony. I know this is a shock to you,

218

but maybe you will understand why it has been so hard for me to open up with you about this. You've been so intense about getting my life story on paper, and I have been dreading getting to this place. I didn't know if I could tell you, but here we are."

"Yes, you are right, and I am still determined to know the truth. Go on with the story."

But she was getting old. When I was only sixteen, she passed away. There was no other family, and I was left to fend for myself. I lived by myself and managed with what was in the house. I quit school and took jobs keeping house and minding children for people. I had nobody at home to answer to, and I did pretty much as I pleased when I wasn't working. I learned early how to arouse young men and get them to give me money and other things I wanted.

When I got older, I started working in eating establishments. I learned how to please customers and get good tips. A white man named Nick Navarre who traveled around in the area and installed and serviced the jukeboxes in all the restaurants in town took notice of me. When a café I was working at went out of business, it was he who got me the job at Dan and Dora's place. He was attractive and interesting. I was in love with popular music at the time. He sometimes gave me old records and then one time he came to my house to fix my record player. He started taking me home from work. We were both flirts, and it was not long till we wound up in bed together. He was separated from his wife at the time. He told me she had moved out and gone to Houston. He had money, and he was always buying things for me, and making my life easier. He came to town for a few days of every month, and he made a habit of staying that time with me. He was a jealous man, and he made it worth my while to be true to him when he was not in town.

"Now, Cousin Randy, surely you are not trying to tell me that man was my father? I am dark. I don't think I could have a drop of white blood in me, could I?"

"No, son, I assured him. He wasn't your father. Just stick with me here; I'm getting there.

219

Like I said, Nick got me the job at Dan and Dora's place partly because he felt sorry for Dora. Dan was kind of cocky and lazy. He acted like he thought Dora should do all the work. Nick didn't like Dan much, and he began to get jealous of him. He was also angry because Dan wouldn't raise my salary. And, yes, Dan had given me those kind of looks, but I never paid any attention to him.

Nick found me a better job downtown in a really fine restaurant, but he continued to see Dan driving around in my neighborhood and to act like he didn't trust me. He carried on about it so much it made me angry with him, and I began to be irritable when he came around.

One night when I was alone, I was not sleeping well because I was turning over in my head what I was going to do about Nick. The neighborhood dogs were barking like crazy. I finally got up, turned on some lights, and looked outside to see what had them so stirred up. I was surprised to see a man lying on my outdoor table. He was so still, I thought he might be dead.

Other than the barking dogs, things seemed pretty still out there. I was a little afraid, but I thought I should get a better look at the man. I wished I had a pistol, but I didn't. Instead, I picked up my broom. I put on my robe and house shoes and slipped out and tiptoed near him. I was so surprised. I knew the man or, actually, he was hardly more than a boy. It was Randy Carter, a young man I knew from Dan and Dora's Café. Randy was the sweet, quiet young man who always treated me so respectfully. I was ever so impressed with his polite, good manners, and he was so good looking.

There was no one else around, so I looked closer and touched him. He was certainly not dead. He was warm, and very soundly asleep. I shook him, and he roused up. I could smell alcohol on his breath. This kid was dead drunk. That was not like the Randy I knew. I thought I'd better get him into the house before somebody else found him. I pushed and pulled him, and he staggered along with me. He was very confused and thought I was someone else. He kept calling me Maggie. He kept hugging me and feeling me and saying he was so glad I found him.

I finally got him into the house and got the door closed and locked again. I was sure no one had seen us come in. He kept groping me roughly, almost angrily. I knew, if I could just get him to the bed, he would fall back asleep, and I could send him home in the morning. I confess I had been drinking some of Nick's wine myself and was feeling rebellious at Nick for his unreasonable jealousy. I don't really understand it myself, but something about this wild behavior in tame young Randy spoke to the wild part of me. I found myself responding to his advances. I don't know what got into me. I just let him, even encouraged him to do as he pleased with me and it seemed like what I wanted, too. Soon we both fell asleep, exhausted.

I awoke some time before daylight and took off Randy's shoes and pants and laid them on the chair beside the bed. I automatically took the contents from his pockets and laid them on my dresser. There was a little money and a pocket watch.

I had just laid back down when a knock came at the door. What now? "Who is that," I called out.

It was Nick. I was not expecting him until the next day. He had unlocked the door with his key, but the screen was locked. I told him he couldn't come here just any hour he pleased and to go away. When he argued with me, I told him a relative was spending the night with me. Nick was furious. He threatened to cut the screen and, if Dan was there, he would shoot him. I knew he always carried a gun in his car.

I told him that Dan was certainly nowhere near. When he stopped talking, I slammed the door shut and put a chair under it and some heavier things behind the chair. I didn't hear any more from Nick, so I assumed he had gone on. I didn't hear a peep out of Randy. He had heard nothing and was still sleeping soundly.

When Randy woke up at the first light of dawn, he was ever so anxious to get home. I didn't want to be alone, and I tried to keep him with me a little longer, but he had to be off. I didn't want to stay in the house. I didn't want to have to deal with Nick. I was afraid of him and his gun and his temper. A friend I used to work with had moved up to Fall County. I knew I could take the train up there and stay with her and find jobs chopping cotton for as many days as I wanted. I needed to do something mindless, so I could think about where my life was going. I just packed up some things and took all the money I had saved up for some time. I soon realized Randy had left without his money and watch. I put them in my suitcase, too. I didn't want to leave them. I would find a way to get them to him sometime. I had padlocks to put on my doors when I was going to be gone overnight. I locked everything up and told the neighbors to watch my place.

The time away did me good. It was good being outdoors, and the farm workers were a fun loving bunch who really livened things up after work. There was drinking and gambling. My friend and I could dress up and get lots of attention at some of the night spots. I was fairly happy, but I was thinking I would go up north soon. I heard there was better money up there.

After a couple of weeks went by, I thought I should go home and check on things. I planned to just spend a night or two and get more of my things and come back to my friend's house. I found the house just as I had left it. I packed up more things, all that I would need to take with me if I decided to go up north.

I was feeling a little melancholy and so unsettled. I got out some of Nick's whisky and started drinking it. I was really not used to drinking much, but I downed about four drinks that I mixed with some Coke. I was not planning to go out anyway, and I wanted to sleep good. Then I heard some sirens and what sounded like a commotion just down the road. I went out to see what was going on. I could see flashing lights not far away, and I walked toward them. Everyone in town seemed to be heading that way. I just fell into the crowd. People were passing the news around that some foolish girl had run Randy Carter down on the road near the ball game. I kept on till I saw that Randy was standing up and not dead. I must have acted pretty foolish myself because someone took me home and got me in bed. I woke up remembering the accident but not anything I had said or done. I had brought Randy's things back with me to Nelsonburg, but I certainly didn't think to tell him so at the time.

The next day I gave my house keys to my neighbor and told them I might not be back for some time. I took the train back to Fall County. I stayed on there still undecided about whether I would move on.

A few weeks later I began to feel ill sometimes. I thought it was just time for my period, but it never started. Surely I could not be pregnant! I had decided long ago that I couldn't get pregnant—all those times when I was young and careless I never did. Surely I was not pregnant with Nick Navarre's baby. I cer-

tainly didn't want to bring a white child into this world. It probably would be white. I am light skinned myself. Such a child would have a hard time in my world or the white world. What was I to do?

It was a good thing I had saved back some money. I had enough to get me up north and get a start. I had put back quite a bit when Nick was helping me out. Everyone said that there were good paying jobs up north and more social programs to help people. It was something I had considered doing even before I got mixed up with Nick. Mary, the friend I was living with, knew someone in Baltimore, Maryland. She called her friend and got assurance I would have some help and guidance once I got up there. A few days after that, I was on a train headed for Baltimore. I decided that there, I would use my real name, Julia Trotter. It was my legal name, after all.

Luckily I had a healthy pregnancy and had no trouble working, and in spite of my small stature, my pregnancy didn't show as early as it does with some people. I got a job right away in a nice restaurant and Mary's friend told me about a home for unwed mothers where I could stay and get advice, medical care, and help along the way. It was one of the best things that had ever happened to me. The women who helped there were so kind and understanding. You know that, Mrs. Williams, because you were one of them. No one was nicer than you.

Those women who helped care for me and the young women who were there in the same predicament as myself were a support community like I had never known before. I felt safe and cared about there. I started going to church with some of my new friends. I began to pray and believe that the Lord heard my prayers. I changed, and felt like I was truly born again.

I still worried about my baby and what to do when it came. It would be hard on a colored woman like me to raise a white baby. I had considered having an abortion, but since I had been going to church and thinking about what was right and wrong, it just didn't seem like the right thing to do. I decided to give the problem to the Lord, and trust there would be a way.

My health stayed good, and the people I worked for were wonderful to me. When I got big, they let me work in the kitchen right up to when the baby was born. The home had arranged for me to have the baby in the hospital, and when the time came, I went there. I had been so frightened of giving birth, but the doctor and nurses kept me comfortable and encouraged and reassured me. It was nothing like I expected, not a fearful thing at all. Once again, I felt the Lord's presence. When the baby was born, the doctor announced that it was a boy. Then they laid him, crying loudly, up on my belly. I looked on him in wonder and got the surprise of my life. The baby was a beautiful dark brown, darker even than me. This was surely not Nick Navarre's baby. It suddenly hit me that this was Randy Carter's baby. That was a possibility I had never considered since I was only with him that one time. This was a gift, an answer to my prayers that I was not expecting, an end, at least, to one of my biggest worries.

Cousin Randy hesitated here, like he knew I would have to say something. I just looked at him. I had not fully taken in what he had just read me, and then suddenly I was overwhelmed. "You, you," I stuttered, "you are my father?"

"Yes, son. I've known it since Nana Ella, your mother, died. I wanted so to tell you, but I just couldn't bring myself to do it. Now I believe I should have told you sooner. Put yourself in my place and try to understand."

"Is it really true?" I was still in a state of shock. All this was too much to take in.

"Yes, it's true. After I read this, I took you to the doctor and had your blood tested. You are definitely my son."

"Why have you waited so long to tell me?"

"I've been trying to tell you that, and you know you adored Aunt Ella and your father so much. I didn't want to take anything away from that. Elberta kept telling me that truth is always the best way to go, and I thought many times I would tell you, but then I just couldn't. Please understand and try not to hate me."

"Of course I don't hate you!" I said. "It is just a shock, and I felt angry when I first realized you could have told me this before." I was beginning to adjust to this new knowledge and even to appreciate what it meant. "I love my life and I'm glad I was born. I can't be angry about the way I got here. I have to be thankful, not only for me but for my children. I can't hate you. I love you. You've always been good to me and treated me like a son. I have to love you. You must understand though that I have to get used to this new knowledge. I'm really glad you are my father. It is just new to me."

"Thank you, my son. You don't know how that relieves my mind. There is just a little left of this story. Shall I read it to the end?"

"Yes, I want to hear it."

I still felt like I couldn't give this baby what he needed. I didn't know if I could afford to pay someone to keep him while I worked, and my life up to now has been so unstable. This baby is a Carter, I thought. That family is well off and well respected. This baby deserves to be part of that.

Mrs. Williams, you and I had talked after I came to the home, enough to know that we were both from Nelsonburg. I thought so highly of you and I made some inquiries of some of my Nelsonburg acquaintances and found out you were Cephus Carter's sister and Randy's aunt. We had talked about how you had longed for children and weren't having any luck at having one of your own. What better home could I give my child than to leave him with you. I knew you would love him and could provide for him. And now you know he is really your family. If anything could possibly make you treasure him more, that would be it. The coincidental circumstances of meeting you in my situation and then finding out that my baby was Randy's was like a message from God. It was like God answered my prayers with you.

It was so hard for me to do, but a few days after I left the hospital, I left the baby on your doorstep. I made sure someone found him before I walked back to the corner where the taxi was waiting to take me home. It was the hardest journey I had ever made. I loved that baby, truly I did. I just loved him so much, I had to give him a better life than the one I had lived. I was full of grief, but I knew I had done the right thing. You were always so kind and understanding. I hope you will understand this and not condemn me.

Julia Trotter

"I can't get over how fantastic this story is. It is hard to

225

believe it all happened as it did. What are some of these other things that you got out of the bag?"

"You know, I really don't know. I thought they were things for you. I never opened them. I knew I would give them to you sometime. Shall we see what they are?"

"I am so curious. Let's look."

"Now you saw this little ring. Nana Ella told me you had it on when you came to her. Lizzie Belle must have bought it for you so you would know she cared about you. Nana Ella must have put it back in the bag for you."

"Open the brown envelope there."

"Why don't you open it. These are your things."

"Look, it is a deed. What is this to?"

"Let me see it. Why that is Lizzie Belle's property that she inherited from her aunt, the one where her house still stands. I didn't even know she owned it. She had just always lived there and it has been empty since she left. I guess that is yours now, too."

"Now here is an envelope that looks like it is an invitation of some kind. It is bulging with something besides paper. It is addressed to her, Lizzie Bell Belle. Look, it is your graduation invitation. It says Randall I. Carter right here. What else is this inside here?

It's a gold chain with RIC on a center plate. She must have bought you a graduation present she never gave you."

"I guess so. We wore chains like that back then. I can't believe she bought me such a nice gift. We sent those invitations to everybody on our church roll. I do remember that she came to church sometimes. She must have been planning to come to my graduation before that fateful night but left town instead.

"There are two things left, a plain envelope and a package. Which one shall I choose first?"

"Open the envelope first."

I opened it and pulled out the contents. My eyes met his knowingly. We both were immediately aware of what this was. "Maybe I am worth at least this much?" I asked wryly as I pulled out a five and a one dollar bill."

"Oh, my son!" I exclaimed passionately. "There is no amount of money that could match your worth to me. You are worth more than millions of dollars, more than the Hope diamond to me. But think about her keeping that little bit of money all that time to give back to me. She could have spent it time and time again. That says something about her character to me. It tells you something about her to be proud of."

"I see that. Her life wasn't easy. She probably did the best that she could, and there was goodness in her. She found Jesus and gave her heart to Him in the end. I have to remember those things about her. You know, Cousin Randy, I think I have guessed what is in the package. Have you?"

"No, I don't know what you mean."

"You open it. I think it is something of yours."

An incredulous look came on his face. He took the little package, a box all wound up in tissue paper, and slowly unwrapped it. "It can't be!" he exclaimed even before he opened the box. When the lid came off he saw his watch and tenderly lifted it out. "My daddy's watch." he declared reverently. "I thought I would never see it again, and it has come back to me. Lizzie Belle sent it back to me. Oh, Mama, please! I pray you are seeing this from Heaven.

He was so overcome with emotion, he had to sit down. Tears came into his eyes. "This is yours now, my son. I pass this on to you so you will remember the love of your family. Someday you will want to tell your children about all this watch symbolizes."

We were both overcome with what seemed like holy silence. "Well, where do we go from here?" I finally asked.

"Well we're going to make sure you are legally my son, for one thing, and you will inherit my property along with my wife and daughters as well as Nana Ella's. We need to have some kind of celebration as a family and let your sisters in on this. We'll have to plan it for when they are home. I am so proud of you. There could be no better son than you!"

"How are they going to take this."

"They are going to be thrilled. You have been raised like brother and sisters. They will be so pleased to know that you are truly their brother."

"Are you going to tell them the whole story. Have you ever told them things about your past like you have told me?"

"No, but I think they will understand. They are very like their mother, and they love both of us like she does. And, for that matter, now that I have told you, I feel like telling my church the story. I want the whole world to know that you are my son. I know I did a wrong thing back then, and I have prayed and prayed to the Lord for forgiveness. I have believed for a long time that I am forgiven, but I have felt I haven't gone as far as I should. I've felt guilty standing up there in the pulpit calling you my cousin when you are my son. I need to confess to my fellow man and feel clean again. I should practice what I preach if I want my reward in heaven, and I do."

Well, Cousin Randy, are you asking my permission?"

"Not entirely, but it does affect you, and I want to know how you feel."

"It is a big step, a very daring step. You really need to weigh and think about the possible consequences. I would not want you to risk your reputation for my sake. I do so appreciate the thought. You have achieved so much in your lifetime. You are a great preacher, a scholar and writer as well as a leader in the community. You are known all over the state. I wouldn't want you to be criticized or ridiculed for my sake. All that can be avoided if you just let it be. I'll gladly stay your cousin for the sake of your reputation. I don't want Cousin Elberta to suffer either."

"Don't worry about Elberta. She is so loyal to me. She will stand by me through anything. She knows what forgiveness is all about. She loves you as much as I do. She has wanted me to claim you as my own. Anyway, it is not just for your sake that I want to do this. I need to do it for myself."

"When do you propose to do this?"

"How about Sunday?" I suggested recklessly.

"I think that is a little soon. I need some time to prepare my family. My children don't even know yet that you are their grandfather." How about the next Sunday, nine days from now. That will be the first Sunday in the New Year. Isn't that a time for making new beginnings?"

"I hadn't thought about that, but you are so right. That is exactly the right time."

"You need that time to prepare yourself, too. You are going to shock some people, and you are going to have to give them time to adjust to that shock just like I am having to. You are going to have to look into their faces and realize that they may not think well of you, especially not right away. You don't have to tell them all the details you have told me, but you need to choose your words very carefully. There are young people in the church, and you teach them to be chaste until they marry."

"They also need to know that they can be forgiven if they fail to be chaste. You are right about me needing some time to think this all through, but I'm willing to risk my job as pastor of the church to set this straight. That would be better than staying a hypocrite. The deacons called me to pastor the church, but the Lord called me to preach. I'll go back to preaching on the streets if I have to."

"For what it's worth, I'm a deacon myself. I think you are being honest and courageous, and in the end, I believe you will be respected and endorsed for it. We all have skeletons in our closets. I intend to stand by you and tell the church and the world how proud I am that you are my father."

CHAPTER 19

Nine Days 'til Sunday

"THERE ARE TWO THINGS that have just occurred to me," I said. "Do you think my poor eyesight was caused by the disease that Lizzie Bell gave you the night you slept together?"

"You know, I asked a doctor about that after I found out about you. He said it was possible."

"I'm not trying to place blame on anyone. It is just something I wonder about since no one else in the family seems to have a problem like it. The other thing is my mother's grave. I would really like to go up to Baltimore and see it. She said she wanted me to do that."

"I'm not surprised to hear you say that. You certainly should go."

"I'm even thinking about having her moved here and buried in Rose Hill Cemetery with all my people. This is where she lived the longest. I would like to bury her beside my other mother, Ella, and have them both near where I will be buried someday. Thanks to the Lord and to you, I have the financial means to do these things. I would like to buy a new stone for it and inscribe something on it from me. What do you think about something like this, "To a mother whose love I cherish. Your loving son."

"I think that is beautiful. I am proud of you for thinking like that. I believe that is the way God wants us to love each other. I would be glad to pay for that myself."

"No, I thank you for offering, but she is my mother. It is my place to do it. She gave birth to me. She could have aborted me, but she didn't, and I love my life."

"I understand. I'm proud that you have the caring and respect to make you want to do it. Would you understand if say I want to go up there with you? Would that be all right with you? After all, she gave me you. I have good reason to pay her tribute."

"I would like that very much. It should be the two of us. I am eager to do it as soon as we can. Not today, of course. We have got to get some rest. When do you think you can go?"

"As soon as Monday morning. Would that work for you?"

"Let's do it," I said eagerly.

"And so mote it be," he said, using an old Masonic expression for finalizing things.

"And so mote it be."

"I think I can rest now," he said. "I need to get up to Elberta. I know she is not sleeping well. I have seen her looking down on us from upstairs several times tonight. She is always looking after me. If I'm not sleeping, she isn't either.

"You know that foot that I injured so badly at the rodeo. It hurts me still. If I hurt before I go to bed or in the night, she has all kinds of things to make it feel better. She'll get up and get me some aspirin. Then she will get that antique pitcher and bowl down. She will fill that bowl with hot water and salts and soak my foot. Then she will rub it over and over with a soothing salve. She doesn't rest until I can. She is so good to me. I thought when I lost Margaret that there would never be another woman for me. I certainly haven't forgotten Margaret, and I remember the powerful love I felt for her. Oh, but I do love Elberta and the wonderful life we have together. She has soothed all the pains and hurts of my life. She has given me two beautiful daughters. She is my love and my friend. I could not do without her or love anyone more than I do her."

"I know. She is a great mother to me, too. I have been a lucky man to have had three mothers to love me and care for me."

"Well, it is time for me to go up to her now. Let's call it a night." He moved slowly getting up, and I stood up to help him but he came on up and stood very straight. "I've just sat in this chair way too long," he said chuckling. "You may have to help in time, but I can make it on my own tonight."

"I just remembered something," I said. "I'm sorry to keep

231

telling you things, but that Sunday when you plan to tell your story, that's the Sunday Mr. Navarre said he'd be there."

"That's all right. He should be there. I hope Maggie Brown and her husband and Vernon Stewart and his wife are there, too. There is no one I would want to stay away. I'm going to be ready for this and glad to tell it to anybody You don't need to worry. It is all going to be all right. You go on home now, and you get some sleep too." With that he started up the steps. His back was straight and his head held high. It occurred to me that he looked so dignified as he went up those steps. I just watched him. When he got to the top, he turned around and put his left hand on the banister and looked down at me. He raised his right hand and waved slightly to me and said. "Nine days 'til Sunday."

"So mote it be," I answered.

Just then Cousin Elberta came out of the bedroom and walked toward him and put her arms around him. She looked down at me lovingly as if she knew what had been going on with us. Cousin Randy met her embrace and then looked down at me again. "Good night, my son," he said.

I felt a lump in my throat and tears came into my eyes. For the first time in my life, I said, "Good night, Dad. I love you, and I love you, too, beautiful lady. I'm not sure what to call you now."

"Call me Mama," she called back to me. "I love you, too, and how glad I am this day has come."

Just then the old clock in the hall struck five times. At that very moment it came to me that he'd told me it was five in the morning on a Friday when he had left my mother, Lizzie Belle's house that night I was conceived so long ago. I could not yet leave to go home. I had to run up the stairs toward them, and they came down partway to meet me. The three of us stood there embracing and crying and saying how we loved each other.

My father finally spoke. How like him to burst out in song at a moment when just words were not enough. No hymn will ever be as lovely to me as that one. "Blessed be the tie that binds our hearts in Christian love," he sang out clearly. Mama and I joined in reverently and sang with him to the end. Then, all together, we said "Amen."

232

www.ingramcontent.com/pod-product-compliance
Lightning Source LLC
Chambersburg PA
CBHW071835020726
47502CB00004B/1367